I0691946

Sary's Diamonds

by

Sharon Shipley

Love, Lust, and Peril:
Sary's Adventure Series, Book 2

This is a work of fiction. Names, characters, places, and incidents are either the product of the author's imagination or are used fictitiously, and any resemblance to actual persons living or dead, business establishments, events, or locales, is entirely coincidental.

Sary's Diamonds

Cover Art by *Debbie Taylor*

The Wild Rose Press, Inc.
PO Box 708
Adams Basin, NY 14410-0708
Visit us at www.thewildrosepress.com

Publishing History
First Mainstream Historical Rose Edition, 2017
Print ISBN 978-1-5092-1345-0
Digital ISBN 978-1-5092-1346-7

Love, Lust, and Peril: Sary's Adventure Series, Book 2
Published in the United States of America

Dedication

For Skip, my most loving adventurer,
and Nan Swanson, editor without peer.

Prologue

As she studied the length of her pale arm, outstretched across sand as cold and unyielding as marble under the starry sky, Sary wondered...

If I had to do it over, would I? Endure the pain, suffering, and terror again?

Yet she knew that hand lying on chilled sand could never draw back the veil to reveal the future. Perhaps, a mercy. She would. Again, and again, because that was who she was.

She tried to call to her companion, her voice a dry whisper, a single grain of sand skittering across a glacial desert under a cold-moon sky. Then Sary felt herself deliriously, miraculously lifted as if by angels, and the man held her close to his delicious warmth, tucking her head to his neck.

His pulse thumped against her temple. Sary's mind winged back to the time when she was so blessedly warm, and wind was a wet friend against her face, and hunger had yet to visit...

Chapter 1
Dark Continent

Sary leaned over the mahogany rail of the sailing ship the *Constanzia*—her white lawn gown, liberally clotted with Battenberg lace, billowed heavily in the humid wind, her petticoats blown to hell and gone, and she neither knew nor cared a fiddler's fig if her legs and ankles were exposed clean to her ruffled bloomers.

Africa!

Her green gaze strained for the matching green of distant vegetation, even though heat shimmered above it like a fecund aura… Actually, swarms of insects of outlandish sizes and shapes, from no-see'ums to enormous beetles, teemed and clouded the fetid air. However, she wasn't to know that. None of her small party did.

She frowned slightly.

A rather poisonous vapor.

As her perfect brow crinkled, Sary's sea-green eyes took on a cloudy cast. *I'll have to tell Tommy the truth—at least part of it—soon.*

She gripped the taffrail tighter—*No bad thoughts now. Put a good face on*—and turned a sparkling countenance to the wind, teeth white between salt-sprayed lips, cheeks rosy with salt wind, hair fighting to fly from her Gibson Girl "do," so popular now, under the extravagant lace hat.

Drat. Where was that Jude? She wished to hold him up on the rail like a miniature figurehead, to view his new home, or at least it would be for a few months. By that time, she would *surely* find the treasure.

Aha. At present her little monkey tested his mama's nerves, it seemed, by reattempting to climb the main mast, his little bottom a quarter of the way up—*way* past the boom.

Sary ran to the foot of the waist-thick mast and hollered, feeling eyes on her. From there Jude had a magnificent view. Her feet itched to climb. *Why not?*

Biting her lip, Sary Swinford plucked skirts with one hand, jumped on the capstan, and with the other hand grasping the ladder, placed one kid-covered foot and followed Jude's chubby bottom up. Quite easy, actually, except for the rolling of the ship.

She glanced down—a few of the swabbies and snotties—*ugly word that*—gaped, showing a fine display of black teeth. *Or no teeth.* She giggled. *Hope they enjoy the view, as I certainly shall.*

"Sary!"

She glanced past her flying Battenberg skirts. *Confound it! Tommy!* A thundercloud below. Back at Jude. He was at the top sail already, or top's'l, as the yeoman called it. "No further, pumpkin! Mommy will be frightened. Aren't you?" His face said it all. Jude looked up, powerfully wishing to continue but awfully glad she was there.

"Umm, no, Mummy. No! W*eawwy. Wanna go up dere!*" He pointed to the crow's nest. It *was* enticing.

Sary breathed deep. As much as she yearned to follow—*Oh, how breathless the view must be!*—she was between the devil and literally the deep blue sea,

3

the devil being Tommy below.

"Follow me down—*now*, you little urchin."

"Sary!"

"Yes, Tommy. Of course. I'm not proceeding further," she called down. "I—I just wished to rescue Jude."

The wind nearly knocked the breath out of her, and the giant sails snapped like bedsheets of the gods on a vast clothesline billowing in the wind. She could see the earth actually did have a curve like her old school globe. *My, it's fascinating up here, though.*

Tommy's voice intruded again, calling her name.

Drat!

She hopped the last few feet, refusing Tommy's arm and letting him catch Jude. "Really, Thomas." She decided to be scandalized and squash him, to no reward.

"Sarabande. *Sweeting.* You do realize you have scarcely a…a *womanly* secret left unbeknownst to the entire crew!" he hissed.

"Why? A sailor's never clapped eyes on a woman's pantaloons? They are unaware we have two legs, separated in the middle?"

Ignoring Tommy's umbrage, she chuckled, pointing at her young son.

"When not attempting to be the world's youngest swabbie, Jude pretends to be an anchor hiding in the anchor rope's enormous coils"—she poked Jude's snubbin' nose—"like a cobra in a pot, when he is not teasing the cook into extra ship's biscuits. Climbing the mast was harmless."

She tickled Jude's tummy till he giggled. "Maybe we should make him eat all the ship's biscuits as punishment, but even I'm not that hardhearted."

Sary babbled and chattered, finally catching a laugh.

"Whatever is up there?"

"Why, the world, Tommy. The entire"—she dropped her voice—"*bloody world.*"

Tommy shook his head. "You could have been flattened across the deck instead. Both of you."

Chapter 2
Goddess of Destruction

Tommy had never seen her so lovely, so damnably appealing. Sary's childlike wonder never ceased, but it concealed a mind as calculating as Catherine De Medici's. Yet she had been so toughened by adversity she seemed one woman hiding behind another—the twin always struggling to step in front.

He spread a bemused grin. Sary always did gild the *gilding* on the lily, and per usual, when one pink silk rose (drooping with salt spray) would suffice, her exquisite bonnet suffered under six bobbing pink confections.

A former actor, Tommy could appreciate the over-the-top elegance, sensing it was born of bone-deep hunger.

However, in Sary's case, she might seem a goddess—but a goddess of destruction. His arresting eyes took on the black of the deeps, scanning the mysterious landmass across increasingly molten-colored waves as they neared equatorial Africa, so different from the steel-gray chop of the English Channel, feeling unbidden fear. What lurked in that wild terrain where even esteemed explorers like Burton and Doyle and Livingston were swallowed whole?

He gazed out at the swell. Dark shapes circled below the chop, matching his own thoughts. What chance did they have—a small female no matter how lovely but with a gimpy arm, a traveling actor who kenned the stage like his own hand yet possessed few survival skills beyond rain-soaked back roads and how to avoid landlords, plus Jude, a small boy who never had to seek out terrifying situations.

Besides, *he* could show her the world. It nettled.

He held little Jude tight. The boy weighed near three stone but squirmed to be let go—otherwise his one goal in life seemed to be that of pitching himself headlong into the sea—to join his mother, most likely.

She too looked halfway pitched over and dunked as she leaned across the taffrail, straining to see the African coast, once more with skirts sailing up in back and affording passing yeomen and swabbies another tantalizing glimpse of her lacy underdrawers.

Tommy took time, mesmerized by her bewitching bottom stretching the fine linen.

He felt a stirring. With her gown stretched tight over brimming bosom, she resembled the lusty straining-forward figurehead of this leaky old bucket of a ship, leading the prow onward to Africa.

Africa. Bloody Africa.

Why? Why the rush? Tommy had pondered it uncounted times. *Something wrong.* He could feel it.

Tommy looked past her bosom, straining ribbons, roses, lace, and ruffles, after a respectable moment of appreciation, and viewed individual palms seeming to encroach stealthily, raggedly, toward a distant coastal village as if devouring it.

Sary joined him. Tommy glumly stared at the distant smudge, his gaze black and thunderous as clouds looming over the distant shore, spitting lightning bolts as if punishing the natives who dwelt there.

Why endanger Jude to entertain such a repellent spot?

Yet Sary had risked all for Jude in the past. Shot, starved, and left to die back in Big Bear, this was one of her many anomalies. Even now her left arm was stiff, and smaller than the other—a fact she concealed by long sleeves and extravagant ruffles. Tommy eyed her slightly bent arm, held close. When she could, she held a fan or gloves to disguise it.

It all began back in England...no, before that, in Big Bear, California, a lone woman amongst brutal, vindictive men where she clawed a massive fortune from an unforgiving mountain. Now what was this fever for more?

His Sary seemed chased by unseen devils.

She was afraid under all that brave tat.

Chapter 3
Bloody Africa

Sary covertly studied what she wouldn't admit *was* a rather revolting shoreline as the *Constanzia* sailed the coast, the length of Africa, toward her goal of Cape Town.

She strained to see a sign of hope, keeping her face expectantly bland. *So green—a lurid, poisonous green.* She had the impression of secrecy, as if the wall of tall thick foliage imprisoned the land, or kept others out with fecund warning.

Stuff and nonsense.

Tommy covertly watched her, too, for reaction. *How irritating.*

"Why aren't we closer?" she demanded perversely. Spray hit her face. *Water is like soup here—warm, heavy, green, and salty.*

Sary knew how feverish she looked—a zealot handing out pamphlets could look no more fanatical. With every bone, she yearned to go ashore and begin her hunt for not only treasure but her own lost pride.

Watching sails droop limp and brine laden, snared in something called the doldrums since yesterday, so their captain informed them, if she could swim and tug the ship at the same time she damn well would.

A hundred times, it was on her tongue to tell Tommy why her abrupt haste and why she had fallen to what surely must seem lunacy.

She, Sary, the level-headed one.

The enduring. The shrewd.

If she could make it right, Tommy need never know her folly.

However, she must bloody well get there!

It was the afternoon of the next day. Wind once again lofted the sails.

"But we are passing it!"

Sary watched the huddled settlement slide by.

"Should we not be landing?"

Raising skirts, she tripped up the ladder to the main deck. From there, there was no beach, or curving inlet. Only unrelieved green pressing the water and cement-colored thunderclouds stabbing the landmass with bright yellow spears and distant *booms.*

Tommy led her from the taffrail. "Perhaps because that's not Cape Town, love. Just an outpost or small village."

"Damnation." Sary peered at the distant village as if it were a hell on earth. Then the storm raced to them, splatting decks with giant tears as they fled to the ship's insalubrious saloon.

Chapter 4
Port Nolloth

Arms wide as if flying, Sary embraced the world when at last they spied a largish colony. Laughing with a glee she knew Tommy didn't understand, Sary fought her voluminous skirts in the lashing spray.

Nettled, Tommy carped, "Once again you're garbed like Mrs. Astor's pet horse. I'm bound they do not dress this way where we are heading." Tommy gestured helplessly at the far shore. "Why?"

"Now, Thomas! We've been through this."

"Have we?"

She looked down at her extravagant dress. "Perhaps you are right. But I can't miss this to change now. Besides, I wish to make a good impression. There are governors' wives and—"

"And they are certain to greet our arrival with full pomp and ceremony. Odd. I don't see the welcoming committee or the marching band," Tommy said with a twitch of his lips.

"Stuff and nonsense!"

Sary didn't see Tommy roll his eyes. She had picked up an All-Sorts of outdated *bon mots* among the London gentry, bits of language no self-respecting Englishman would now utter.

She thudded down the gangplank, propelled by momentum, leaving Tommy pacing sedately behind with Jude. He lagged to irritate, she just knew. Tommy'd be along, and she could not wait!

She slowed. It didn't look pleasant. She tried to ignore a sky drooling rain, but it was no use pretending. Even little Jude looked askance at the huddle of storm-ravaged huts, tucking his head in Tommy's neck. Jude, who chortled with glee at the ship's violent wallowing, when waves clawed the mast clean to the crow's nest. It vexed. She felt peevish at both of them. Or guilty?

Her steps faltered. The eddy of rough passengers and common sailors flooding past in the drizzle pushed her sideways.

So bleak and ugly since we rounded the jetty. Huge piles of mine tailings, rail lines, enormous copper barrels, a hodgepodge of odd buildings, some squat and stunted, others towering and narrow. She had thought from aboard ship they were office buildings or homes— all bespoke a grim mining town.

"All ashore, goin' ashore."

A cheeky young swabbie grabbed her hips "to steady you, miss," winked, and was soon lost in the throngs.

Sary slogged through mud near an island of dry space and looked for Tommy. Why was he lagging? Still among sailors shuttling down the plank, head bent, gravely listening to the captain.

He followed slowly. Not smiling. *I will not ask. No quarrels now.* First, food and hot tea, and await their baggage. There must be the town proper further on. She'd expected Africa to be a frontier of sorts, hadn't she? *But this?*

She fanned. Her corset pinched. Without even the slight ocean breeze to cool her, perspiration trickled between her breasts, soaking her chemise despite the rain. How could it be both rainy and humid? It was like breathing through a damp tea towel.

She raised priceless lace above dung and dock garbage as she went. At last, *Sir* Thomas picked his way through stevedores swinging nets of haulage and rough men with kit bags waiting to board ship.

Along with unnamed dread came an urgent thought. Sary yearned to join them.

Instead, she picked her way to a raffia and tin-roof establishment; its corrugated roof shone, and it was floored by mud tamped to concrete. She eyed planks sticky with drinks' rings and old food, and benches worn to a sheen from dirty boots.

Ah, well, I've seen worse—far worse…

A boy squatted lazily, waving a palmetto, eyelids drooping. Flies settled on his face unheeded. She sat close for the faint breath the fan provided, nudging flies a few feet until they dodged the fan and darted back into her face. Assuming an "all's well" look, Sary beckoned Tommy.

Tommy quirked the gorgeous cleft beside his mouth, black eyes shining with wickedness. He settled Jude and glanced at another table.

"Vittles beyond ship's biscuits." He nodded at what looked like the hind leg of a pig hiding a man's face, grease dripping down his chin.

It smelled perversely wonderful. Her gaze caught on a squabble of monkeys in a cage, mentally assessing their hindquarters.

Perhaps not after all. "Best drink beer here, ma'am. Might make pitchforks in the belly. I mean the water."

Sary nodded, hoping the captain wouldn't sit. Still hungry, she had to get Jude settled and needed a suitable but cheap place to stay before she got down to business.

"Sary has the constitution of a goat."

Sary kicked Tommy under the plank.

"You, ah, might wish to re-board, madam."

"Re-board? Of course not. Why ever should we?"

"In light of…"

Tommy hid a grin.

The captain shrugged. "Safe enough, I s'pose, for now," he said somewhat evasively, if Sary noticed. Settling his broad thighs with a grunt and a plop, he snagged a server. "Allow me," the captain oozed, speaking to the delicious swells visible through Sary's damp, near-transparent chemise. She had dared undo the top clasps due to the dripping humidity.

She glanced at Tommy. Her detestable male wallowed in some small gratification from the captain's attentions in a male bonding.

"Perhaps you should see to our trunks, Tommy," Sary snapped. "While I—" She rose.

The captain drew brows that went every-which-way in a confused brown squint.

"How's 'at? Just have ta shuttle 'em back, ma'am."

"Don't see why. We—"

"Yer debarkin' in Cape Town."

"Of course. This is—?"

"Hell's bells! This ain't Cape Town, ye idjit female."

Tommy started up like in a bad play. "See here, now…"

Nevertheless, Thomas had a grin lurking.

Drat, Tommy.

"Meant it kindly, girly. I mean, ma'am."

The captain touched his greasy cap and took another peek at her bosom.

She refused to cover. She sweltered.

Jude had bare legs and arms.

Tommy's coat was off, with his fine linen sleeves rolled to his biceps, and Cap's shirt was open to the apex of a brown belly, displaying a mat of chest hair that would do a gorilla proud.

"Call all my sweethearts sweet idjits." He doffed the dirty cap with "CAPTAIN" in tarnished braid. "Meant no disrespect."

"Wait. Then, where are we? I wondered if this filthy hole were indeed Cape Town."

"Ha. 'At's an even bigger filthy 'ole, ma'am, beggin' yer pardon. Take District Six. No decent lady wanders near 'The Six.' Used ta be quite nice. Streams runnin' to the sea where Malays washed their clothes. Now just muck, soon to be covered over."

"This here's Port Nolloth. Copper smelterin' and all." The captain oozed complacency and sweat. "And, since this is now the captain's table?" He snapped dirty thumbs. "Allow me to treat you as the honored passengers you are. Rum all around, and none of that tiger pi-"—he glanced at Sary—"juice."

"I dare say," Tommy hissed to Sary, "we're the most elite passengers since the ship's christening, back when Moses was a baby."

"Shush, Tommy!" She wondered when he'd comment on the poverty of the other passengers—a down-on-his-heels, by way of whiskey, coffee grower, a wan clutch of kindly missionaries, and a woman with

15

darned stockings and rundown slippers, plus a scruffy lawyer, to name a few.

"Most terribly kind," Sary said in her new toff's voice. After their emersion in English rarified society, she could turn it on and off as suited.

Tommy rolled his eyes again. "In-*dooooob*itably. Oh, most gracious—" He earned another swift kick under the table.

Rum made her forget Africa's torrid climate even though the sun was now out, melting frustration to vague concern; Sary giggled like an unwed missionary lady at the captain's scandalous tales, at one point, slurring, "But why *have* we docked?"

"Stopped to give the swabbies…" the captain mumbled, "a chance to blow off"—he winked—"a little steam with some of the lasses, and to take on water. Hard slog, roundin' the Cape a Good Hope."

Sary wasn't listening, subconsciously sensing a ripple like a tremor that caused birds to scatter before an earthquake.

An odd prickle that wasn't sweat lay on her neck. Her eye caught a scurry of native workers. Worried faces. Her mind picked up a Morse code of doubt and sudden fear. She looked instinctively at Jude lolling asleep in Tommy's arms.

The captain was suddenly all business. "Crew may not be shipshape, but I'll be. Ma'am—sir?" The captain drained his rum.

"Of course," she said vaguely. A general turmoil like the track of a shark still distracted her.

He wobbled to a halt and lurched at Tommy's face. "S'truth might be a bit a sickness here." He placed his finger beside his nose, or meant to, missing his nose and nearly gouging his eye.

She spun. "Tommy? What does he mean? Sickness!"

"Dunno. Some illness peculiar to natives?" He shrugged, hefting Jude.

Sary felt a chill run down her spine in spite of the heat.

"And why didn't he make it clear this wasn't Cape Town?"

Tommy swallowed a grin.

"You knew," she accused.

"Too right. Gets weary, you playing General Grant, Lee, *and* Sara Bernhardt all at the same time."

"Old drinking buddies now, are we?"

"It proves a point. One day you planned to buy a country estate in Cornwall, the next, you drag us off in our bedclothes as if bailiffs hounded our heels. Fact is, you don't have a bloody clue where we are, and I sure as Hades don't know why we are here!"

Fortunately, the captain returned before Sary needed to answer.

****

Relieved to keep the squalid town of Port Nolloth in their wake, Sary sped along the ship's passageway with Jude's discarded toys, including the fish carved from whalebone by a mate, that had been left scattered on deck. She skidded to a stop in her search to find her hoodlum-in-the-making.

"Welcome, mistress."

Their cabin door swayed with the ship's wallow, like a stage curtain. Tommy was gesturing before the looking glass, leering, grimacing, and intoning lines from *Othello*.

"Let it not gall your patience, good Iago!" Tommy tossed an imaginary cape. "That I extend my manners; 'tis my breeding—that gives me this bold show of courtesy."

Tommy flourished a bow, kissing an imaginary hand. He then changed his voice to a rumble. "Sir, would she give you so much of her lips, as of her tongue she oft bestows on me."

A deep laugh came from Tommy's stomach, if not his toes. Then, mincing, peering sideways, he batted long black lashes as, presumably, Desdemona.

Sighing, Sary eyed the trunks and the scattered wigs and props.

"Alas, she has no speech," Tommy bellowed.

"In faith, too much;

I find it still, when I have list to sleep:

Marry, before your ladyship, I grant,

She puts her tongue a little in her heart,

O thou foul thief, where hast thou stow'd my daughter?

Damn'd as thou art, thou hast enchanted her;

That thou hast practiced on her with foul charms,

Abused her delicate youth with drugs or minerals

And chides with…"

Sary entered and chimed in, giggling, "and chides with…"

Tommy stiffened.

Slowly applauding, Sary walked up, green eyes dancing.

"Very good, my lord! We didn't play it much."

"Our audiences relished bawdy comedy like your Kate of the *Shrew*. They didn't cotton much to Desdemona being throttled. Only *me*," he said heavily.

"Miss it, don't you?"

He turned with his dangerous black eyes.

"If I knew why we were here, it would make a difference."

This is getting old.

Then her Tommy brooded dramatically out the porthole. *Like Lord Byron.* "Some'at, I miss it. I kenned who I was there, Sary-lass. On the road, managing my own…" Tommy gestured with a sad hopelessness. "I was *something.* Here? What am I?" He flopped on the bunk, drawing her down. She landed, inserting her hand under his shirt.

It has been too long.

"You are my manager," she dissembled, glancing under lashes and planting soft butterfly kisses on his chest.

He attempted to shove her off. Not too hard, though. "I've devolved into nursemaid and playmate for Jude."

"A full-time job, then," she murmured, kissing his neck, biting his chin, playing with his absurd little nipples.

"Indeed." He drew her onto the bunk and nuzzled her breasts in turn, murmuring between kisses, "Why not make us another little Jude?" he said huskily, drawing up her gown—not much to raise, for the ship was in the doldrums again and heat heavy.

Sary wore only one thin petticoat and, to his delight, no knickers. He reached for her moist epicenter and soft curls and, with the other hand, slammed the cabin door.

She rose as if his touch burned.

Lord—so difficult, not to lay languid, drowsy, and

19

let Tommy have his own sweet way.

Instead, she shot up, re-pinning her hair, breathing hard…

"Hot, Tommy," Sary snapped, alarmed. *A child? Now?*

She avoided the subject with jests, demurs, and playfulness. At wit's end, Sary optioned for the black-silk-thread affair tied to a vinegar-soaked sponge and placed where it counted. She had learnt the secret from a demimondaine in a gossipy huddle in a retiring room at one of London's nameless sumptuous parties.

Apparently, the vinegar-sponge affair was indeed effective, and Sary did not need the ignominy of asking Tommy to use the odious sheep-gut things. One of the titled ladies coolly dipped into her reticule and showed her one of those, explaining their use, as if the general shape would not have educated Sary quite enough.

Intuitively she recognized Tommy would never use them, not that she wished him to.

She felt Tommy's eyes speculating with hot appeal. Sary went to the passageway.

"Where is that scamp?" *I can always use Jude as excuse.*

"Devil take it!" She ran.

There was Jude, bottom up, draped over the railing, helping cook empty swill over the side and doing his damnedest to be part of a shark's dinner himself.

Sary crept up roughly and snatched him. Her eyes blazed at Tommy when she returned. "Another child?" she accused. "You can scarcely look after this one." And swept off.

Oh. So unfair. Why did I do it? Hurt Tommy so?

****

Later Sary crept into their cabin, sleeping Jude nestled under her neck. In penance, she played with him the rest of the day in the ship's confines and laid him somnolent in his hammock. She could scarce manage with the stiff arm.

Tommy lounged in the bottom berth, brewing a storm.

"Sary, if it is indeed adventure..." he began. "Marry me, Sary. There will not be one scrap of the world safe from us."

"Are we not doing precisely that?"

Tommy looked off, tight jawed. "Of course, if one fancies torrid climes, or a boorish populace who wouldn't appreciate King Lear from *Charlie's Aunt*." He sulked. "I don't want your money, Sary, if that is what you fear. I mean about us getting wed."

Sary felt an ice dagger in her heart.

She wanted to scream.

Oh, Tommy. We have no money!

"No one this side of heaven knows we are not married, or cares, Tommy."

"In this godforsaken hellish netherworld, I would imagine not. There are no *mores* here." He brooded. "And what about Jude?"

"Oh, Thomas! What part do you play now?"

"Recall Malcom?" He named his all-purpose dwarf actor, who played anything from orphans in the storm and young girls to the odd sinister character—and who was now proud owner of Tommy's old band of gypsy-traveling thespians.

"Such a fount of gossip concerning your forays into the world of morality, as I recall," she teased.

Tommy inspected a nail. "Call it what you will."

"How many farm girls, shopkeeper's daughters, and eldest unmarried spinsters did you have in backs of wagons, behind hedgerows, in haymows, or—during rainstorms—in abandoned barns?" Sary guffawed.

Tommy had the grace to looking contrite. "You win." He eyed her closely.

"Sary? Have you gone…all *womanly* on me? I mean, is this…?"

His Irish cameo-pale skin flushed, and Sary knew well that which he supposed.

That her monthly visit from "Auntie Scarlet" had descended like an Egyptian plague. That she could not have a rational thought in her silly head when her notions did not match his.

"Or are you…?" His eyes softened. She wanted to smack him.

"I am neither crazy nor with child!"

How dare he? With child? On a rolling ship on the high sea? Doesn't bear thinking of. 'Sides, I made certain—didn't I?

Sary bit her lip. She must be careful. So much at stake. If Tommy only knew what frail horse they rode.

Sary dipped her face and swiped arms, neck, and chest in the tiny china basin to cool her temper. The box of hot cabin air weighted her after their quarrel.

****

Sary couldn't sleep.

Suicidal insects banged against the lantern still burning below.

Tommy slept the sleep of the innocent in his under-breeches, his handsome actor's face in repose—jet hair falling wildly across the pillow, lashes iridescent as crows' wings fanned on his pale sculpted cheeks. Her

22

eyes rested on that perfect mouth, both soft and hard.

Sary wanted him.

It would be a cheap forgiveness.

She must not have these hot wet thoughts in this humid night, yet her body goaded her. Drawing her shift to her knees, Sary eased her damp legs on either side and scrunched down on the comfortable bulge in his underclothes. As always, Tommy was instantly awake in more ways than one. She grinned. "I'm a good girl, I am."

Tommy's mouth was open and moist. Eyes hooded, unreadable, but his body betrayed him. "Very good," he muttered thickly.

Slowly, she shirred the fabric of her shift, drawing the cotton up to her little V of pubis silked with blonde down.

Just as Tommy reached, Sary skittered off—not far; their cabin was small. Clutching her shift tight to her thighs, she shimmied, wriggling her bottom in a slow, gyrating dance.

He watched her pale peach fanny though the flimsy cotton like a reclining sultan.

Still shimmying, she raised the shift, revealing her smooth bottom; looking over her shoulder, she swung the weight of her hair as her shift puddled at her feet.

She turned and lifted her hair, fully revealing her high firm breasts, fuller after her child, the taut belly and rounded hips and long, slim but muscular legs. Tommy restrained himself, motioning for her to stand before the lantern, his eyes devouring every inch of her.

She could scarce wait until he did it for real.

The lantern made her hair gleam like white gold and smoothed the bullet scars, while Sary unconsciously hid the slightly bent arm.

Raising a foot, she toed the hardness in Tommy's lap.

He made to grab the teasing limb, but she jerked away, cupping her full, ripe breasts.

She could do or ask anything, but she wouldn't. It wasn't right. Besides, she was aching, near shaking with longing.

She pressed his face into her belly, draping a curtain of pale hair smelling of Guerlaine over him. He clutched her hips, breathing her in, lowered his face to nuzzle her delta, running his tongue in circles until she arched in ecstasy—*oh, how the farm girl has changed*—and pulled her to the floor and put his full weight on top, groaning, "Sary, Sary."

Chapter 5
Reduced Circumstances

The next morn, magic melted with the heat, the ship still wallowing in sultry temperature and heavy green seas. Sary twisted her weighty hair in what she hoped was a becoming and cool knot.

"Spoiled," she grumbled to the looking glass. "Won't be slave to a hairdresser." She tossed the pig-bristle brush, near-missing Tommy. "And when *will* we sail?"

"Have a care!" Tommy sidestepped.

"Then stay out of my way!" she grumped, leaning to make complicated-looking but simple arrangements with a few spirals and hairpins…and then the ship wallowed.

Tommy stumbled, knocking the whole assembly askew, and huge lollops fell in her face. Sary spun as fast as the tiny cabin allowed, glaring with the one eye showing past the messy waterfall of hair. Her elbow hit his eye.

"Tommy! Must you take up the entire space!"

"Ow! Do have a care!" Tommy very showily stirred his shaving cup and hipped her aside. "Oh, so sorry!" He vigorously daubed the brush on his chin.

"Yes! Yes, Thomas! I'll finish soon." She hipped him back, with the help of an elbow shoving the soapy brush up his nose.

Thomas's reflection scowled through a white foam beard. "Time's up. You look no worse than you usually do," he said carelessly.

So it's going to be that sort of day.

"A more gracious cabin might have done!" He dug in.

Not that again.

Tommy held her eye with pique. Sweat ran into his soap foam. The ship gave another lurch.

"If we had a more plentiful space?" he nagged, crowding her shoulder, and wildly applied the straight razor with a sharp upraised elbow and menacing manner.

"My. Aren't we turning grand?"

Tommy stared with eyes black as tar pits. "As a matter of fact, yes. Thanks to you and your fabled riches, I did rather enjoy the amenities. Why? Was I to despise them?"

He reddened, resuming straight-razoring his throat, wiping soap on a towel.

He finally blew out, laying the razor down. "I've not given a fig if we're paupers or one of the bloody Four Hundred. You know that, Sary!"

He glanced helplessly around the cabin from the mirror.

"Yet couldn't we have mustered a *tad* better? I don't mean to mention it over much."

Oh, no? Only every day.

"Three of us crammed in here, with our entire luggage."

Useless props.

"And there are larger cabins available, even now." He stared perplexed. "You'd only need ask," he added, hopeful.

He whines plaintively. Sary daubed sweet talcum under her arms. *He won't let it rest.*

"This old girl is not precisely an unblemished maiden on her first voyage. The rigging looks like my great aunt's crochet. The decks are splinters. In addition, the top gallant is more rag than sail—and *mon Capitan* is definitely third-rate," Tommy said, "but a first class tippler," he muttered, deliberately turning into her.

Sary thrust home a last pin in a losing battle with the shining cascade and in so doing knocked Tommy off balance, and he sat heavily on the bunk behind her.

He wiped off the last of the foam, slapped on an expensive Parisian concoction smelling of lemons, making the cabin reek an intoxicating fug, and looked sadly at the almost empty flask.

Sary recalled their spendthrift orgy when they first arrived in London and Paris. Carriages, tailors, dressmakers, expensive toys for Jude…the most elegant hotels when not "fortnighting" at glorious estates.

All gone.

Sary eyed him as he dressed, eyed the billowy linen shirt that showed his chest. She shook the notion off.

"What have you done with your fortune? Your gold? Have you bought a castle in Spain? The whole village? A hippopotamus for Jude? Enameled, diamond-encrusted knickers for me, my initials writ in gilt embroidery?"

Something like that.

He tucked his actor's shirt into his trousers, crooked his arm, and said, "Come, my darling. Let us go forth to the cap's table for our morning swill."

Perhaps she had been a bit indulgent. Maybe six rose-bedecked velvet dresses were over much, but the ladies all wore laces over veils, over silks, over damask, every inch embroidered, rucked, embossed, cut out, ruffled, and fringed.

Jewels in the hair, at earlobes, necks, bosoms, and wrists. And the hair! What teetering confections. It seemed whimsy ruled the day. Capes, flounces, chokers, yards of pearls, parasols that whirled and fluttered useless in the breeze. A glove in every color for each occasion. A lady was naked without them apparently.

Sary hated gloves. She felt suffocated.

Yet—these ladies seemed to know how to proportion just the right amount of furbelows and tat, before it was over much. Sary hadn't educated herself at what point to stop ladling the frosting, until she resembled a layered gateaux, topped with marzipan and candied fruit trembling on every hat brim.

Sary laughed, suddenly starving even for swill.

Chapter 6
Cape Town!

After the ship emerged ghostlike from fog and they could see the coast at last, the *Constanzia* rounded wind- and sea-bashed rock.

Sary, twitchy as a cat on a hot tin roof, willed the ship forward, annoyed each time a sounder lifted the knotted rope and a foghorn bleated for its echo.

As the *Constanzia* pitched upward, she spied a clock tower and a thoroughfare winding up a hill lined with electric poles and was vaguely disappointed it seemed so modern.

Battling salt spray, she leaned over the rail, the better to see.

"Devil's Peak," she heard the captain say at her side, "and there's the old fort…"

A stark stone wall squatted at water's edge—an odd tower resembling a marriage between a wedding cake and the Tower of Pisa. Yet the closer the ship sailed, the more disappointed she became. The buildings were all Victorian—almost like England.

She had expected something more exotic—foreign.

Does it matter if Cape Town is a flesh pot or a stew pot? It all ends or begins here. Impatiently raising her spyglass, she saw some houses were queer mixtures of domes, scaled like armor and gables. A few sported Stars of David, and on the front of one, a red-and-gold

29

baronet's crest. *What did you expect? Grass and mud huts? Well—yes.*

"Me too, Mummy, me see."

"Nothing to see yet, Baby Bear."

Jude contented himself squatting at the railing and trying to get his head stuck, and getting drenched in the bargain. From his giggles, he enjoyed himself.

An odd hustle and bustle here too, from the distance. Folks of dark skin and light scurried like ants, with no set pattern. Didn't help the ship rode like a rocking horse, as waves brushed them close to boulders fallen away from the headland like a curving cat's tail.

Sary passed the glass to Tommy.

At last, the ship maneuvered past a granite outcrop and they drifted to the wharf, where a cacophony of noise, orders, and what sounded like the cracking of gunfire—but it could have been the rattle of waist-thick anchor chains, or sails thudding—curses, and Cap's bellows over the horn.

Sary didn't need the glass now.

Police in toupees and leggings chased natives scattering like water bugs. Soldiers herded one angry group behind a barrier, while two stayed on guard with bayoneted rifles.

Odd.

She hoped it was not an uprising or other bother.

As quickly as it began, it was over. Once they had cleared the natives behind the barriers, the soldiers vanished. Once more streets were crowded with commerce.

Tommy shrugged. "Perhaps someone important's arriving. Certainly not us." He noted pointedly, "We are hardly a first-class ship."

Sary felt the familiar flush of anger, biting her lip. She turned on him, but Tommy's hair was glossy in the sun, like anthracite coal. Silky not-quite-curls whipped a weathercock around a sculpted face, all sharp edges and hollows beneath a fine layer of muscle. She couldn't be annoyed with him. Spinning abruptly back, she was startled at how close to shore they were. All around her, ropes were tossed. Sails dropped.

Her skin turned cold.

Chapter 7
Plague

Sary unsnapped her fan and raised her parasol.

While they waited for their luggage, a hot breeze blasted offshore, heavy with fish, unguents, spices, fruit, and the tar oozing in black oily puddles. The wharf was alive with commerce and hawkers, food stalls, and people of all races, ages, and station.

A kaleidoscope of colors, with ebony, milky white, lovely golden mulatto skin tones; beautiful gowns and matching turbans and, even in the heat, puce taffeta and green moiré; a few people in Arab garb, the long nun-like gown concealing the whole figure.

A hundred voices and dialects, from Boers red-faced under pith helmets to ebony bull-like men, with only teeth and eyes showing their features, toting enormous stalks of green bananas, and bearers with bales that dwarfed them. Children splashed barefoot through oxen, horse, and goat dung.

Sary glanced at wicker cages of monkeys and jewel-bright birds screeching a cheerful racket.

"Off you go, Jude. Pester the monkeys. But don't touch anything."

Between the colors, heat, noise, scents, and activity, Sary felt growing excitement. This was more like it. Yet nowhere seen were the mustachioed hunters and explorers of her imaginings.

Jude plucked a tiny banana hanging low by their table. "Oh, go on with you, but not too close. Don't feed them. Here."

Perversely, Sary proffered another banana. "Don't let them touch you—toss it in, you little monkey yourself." Then she turned and declared, "Oh, Tommy. I did it wrong again."

Yet he's so big for his age. She shuddered with a flash of his father, her attacker, the huge barn-like Ev'ret. Unlike Ev'ret, Jude was sharp as a scythe.

For an icy moment, she lost sight of him in an abrupt swirl of color, thick calloused feet, laced boots, bare calves, and thong-like sandals. European women openly smoking white cigarettes shortly distracted her.

When she looked back, Sary noted a light-skinned girl, comely if her face weren't so drawn. Sary's gaze flashed to Jude, vaguely troubled.

When she glanced back, the girl, a gorgeous octoroon with reddish curls, sagged, still holding her tray of bright things, and sat or slid to the bottom of a post.

Oh. That was all—she's selling sweets, or toys.

Still Sary had an unsettled sense of something very wrong...

Odd.

The young girl lay full on the ground now, sweets and toys scattered. No one picked them up.

Sary half-rose and finally saw Jude standing respectfully at the monkey's cage.

"More impossible each day!" She sat rapidly fanning.

"Me or Jude?"

"Both pests of the first order."

"Sorry I came?"

"'Course not." Sary searched Tommy's arresting face. "But must you drag behind like a cart full of rocks?"

"Don't put quarrels on my tongue. Admit it. This isn't what you thought it would be, whatever you supposed. Shakespeare said it better. 'Let us make an honorable retreat.' Besides"—he flashed white teeth—"if I drag behind, it is only to behold your bewitching arse."

"Stuff Shakespeare and his horse! This will be a *grand* adventure!"

Tommy bit his lip, studying Jude. "For him too?"

"Jude will learn the world."

"At present, Jude's on the verge of being turned into minced meat, and it isn't even Christmas," Tommy drawled.

Her gaze flicked to another cage, concealed until now, and an ape's sharp yellow incisors in a wicked gummy grin.

Jude, smart lad, backed off, chubby hands behind him.

She looked again at the post. The girl had vanished.

Sary caught a flash of Jude shaking hands with the monkeys, little beggars clutching his shirt for food. Tommy dashed across the distance and grabbed him, screeching to wake the dead, from a larger chimp's grasp that had dragged the little boy close to the bars while violently shaking him.

Tommy carted Jude, still bawling, over his shoulder. "'et me *down*. Pway wiv *monkeys.*"

"See? Even in the most benign settings there's danger," Tommy carped. "You don't play with monkeys. They will eat you!" He grimaced at Sary over the lie.

"He can walk now," Sary scoffed, making a great motherly fuss.

If you weren't distracted by your *secret* endeavors..." Tommy said heavily.

"Why ever do you wish to marry someone so flawed as I?"

"You change the subject. I have not asked for your hand since breakfast. Speaking of which, I'm peckish." He looked for a waiter, chewing his thumb.

****

"We should hire a nanny. For Jude's sake," he announced.

Sary looked away.

"Sary? We've hired nannies and governesses, various nursemaids, baggage handlers, ladies' maids, manicurists, hairdressers, and dress makers, and stayed in the best hotels since landing in England. You even foisted a valet on me. Something has changed. It was at that last house party," he said slowly, staring into the distance as if seeing a play. "*You* changed after that."

He pushed his plate away, with its cracked, greasy, chipped edges. "And this cheap fare. *More* beans, rice, some kind of gristly pig—or goat. Can't actually tell."

Sary opened her reticule, mentally calculated change, and slipped small coins to the waiter, with a worried glance into her purse for a second before she snapped it safely shut.

"The troupe ate better at every village and two-barrel tavern," Tommy continued grumbling.

"You've grown soft, living off me."

"We are richer than God, Sary! Why this punitive

parsimony?" Tommy trotted out his playwright skills again.

Sary bit her inner lip—hard. *Oh, Tommy, we are not "richer than God"—not any more.*

"Quite," he snapped.

"Keep the drama for the stage. This is good, nourishing fare. Jude can't be strong if we coddle him."

"Does that include tainted meat?" Tommy asked quietly.

Sary's stomach flipped. Flies seemed to take particular delight in their all-gray meal, and she shoved it aside.

He peeled the little boy another banana. Jude happily smashed a boiled egg to oblivion, crunching the bits and pieces.

"Cap said we could spend a few nights on board ship while he conducts some business or other, until we find suitable lodging. That should save us a few coin."

"Yes," she said quietly. *And fall neatly into my plans. It must be a sign.* "Of course. How kind."

"Thought you were so desperate to get on with your—*whatever* it is."

Across from them, activity took a fevered turn, lurid and alien, saving her from answering. She flashed a look for Jude, who'd wiggled off Tommy's lap, chortling, "Birds!" Only he still said, "Buds!"

Her eye snagged on the girl again. She'd crawled some way, wooden toys broken underfoot.

"Tommy, get Jude!"

Sary moved toward the girl, or rather the tide pulled her, whirling her about with a rip of lace and yank of skirt as the crowd whipsawed Sary closer until she and the girl were the epicenter.

"Oh!"

Purple lumps covered the girl's neck and chest. Her lips were cracked, and her neck puffed like an adder.

"*Water*..." she moaned, so faint it was tissue paper on a Christmas cracker.

Bedamned to her lace, Sary knelt and put her hand out to feel the girl's forehead. It radiated heat before she ever made contact. She pulled back.

Then Jude screamed, "Mummy," his normal lusty bellow a timid wail, and Tommy yanked her by an arm.

"Inappropriate charity, love." Dragging her from the doomed young woman through a retreating crowd, and jouncing Jude on his shoulder, he ran with her back to the *Constanzia*.

Chapter 8
The One-Eyed Man

One man watched their domestic exchange with a snigger, even that hidden behind a clay shot glass. He was drinking steadily now. It quenched impatience, and the heat, and the agony in his leg.

Murdering bitch!

He studied Jude over Tommy's shoulder with bright-eyed interest, chuckling. *"Well, I'll be hanged."* It seemed a private joke.

Enjoy your fancy dress, Sary Swinford. You'll pay. I'll make it long and drawn out. I'm waiting.

Sary turned a second before her eyes rested on the man. Not that he'd care, but it would be meddlesome until he had the lay of the land. He was Ratchet, after all, and liked to have his plans well set.

As he sullenly scanned the mob, he found them too alien. The bitch sure could pick uncommonly loathsome places, the one-eyed man decided.

Hell's fire and spare the matches. Sary had vanished. He needed to see where the murdering bitch went.

His long-fingered hands tightened until bones popped like knobs. "I got you like a kitten in a sack headin' to the river," he claimed as he dug out another fruit. A *morula*, had he known, but juicy, just like the oranges he loved.

****

"But when will we get to depart?" one of the missionary ladies asked timidly.

The captain kept his eyes on his pea soup, grunting something vague.

"Three days, I 'spect. Awaiting a, ah, shipment."

"And your crew will have their fun?" Sary earned a look from another of the missionary ladies. Her companion, a bright-eyed octogenarian, winked.

"'Spect they'll be stayin' aboard too. No more questions!" He studiously kept his eyes on his soup.

Sary noticed the sailors looking morosely at Cape Town, and they did indeed remain on board.

Chapter 9
Erstwhile Duke

Sary paced, longing to be free of desire—she had to find that blasted duke. The quarrels with Tommy heightened both their blood, Sary knew from familiarity. Even now Tommy gazed at her from under hooded lids.

She nodded reproof. Jude was yet awake.

Urgency flooded her whenever she was near Tommy. Her need intensified with intimacy—a malady whose fever never broke. Intimacy was addiction.

Tommy's black gaze burned as if reading her lusty thoughts, but his expression was yet sulky as ever.

"I apologize, Sary. Thrift is rarely a fault," he said stiffly.

"And I suppose you are the long-lost bastard son of a now-penniless lord."

"Only in plays, my overwrought Bernhardt."

Tommy, confound you. Take me! Don't wait for me. Lay me down. Let me feel the comfort, the weight of your body.

Her own body willed forward as if pulled by petticoat strings, she plucked up the dozing Jude, savoring for the moment his warm, sweet body, checked him swiftly for bites and the mosquito netting over his hammock for holes, and tucked him in.

She approached Tommy again, timidly, as if an

untried bride. Her breathing quickened. His mouth in repose was sculpted by Michelangelo, and she knew what those lips could do. *Oh, yes.*

She unfurled half-naked against his body, fragrant and musky all the same. Tommy had his own special animal perfume, clean as new soap.

She brushed his smooth muscled back, rippling long fingers, their work-reddened state long past. Gently tweaked his ear.

He turned with immediacy, staying her hand, as though hating her for her power over him. He pressed her close, never mind the heat. Never mind sweat-slick bodies and that she could not breathe when he was kissing her so thoroughly, roughly tugging her pantaloons down.

"Another magic trick," she murmured. "Where did you learn that?"

"Houdini's knee," he rumbled between deep wet kisses.

"Wicked. No one *ever* undressed me so swiftly as you, Houdini of the Boudoir." Sary giggled. It felt so good. They couldn't stay angry so long as blood and bodies pulled them like lodestones.

"I have other tricks too," he whispered, his breath hot in her ear.

He murmured between her slick breasts and down the soft line of pale silk sketching her flat belly, gripping her as if he wanted to press to the other side and devour her until she moaned with pleasure, or pain.

She wanted to cry out, aware of Jude sleeping his usual sleep of the innocent. Confined to the narrow berth, she gripped Tommy, forcing him deeper still, holding her in place. He eased them both to the floor, thrusting himself down, then up as far as he could to secure her as she thrashed and moaned, and then they were truly one again.

Later, cooling, feeling the oily sweat of their bodies tickle as flesh dried, she stroked him, gasping. "I rather liked that trick."

"Don't be greedy." He nuzzled her hair.

"I wonder you could breathe," she teased.

"I have others," he told her, "even more death-defying, electrifying, and diving even deeper."

"Then I shall have to wait." She climbed on top, framing them both with tumbles of golden hair, countering her words.

She felt his strength return—all tricks and lightness gone, and he was with her and in her as if for the first time…*Could she ever get enough?*

Chapter 10
Sir Dudley's Gambling Den, Cape Town

Later, Sary stealthily reached for her clothing, watching Tommy slumber the sleep of surfeited angels. Tommy was right; it *was* hard making oneself presentable in the tiny cabin. *Where are my shoes?*

She chose a gown buttoned down the front, and hiked up a single petticoat from the floor. She didn't realize it, but she had never looked lovelier, with flushed cheeks, crimson lips swollen, and eyes bright as if fevered.

She checked Jude, his flat little nose flaring; his sweet mouth pursed. Gently Sary eased the door open. It swung from her hand, banging in the hallway. She tensed. Tommy stirred, turning over, and Sary slipped away.

Chapter 11
Secrets and Denial

Tommy met her at the bottom of the gangplank, storm clouds brewing, brows drawn, eyes shooting black lightning.

"I needed air," Sary challenged before he could speak.

"Alone? At night? I find that hard—"

"Keep your voice down, sir! Don't question me. I'm not a child. It was stuffy. As are you! I went a bit farther…"

"Jude has more wits when it comes to common sense."

"I'm tired…" She tried to brush past.

He vainly searched the empty waterfront for answers. "I was concerned, you blasted woman!"

"I won't do it again." Sary lowered her gaze and demurely pressed her hands together.

The next night, Sary drank little; assuring Tommy's glass was perpetually filled, even though with cheap *plonk*. Jude played himself silly amid the sailors, clambering over every rigging the *Constanzia* owned, until finally he fell into the arms of a very weary Morpheus.

She hadn't time for games or truth. Sary swept down the gangplank without challenge this time, armed in the same drab gown, of brown muslin snatched off the missionaries' laundry line, one she vowed to return. *Soon.* Sary fancied she conjured up a church lady, which might explain an errand of mercy late at night, alone.

Sary slipped a small psalter into her reticule, a plain black leather one, as further armor.

If not tonight, the next, and the next. Until she ferreted out the duke and his infamous gambling establishment.

She had two more days before the *Constanzia* sailed. Surely, in that time…

The ship's watch, a lowly yeoman, haggled with a native. The girl saw Sary, dipped liquid eyes in secret message—*you are invisible*—and so Sary slipped from the safety of the good ship *Constanzia* into the dark.

The vast market, littered with bales, barrels, cranes, pulleys, and a clutter of stalls crowded about the wharf, was eerily quiet. Even haunted. She studied the vast dark square—nothing but a scuttling rat to stir its rubbish. Each innocent bale gleamed like a dead fish under the moon casting ghostly shadows. Cranes of the mechanical variety were crook-necked monstrosities, as if reaching across the plaza to pluck her up.

Skirting the maze of silent shapes, Sary looked back to mark the ship, as she had the night before. Even this short way, the forest of masts poking the night sky, bobbing in gentle tide, was bewildering. The *Constanzia*'s pinched figurehead with the cracked wooden face rocked forward. She'd easily spot it again.

Last night, Sary had asked discreetly of the ship's crew, who must suppose Sary an addicted gambler, trying to ferret out the location of the most notorious establishment in Cape Town.

"Gov's anti-gamblin'," one seaman grumbled. Cap was apparently against anything hinting of pleasure—the fines were daunting.

"On the side of the market," they all agreed, "right orf the square, but not so's you'd a know'd it iffen you ware ta see it."

Sary peered into the dark. Unfortunately, she hadn't asked which side. She'd go left.

What did you expect? Monaco's Grand Casino, glittering with Belle Époque elegance?

She scrutinized the ragged string of raffia shops, rattling dry bones in the slight breeze, all much the same in the dark except for pale light in living quarters behind.

"To the left, right at the edge." *Whatever that means.*

Sary checked behind her at a skittering, but it was only a palm leaf rustling across grit, and a sough of wind through banana palms.

She crossed by the primate cages. One ape studied her with intelligent yellow eyes. Rushing past, Sary peered up side paths, dreading the dark tangle of walkways leading deeper into the city, obscured by awnings where no lamps flickered.

Low talk and spurts of guttural laughter. Light flickering behind shutters. In the distance, her ear caught strange wailing. Sobs or cries. She dismissed them. Possibly an animal, or lovers, or an angry child. Nothing to do with her.

Sary looked across the plaza. Yes. The *Constanzia* still bobbed peacefully—no outcries of sailors searching.

She rushed past more shuttered stalls, another ten

minutes. She could no longer make out the ship. She heard footsteps and ducked between stalls. Two natives padded silently past, footsteps fading.

Perhaps the gambling establishment wasn't on the square but further in. Somehow, such an edifice should stick out, shouldn't it? Have *some* activity? Gamblers congregating as they came and went?

Okay, Perhaps famous, but nefarious and discreet.

Sary paced faster as she turned in farther from the wharf at the end of the north side of the open market, frantically peering down each offshoot for fear she might miss her goal. Outside of three mingy native bars she avoided—*nothing*. She dipped under a dry palm. Her hair snagged, releasing a heavy shining curtain. She couldn't see. "Drat!" Twisting her thick tresses back in a messy bun, Sary checked her light slippers—one sole had come loose and was flapping. A *fine sight to impress anyone.* She was poised to turn back when she detected a glow accompanied by a faint clink and murmur where the square cornered.

"I'll go that far," Sary muttered.

Chapter 12
Den of Iniquity

Two-story. Wood. Corrugated iron. Not grand, but Sary knew this was the place. Shuttered windows even in topical heat. Unprepossessing, but through a cracked shutter on an upper floor she saw a hand, a card flying across an unseen table. She heard curses, laughter, the *clat-clat* of chips.

She slipped unnoticed into the bar below. Gripping the prayer book as cover, she looked for a way up, after scanning the room. No one resembled a king pin—a Delacorte. Subconsciously, she recalled Julian Delacorte's chilling regal presence in his own Big Bear saloon.

Electric sconces lit the room. The bar was Belle Époque elegance, if a bit tarnished. The men, a shabby bunch—bush hats, short pants on scarred, snake-bitten legs—were brothers to Big Bear panners she knew so well, with their rough canvas breeches or Levi's, hobnail boots, woolen coats, and all manner of headgear from bearskins to earflaps. Spiritual kinsmen.

In addition, the usual dandies, here in fine tropical suits in place of the heavy worsteds and silk vests of Big Bear.

Now, how to find the so-called duke. He has to be here. Oh? Why is that? Thousands of leagues across a sea on the strength of a shyster?

Her female presence was still undetected, as her drab dress faded into varnished wood walls. Two women, one the shade of nutmeg, the other mellow as a ripe peach, toyed with companions at the far end. Sary was a brown ghost. No one gave her a first glance.

At the top of the stairs, her image stared back in a smoky mirror. *Who was that woman with the yellow tinge?* No. That was the mirror. Her face was a disembodied oval, ethereal as a madonna, floating in a smog of smoke.

She looked back down. No one noticed her at the top in the dark. She could still leave.

A gallery ran four-square around the room below. The door to the room glimpsed from the street lay two paces to her right. Her hand was on the latch when, once more, her hair fell from the loose bun, tumbling about Sary's face. *So much for the missionary look.*

Too late. She had opened the door.

A loud clatter of chips erupted. Deeply concentrating men frowned at cards. Pungent cigars and stale rum. The only sound was the rustle of money and *snick-snick* of cards and chips.

The entire scheme seemed built of moonbeams. Sary hoped she was not dropping a bucket into an empty well.

A player leaned over green baize, raking chips—and she saw him, dressed in the quaint, courtly garb of twenty years ago as if the man had fled in the ducal clothes on his back and loathed relinquishing them.

Part pirate, too—red bandana knotted around a wattled neck. It wasn't the huge signet ring but his manner, sitting like a lord to the manor born, surveying his dukedom with bemusement. The duke held a lace handkerchief against his nose as he avidly hawked the players.

Lord Dudley.

Breathing deeply, Sary threaded across the room as it became a silent tableau in waves: players turned, hands stilled with chips and cards, all eyes on her, confounded by the female unadorned by paint or jewels.

The missionary lady had been at least a size smaller. Sary's high, full breasts threatened to break the hooks and eyes of the sparrow-drab cotton dress the shade of dust. The disheveled, just-out-of-bed hair contrasted greatly. As one, the men imagined her long legs beneath the dun skirts.

Sary noted their confusion, regretting her camouflage. She should have worn willow-green satin, lowcut, her most flattering color.

Sary's lips burst with amusement, her eyes sparkling emerald glints.

The chase is on.

Shaking her head in gleeful abandonment, ringlets cascading in haphazard style over her front and down her back, Sary fixed on Lord Dudley until she stood before him, hands prim in front, unconscious she yet held the prayer book.

His ducal tutelage lent him a feigned ennui; perhaps he *had* seen it all. He cocked his head and grated, "You are not as you portray, madam. Why the disguise?"

"Sir—"

He waved away her answer as too wearisome to bother. "If you are a psalm-singing Sally, I want none of it. Left the C of E behind with my good name." A hint of smile beneath a thin nose. Sary saw vestiges of a handsome man, though gray, with bloodshot eyes, ascetic face, a lion's mane of silver hair that could do with a wash.

"I merely hoped for safe passage." Sary dipped her eyes demurely, indicating the book and her drab gown.

She shook her hair again, sending waves of lavender, jasmine and musk through the air, with a slow smile that promised all and nothing.

He sat back. "You're from the colonies. Moreover, nothing would give you safe passage through this company, I fear, looking as you do. You must have a better shield than a prayer book, my delicious American cousin."

"Indeed. Africa by way of England and places too many now to relate. I have business, nevertheless. I haven't much time." Her eyes spoke unfathomable regret.

"I don't take long," he leered, but Sary saw he was vaguely alarmed. *What else had he fled*? The room stilled.

"Let us retire. A female of your evident good character will put my disreputable reputation in shambles. Nevertheless..." He rose, waving to a door with iron locks and braces.

"Indeed." Sary sucked deep. "'Tis best to conduct business in private." *Is that door as difficult to leave as to enter?*

"Oh? Do we have commerce?" He jerked his head, giving roguish glances at his audience. "Let us retire soonest, then."

Chapter 13
Duke's Sanctum Sanctorum

The room was austere, as opposed to the tatty elegance below, with crudely painted oils of titled nobility, grimy chandeliers—half the crystals missing as if used for targets—and knots of frayed armchairs imitating a gentlemen's club.

Here were slatted windows. A scarred desk. One velvet wingchair, spotted and worn, once bottle green, with a pair of shabby bed slippers kicked aside. A chandelier with yellowed tallows hung over a costly but threadbare Persian carpet.

"Well?" He peeled a large green fruit. He offered her none.

"I address Sir Dudley?"

"You have him," he said, concealing his wistful smile.

"And I have a dirty scrap of what I believe is a map…"

His face smoothed to blankness, eyes cold and inward.

A map indeed. The man in England was a cheat. Taunting her. A last con. All a delicious game. And, this Sir Dudley of Nothing and Nowhere, is no better. Sary was angrier with herself than with the erstwhile duke.

"Sit, madam."

Acutely conscious of how long she tarried, Sary

saw the ship leaving without her.

Which is silly. Wasn't it?

"Sir. I haven't time for pleasantries."

"Might be a good thing. Odd happenings here. Governor keeping it all close to his vest," he said, enigmatic.

Whatever. It didn't concern her.

"Let's have a look." He extended his palm.

She did not wish to surrender the map, but slowly she unrolled the stiff leather.

While the clock ticked, Sir Dudley took a magnifying glass and a cut-glass carafe. Sary noted the crest indicating former glory and a huge nick showing his downfall.

He poured whiskey, nodding to Sary as if divining her weakness.

"I don't mind." She forced herself not to toss it back like a back-street doxie. The duke, or earl, whatever he was, settled in his worn chair as if for a cozy chat.

"I see." He checked the filthy hide with his glass. "You've met my old *confrère*. He still alive? Be keen as mustard to hear that particular tale."

Sary stared. She felt sweat trickle on her forehead. She clenched her fists. *Get on with it!*

He flipped his hand with the huge signet ring at the scrap.

"Oh, it's genuine all right. A map not made up for the, ah—gullible." He gave her a smirk.

Therefore, it is real.

"Though near useless. Floating around for years, man to man, like a used-up harlot."

"But surely—"

"I fear my old friend is a sublime hoaxer, an *artiste*."

He watched her over the rim. "I wonder if his magic will be as potent when he loses his looks? Yet"—he contemplated his glass—"he always managed to put the saddle on the right horse, or someone else's, and gallop off safely. The amusing part is whether he realizes or not that *this*"—he indicated the scrap— "wasn't a swindle. The map's real, as I recall. Be deuced if I remember details on how the rascal cabbaged on to it."

"He cleaned his boots," Sary said dryly, beginning to enjoy herself, prompted by the whiskey.

"You chased the fox up the right tree there. My friend wiped his boots and managed to keep it."

The duke looked into the past, then glanced up as though surprised to see her. "Why are you here?"

"I would buy the other half of this map or obtain information on a certain trader, or any information you might offer. A folly of mine."

"Of course it is," he mocked. "I see you wish to play 'The Great White Huntress.' "

Yes, that was exactly it. "My time is unhappily over, Sir Dudley. If you…?" She reached for the map.

He ignored her.

"If the other section exists, or ever did, I obtained this bit in Port Elizabeth. I had pity on a wretch down to his knickers in debt, losing pot after pot. He threw in this"—he indicated the leather scrap—"on his last ante, along with a knackered horse. Importer of tea, I believe," he finished vaguely.

That part matched.

"So this tea-swilling gambler lost?"

"No, by jingo! Won the entire lot and prudently left with his winnings. Not very sporting. He left the map as a jest. He was drunk, of course. I told him, when he sobered, I had no idea where it got to."

He ruminated. "No. Port Elizabeth, if I were a betting man. Might ferret him out of some rum pot."

"Port Elizabeth." *There's no money to go further.* "Does he have a name?"

"Damn me. Cudgeling my brain this whole time. Called him? Oh, what was it? '*Groot!*' Kept mumbling something, something—'*sweet little Kay,*' over and over, whoever *she* was."

"Groot? Dutch?"

"Oh, 'tis. Real name's not 'Groot.' He's just very fat." The duke barreled his arms. "Can't miss him."

She reached again. His hand was close. She could see the map vanishing up his sleeve.

He trapped her hand, murmuring seductively, "You must know some tidbit, to come all this way."

No, I don't!

"Or perhaps, simply, to see me?"

He pursed his lips, moist, red as a plum, slowly raising bloodshot eyes with naked lust under the heavy folds. She saw they matched the veins in his nose. Odd she had deemed him handsome, if worn, when she first entered. He scrabbled for her hand.

"Sir." She tried offense. "You astound me—"

"I doubt it. You hide that delicious frame behind plain brown cotton armor. Do you have other protection? Most of you do."

He raised her hand to his lips.

She smelt whiskey and poor hygiene. "What? Do what?"

"Are you a—*maiden*?" He rushed. "Perhaps you need a protector?"

The words tumbled as he fumbled her hand eagerly, turning her wrist, running his mouth along it as she awkwardly struggled, bent over as she was with his head close to hers.

Still imprisoning her wrist, the duke rounded the desk. "What do you pay for such information? Some token? I bolted the door. No one need hear unless you scream overmuch in your delight over my skills and gifted physique. I am indeed a rapier. I thrust fast and hard, madam." His face was hard and determined.

Sary stifled giggles. Now was not the time to make fun of outdated ploys.

"Here, let me relieve you of that drab protection and taste your delicious sweetmeats."

Sary didn't laugh. He could do harm. He could warn the fat man.

He grabbed her waist, dragging her to him. Sary felt his full length as he sculpted his hand across her bottom and up her spine, pressing wet lips on Sary's neck, murmuring deep in her shoulder and working down.

"Your flesh is marzipan and just as honeyed, I wager." With his other hand, he ripped the first two hooks and eyes, pressing his mouth deeper into the cleft of her two soft mounds.

Sary gagged, bending backward. She reached blindly, touching the ragged edges of the decanter and swinging it wildly overhead, checked the swing, felt the connecting *bonk*, and heard the startled cry. He fell back, eyes bulging.

"You bawd!" he howled, coming after her, blood

running into his bushy brows.

Sary wielded the hefty bottle, cruel with edges, in front of her.

He eyed her warily.

Sick in her heart, Sary heard the echo of that connection of bottle to head, when she had accidently hit Tommy, so long ago in that cheap boarding room.

"Oh, go on," he snarled, hurling the key. "Get out!" He was embarrassed, it seemed.

She knelt, never taking her eyes off him, twisted the key, and fled, leaving him humiliated and with a cut above his eye as Sary blazed through the card players, hair streaming and with his furious eyes burning holes in her back.

"You may need more friends than you appreciate, madam!" the duke hurled from the doorway.

How prophetic that was, she had no reason to doubt.

Chapter 14
Comeuppance

Tommy's eyes were burning coals, turning explanations to cinders.

Sary had awakened that morn, stretched and yawned, unaccountably at ease. Still cool for Africa. The sun hadn't beaten them all into melted butter—and then she recalled the night.

Tommy's berth was empty. He had taken Jude for breakfast. She could avoid him for the while.

Last night she had slipped into the room, wanting nothing more than healing sleep, balled the torn dress, and tossed it out the porthole. Naked, Sary crept into the bottom berth as grateful as a skiff sailing into safe harbor after a storm.

Her last thought—she knew where to go next. Come what may, she'd find a way to Port Elizabeth.

As it turned out, fate, yet none that Sary would wish on her worst enemy, made that possible.

****

Two missionary ladies said silent grace, extremely grateful to stay on board with free lodgings and sustenance. They did not wonder at their providence, or why the captain kept them there. The business man shoveled porridge in without question.

Sary entered with a smiling mask. Surely Tommy would not put up a fuss here. One of the ladies was speaking softly to a burbling Jude.

She touched Tommy's shoulder, and he flinched. The missionary lady took interest.

"Tommy?"

"We have nothing to say"—Tommy wiped his lips—"*here.*"

"Tommy, I just want to…"

Tommy whispered, "I neither know nor care how you spent your evening, *madam.*"

He left.

Sary spooned tasteless oatmeal, mechanically answering Jude and desperately thinking of a way to break down the fortress.

Chapter 15
Confessional

Tommy grasped Sary with a murderous look the instant she entered their cabin.

"Tommy! Let go."

He snarled in her ear, "A man in passion rides a crazed horse, Sarabande…I missed you last night!"

His hot breath was on her cheek, brutal kisses on her throat, her breasts—then he lifted her to the top bunk, raising her skirts.

"Is he better than me?"

His eyes held hate and hunger. "When we quarrel, a fire burns till only you can douse it. Why do I need you so? I despise you. You are an effing Salome—a Delilah cutting my hair and sapping my strength."

As usual, he was dramatic. "Tommy, don't be absurd." Nevertheless, she shivered. Tommy had taught her many new beguilements, and she loved it.

"Where's Jude?" he asked, muffled beneath her skirts, lifting his head, his voice all husky.

Do get on with it, Tommy. I can't wait. "The missionary lady has him. He's safe."

He dived back.

"But is the missionary lady safe?" She giggled.

"Don't change the subject," he advised, lifting her skirts again. "Now where was I?"

"Seducing me." Sary gasped with pleasure.

"That's where he should stay, knowing the kind of mother—"

In answer, she clenched his curls, bending him to his task.

Later, they held each other's gaze in a standoff. A small crinkle erupted at the ends of Tommy's beautiful mouth.

Sary bit back a grin.

She was safe for a while.

Chapter 16
Afterglow

Tommy and Sary sprawled on the bottom bunk with heat melting off their bodies after sampling most of the cabin—including the bulkhead and floor—satiated, yet their bodies still throbbed till blood ebbed at a more sedate pace.

Just in time, too. And before Tommy could question her.

"Mummy!" A loud bang, followed by small boots vigorously kicking the door. Jude barged in. "'Ook what I made you!"

Excitedly Jude clambered onto the berth, shoving Sary a crumbling scone lumpy with raisins. "I made it for you! Tommy, you have some too."

Sary studied the gray, uneven thing. "It's lovely, Jude. Looks delicious!" She took a bite. "Let's give Tommy the rest. He's bigger than Mummy."

Tommy looked askance at the crumbling scone. "Already had my sweets," he murmured with a wicked glint.

"Okay." Jude crammed half the scone in his mouth, then, chastened, said, "Sorry, Mummy," and fed the rest to Sary in small crumbs she gamely nibbled.

"Mmmmm." At that moment, Sary would trade all her tomorrows for more of the same with Tommy and Jude.

Chapter 17
Arctic Winds

After ardor cooled, there was yet frost in the air as Tommy followed her about with his black, questioning eyes.

Sary checked Jude in his hammock. He was fretful. A clammy wind blew in with choppy seas; she couldn't blame his hot forehead on heat. At last, he dozed.

She whirled. Her skin felt as tight as her nerves.

"All right, Tommy. Why can't you trust me? Now you will get the entire scandal!" Sary's fists clenched to keep from trembling.

Tommy, back against the bulkhead, pulled her to the looking glass, under the whale oil lamp. He studied her.

"I want to see your lies."

Tommy slowly released her, looking at twin reflections in place of each other. She caught her face—eyes as green and stormy as Tommy's were black as the seas. Her mouth was dry as a ship's biscuit.

Did she detect the first attenuation of flesh? A shade under her eyes? *How much longer will Tommy love me, if he does now? Still, he should trust me! Believe in me.* She felt both angry and contrite.

"You were going to come clean, I believe." Tommy interrupted her thoughts.

Her looking-glass reflection spoke.

Chapter 18
Shortfall

"I lost"—she swallowed—"some of it."
Bad beginning. Be strong.
"Whatever did you misplace?" Tommy's brows were so lowered she could scarcely see his eyes. His beautiful mouth was white from compression.
"I lost it, Tommy. The money. Our money." Sary watched him with steely challenge.
"Lost? What do you mean? It's in your—banks. Scattered all over the bloody place." His face took on a little-boy bewilderment.
Oh, Tommy!
Truth, Tommy never questioned her hard-fought-and-won wealth from the gold mine, or her desperate escape from the ruthless men of Big Bear, despite her scars and bullet wounds. He never let it show he was discomfited by the inequality of their circumstances. A realist yet, he never expected or asked for anything. It did not mean he had not become used to their magnificent new life.
"But...?" He shook his head. "You don't—*gamble*."
"Apparently I do."
Tommy assessed her with a chill glint.
She spun, despite her chin clenched in his hand. A pale and delicate hand from Tommy's legacy of lusty

Spanish sailors plying Ireland's coast. Yet a hand that could manhandle props and pry horses from many a mud wallow.

"What are you on about? *All?*" His gaze turned onyx hard.

Green flint sparked in turn. "Does wealth mean so much, despite your protest? Is that what I am? A fat wallet?" Her eyes stung. Her mouth trembled. She jerked her chin free.

"Sary! Unfair." His hurt cut worse than a knife.

"No. Not all.*"*

"Then what?"

*"*Yet—I feel ever so foolish," she tried.

" 'Ever so.' And where did you pick up that? Drop the simpering milkmaid act."

"I feel like a whiskey."

He poured.

"Have one with me?"

"Will I need it?"

"Yes."

She tossed the drink back and clasped her hands in front so they didn't shake. "Tommy?" she began. "Do you recall? The ball?"

"Which one?" He snorted.

"The one with all the ugly masks. Men with beaks, women like harpies, Medusas, witches, Cleopatra, Josephine, Roman matrons—for heaven's sake! What does it matter?"

"You never looked lovelier than in that pink satin mask matching your gown. You put the harpies to shame. I wanted to have you without delay," he reminisced. "Green eyes simmering behind that pink…"

"Peach," she said automatically, waving it away.

"Damn it, Sary. Have you taken to dice? Whiling your way with whist? Isn't our *life* a game of chance?"

"The, ah—gentleman," she said, with a moue of distaste. *Incredibly handsome in the light of the candelabras...*

"Go on." Grim.

"In the ridiculous kilt? I found later it was counterfeit, as was he." She tried rueful. "Wasn't Scottish at all." As if she and Tommy hadn't worn costumes far gaudier on the road.

"Sarabande."

She glanced anywhere but at him, as if an incident might occur—the ship capsize, or…

"We danced. Recall? He asked me to dance, and you said…"

"You enthrall me with your storytelling. Do continue."

How possessively and proudly Tommy had watched her that fateful evening. Easily the most striking man, with his simple black velvet mask and raven hair, as the room's other dashing man led her off with swaying kilts.

Usually Sary saw through men more in love with their own looking glass than with the reflections of fifteen-year-old debutantes seeking suitable mates.

"Could've used him as alternate lead. Is that what he was? An alternate?"

Sary reached for the whiskey.

"Get on with your salacious tale. What *did* this God's grace of a male *do?* Force your knickers down?" His eyes were chips of black ice.

"I despise that kind of talk."

For her sins, the wretch *had* almost "forced her knickers down."

Sary looked deep in the mirror, remembering the rush to the maze—other lovers' distant giggles lending to the illicit thrill. She'd felt young as she never had—wed at sixteen after courtship by Jonathon, her sweet inexperienced husband, all exciting because of his need and her innocence.

At the ball, breathless from flute after flute of champagne, she wanted this gorgeous, exotic man to take her. Bubbling with champagne fizz, her willpower was as fragile as the glass flute she'd held, with the effervescence of novelty rushing to her head.

The masked man in kilts thrust her into the maze of yews, each hanging on to the other, darting inaccurate kisses as they staggered along, he helping her unsnag her gown, she running ahead, hiding in clipped shrubbery.

Oooph! Mortifying!

And then he hauled her to the ground in an alcove with a statue of Pan.

Just as she melted and would have given herself there in the damp moss beside the salacious statue—clammy, scratched by yews, looked down upon by a ridiculous statue and the self-satisfied smirk in the kilted man's eye as he was about to complete his conquest—she saw she was a pawn—a notch, as the men back in Big Bear were fond of saying, in his belt.

Sary's face clouded with remembrance.

Sary had wanted to have it out with the kilted man and drown his assumptions. In daylight, without the mask, he was stuffy as a men's smoking lounge, saying he regretted his importunity of the night before.

To show contrition, he would let her in on a fortuitous deal he'd overheard. He knew an interesting chap who was to be at the Hunt Ball next week; she must meet him.

But what she told Tommy was: "I simply wanted to fill the well again." She knew that if simple was embodied in a country priest, she was the Pope.

"The well. And this leads where?" Tommy had that dangerous look again.

"He told me 'to keep my pretty ears sharp'—something about railroads and diamond mines…famous diamond mines." Sary looked in the mirror, seeing on her face how irresponsible that sounded.

"Diamond mines?" Tommy spoke as if she had said, "a crate full of cats."

Sary thought back. How to explain what had seemed so prudent…so clever…

Chapter 19
The Conman's Ball

Sary had been the epicenter as the throng intuited she was an exotic—a rustic—the divertissement of the moment. A sop to ennui for the glitterati, the demimonde, the rarified strata of aristocracy at the glut of fetes, affairs, masques, and balls in which Sary reveled. At first.

Initially dazzled, Sary found no gristle of gossip escaped being munched upon until sucked dry of what minor juices it may have held.

Yes, they flattered, stared, and also whispered.

"What do they expect—a coonskin cap, blunderbuss, and petticoats made of gunny sacks?" Sary grumped with Tommy alone in their host's sumptuous rooms. She had smudged her eyes with candle soot, dusted her face with a powder made of pearls, and carmined her lips and cheeks with a paste of beets and cream. Even she thought she looked beautiful that evening.

Yet as the shoals of society flowed past seeking new fish to fry, Sary was strangely alone that fatal night at the Hunt Ball.

She snatched another stem of champagne, aware she shouldn't—loath to ask where the water closet might be. She understood the owner was proud of this modern invention, rumored to be a sight of gilded perfection. Perhaps she might follow some ladies, champagne flute in hand.

Such was her mission when the word—the *two* galvanic words—speared her.

"Railroads" and "diamonds."

Just the second word was enough, sparkling, clear cut, and hard as the stuff itself. She spun to find the author.

There he was in his own epicenter, smoking on the terrace with the men. The man owned flaming hair the color of autumn leaves just turning to wine.

"You can't miss him," her kilted admirer had told her. "A real carrot top."

Sary fanned herself to the far edge of the balustrade as if to cool from the dance. She turned idly, catching a breeze or sniffing a rose. *Or whatever one does alone on a terrace.*

The tall man looked over the crush of men, eyeing her with bemusement. Moreover, with invitation—what invitation she later discovered to her regret.

"Yes, my dear fellow," she overheard. "I have a *soupçon* of shares left—embarrassments, really, not even a full morsel to offer for my nearest and dearest. Especially my nearest and dearest." He grinned. "I already sold the lion's share."

"They are enemies," one roared. "Adversaries."

"Rivals!"

"Nemeses!"

The gentlemen, smoking and red-faced from a surfeit of food and more courses of wine than Sary could bathe in, fought for ascendancy, each clamoring for a larger slice of the cake.

"Gordon! Have heart!" one called.

"Oh, surely. Why tell us of this fine venture if you don't wish us to share in your good fortune?"

The red-haired man shrugged, charmingly embarrassed. "The fox has been treed!" He laughed. "I do have a few choice shares left. Saving them, gentlemen, because frankly, I wish *a premium*. I'll chat with you all later, individually."

She saw them licking lips as if spying the last slice of chocolate cake and eyeing each other for fear each one held a longer fork.

From the corner of her eye, Sary watched the redhead pat shoulders and shake hands until they reluctantly drifted off. Then he was alone.

She thought he'd approach.

He swept past without a care.

Dash it! I'll have to speak.

"Sir?" Sary asked, sprightly. He studied her, blank-faced.

"Diamonds," she said prettily as any blushing debutante. "A magic open-sesame for any conversation."

She fanned and flirted, watching with what she hoped was vacuous interest copied from several ladies—*Oh, me, oh, my. I do not own a single brain in my poor silly head. I just borrow them from all you brilliant cunning men.*

His gaze had swept her discreetly.

Sary looked miserably in the mirror at Tommy, recalling how she had shrugged enchantingly.

"I couldn't fail to…" She had rapped the red-haired man lightly with her fan.

He cut her off. "Do I know you? I fear this would be of little interest…" *To such as you* was the unspoken

71

phrase.

She stared him down, then dipped her lashes and looked off, pouting.

"Oh! It's railways, my dear silly girl!" He turned, exasperated. She just caught the tail end of a smile. *Silly!*

"I, as it happens, do know—railroads, that is." *Yes, I rode one from Big Bear to San Francisco, another lifetime ago.*

"Perhaps an engineer? Mayhap you shoveled coal. Or you mined coal." He gave her an amused flick.

Sary froze. *Too close to home.* "Don't turn from me!" She bit her lip. "I mean, I could so awfully learn from you, sir, and it seems since my twenty-first birthday I have such *oodles* of money…"

He swiveled clockwise in a complete circle with genuine emotion—*surprise—avarice*?

"I may have only been a passenger, but I do have some knowledge of how essential railroads are," she gushed and dipped her lashes again. *Ooph! Had she really done that?*

The ginger-haired man flicked his barely lit cigar into rhododendron bushes and studied her. "Don't know why I bother." He lit another. "Very well. Might be amusing." He perched on the balustrade. "Africa. You do know of a continent named Africa—rather huge—can't miss it."

She waited, making her eyes round. "Yes! Isn't that where that explorer, Stanley, and what was his name—Livingston? And of course, Sir Burton…"

"Yes, well, you see, my *entities*—who shall remain nameless—let's say wish to build a railway to the Kimberley Diamond Mine, cross country, that is.

Nothing to do with you."

"What if I wish to buy in?" *Dumb, dumb*!

"Buy—in." He bit the words as if they were unsavory tidbits of unknown origin. "Each share is the piddling sum of fifty thousand pounds." He watched her and blew a perfect smoke ring.

"Oh! Is that all!" Sary put her finger on her chin as if thinking hard and very unused to it. *Arrogant beast. She'd show him*.

"I wish..." She barely hesitated. "Ten of those shares," she blurted, clapping delightedly like a silly schoolgirl. She would have danced up and down if she'd not thought it would be excessive.

She thought she saw him blink, his mouth drop. *Good*. The cigar dangled, but his face smoothed to the same mask.

"How tedious. You did hear me mention, I dare say, I have precious few certificates left. You were listening—oh, so covertly. And I did mention fifty *thousand*—not shillings but *pounds*—sterling."

"How else would I know, unless I listened? And shillings or pounds makes little difference. Since my financial advisor passed on, I don't know what to do with—all my inheritance. It would be such a relief to place it somewhere safe."

Sary bridled, blushed, and checked the inside of her fan, which was green, with cavorting violets. She pondered what language of flowers or fans she conveyed to the insufferable gentleman lounging against the balustrade.

"Wealthy pitchers have pretty little ears." He cocked his head. "You are a lovely thing. A bit rough-cut. Dreadful gown. Yet you have the bonds, I do vow.

73

You *are* from the wilds of California. I heard the scuttlebutt."

"I am surprised you risk my proximity." She could have stopped the charade then before it was too late. Before ignominy and ruin.

He shrugged. "Hang on!"

And, fatally, Sary halted on her way back to the dance floor.

"It'll set old MacComber back on his heels. Crafty, greedy, old reprobate might even have a stroke. Now, there's an idea." And the red-haired man held out a soft hand. "Done." He stuck out the careless hand before she could react, dragging hers into his, and as her fingers hesitantly touched, he shook it.

And just like that, her doom was sealed.

He even bent and whispered, "If you venture to my room tonight—I have all the necessary papers there—I might even have a small *cadeau*...a secret."

He made his hands into stars, like a magician, opening his eyes wide as if she were a child. "Unless you don't have the wherewithal?"

What have I done? Five hundred thousand pounds! Because of pride? "I will be there."

"Don't tell a soul. There would be a terrible rush on me."

Like that, he was gone.

****

Now, in their cabin, Sary drank to stall. *How much should I reveal?* "And that was the beginning, Tommy," she finally said.

"And you purchased these—shares? How much? All of it?"

"No," she mumbled.

He scratched his head. "I suppose now I understand this decrepit ship—this *Constanzia* with its third-rate captain, but why—"

"Africa?" Sary continued her story.

A few hours later in the man's room…a tad more sober. "I can't stay," Sary had told the handsome fox-haired con artist. "I trust all is ready." She half hoped it wasn't.

The con spread rich, cream-colored papers with intricate green flourishes.

She tentatively riffled her reticule, withdrawing a stiff folded paper with her signature.

He pinched half-moon glasses to his nose, read her promissory note, and with great flourish signed an impressive stack of papers: thick creamy vellum full of gold leaf, spidery green-and-red scroll work, hand calligraphy, and each with an impressive, gold-embossed seal.

"Shall I register it with the consortium? On the other hand, would you rather? Yet I am going in the morning. You do have that as warranty."

He nodded to the imposing deed.

"Of course." And she actually smiled at the snake, sensing a giddy gladness as she held the thick, rich, embellished vellum.

Ten shares of a whole railroad. Won't Tommy be amazed! After all, if we are not afraid, it is not worth doing.

He bowed. "My dear, since we are now official business partners, out of propriety I'll forego that kiss of amity with promises of further delights"—the wretch rounded the desk and pressed his body close, bussing her in the French fashion—"of the flesh," he whispered in her ear.

Dimples flashed as he flirted beneath long sandy lashes. That was when she knew. Every inch of her wanted to snatch the promissory note back. Her hands curled.

At her scrutiny, he turned serious, thrusting fingers through his fox-red hair. "Oh, pray, don't mind me, closeted with stuffy bankers and odious lawyers the livelong day, and when I beheld you…? Forgive my impertinence." His eyes crinkled. "I suppose that is all. We are done here, madam, except when those dividends start rolling in." With that he busied himself at his desk.

At the door, Sary glanced with regret, hoping he'd ask her to linger. Wondering even then if his look of fervent desire was over the acquisition of money— preferably not his own. She halted, biting her lip, and slowly returned.

"You did say—a *cadeau*?"

She stood hesitant.

What a flaming fool I must seem. Perhaps he supposes I returned for—that.

He blinked as if wondering who Sary was. She felt her face flame, undoubtedly red as her gown.

"Oh, yes. That!" he said with a hint of irritation. Rummaging his desk, he dragged out a stiff, ragged roll of hide tied in dirty string.

"An intriguing scrap, actually. Goatskin, I believe." He sniffed it, tossed it across. "Foul thing. Written in *blood*, I venture." He rubbed his fingers with distaste, checking her with a cocked eyebrow. "Good to get rid of it."

She stared back, stoic.

"Ah, well. It seemed there was this *mission* or

monastery," he said as if it was a brothel or an opium den, "close to the Kimberley mines, for donkey's years. Dutch, I believe, or Portuguese." He waved a negligent hand. "Portuguese are more likely martyrs to the faith."

Sary sank unbidden into a brocade chair.

"This map, so the bush-telegraph whispered, was scribbled by some bedighted monk, or other do-gooder making natives wear corsets or pantaloons and sing psalms in Swahili or bongo-bongo—or whatever nonsense gabble in which they communicate." He thought a moment. "They burnt the mission down—at least that's the tale."

"Continue, please."

"This trader—how he got it is anyone's guess— lost it in, what else, a game of chance. Only trouble, it isn't whole. The other half he kept for *further* wagers. He died, or disappeared, and now only God knows how old Sir Dudley obtained *this*."

"Sir Dudley?"

He flapped the skin. Large as a man's handkerchief, vaguely diagonal.

"Dudley owned a shipping fleet. The rogue tossed it to me one night in the Savoy Club when I'd tracked in mud..." He shrugged.

"I cleaned my boots with it, sticking this thing in my pocket. Later, we had a fine cognac and forgot all about it. Yours now."

He nodded over his desk. "I pass it into your keeping." And laughed.

With mock ceremony, the con passed the filthy, stained, browning vellum to Sary's waiting hands.

Sary sniffed the pong of opium.

His eyes were bloodshot, pupils down to a fine dot.

An elaborate Chinese meerschaum lay carelessly under piles of hastily laid papers.

She wondered if he'd even recall he gave her the map. In that, she was wrong. The map, noisome as it was, held an odd aura, like a talisman.

"And this Lord Dudley?" Sary probed.

"Only *Sir* Dudley. Some scandal involving a lady, or could've been a lad masquerading as a lady—old Dudley wasn't particular. He hightailed it, forming a silent partnership in the most nefarious gambling den in Cape Town, right under Good Queen Vic's—*oops,* our Good King *Edward's* District Commissioner's very nose." He chuckled. "Ah, yes. Old Dudley. Wonder if he's still kicking, the old goat. I heard he eliminated his rivals. Conned, fleeced, bought out, who knows?"

He spoke with admiration.

"This *trader*, then, did he have a name?"

"Something—something. No—lost it. Had a tea export business, or was it teak? My, you are interested. You don't let a thing go, do you? S'pose all women are susceptible when it comes to hidden treasure. However, you wouldn't wish to venture there."

Oh, no?

He stubbed a cigar. "Not a single bonnet shop in sight."

Unconsciously she pressed her stiff arm close. "Perhaps I'll find out."

The man yawned deeply and cast longing looks at the hidden opium pipe. Best leave with the scrap before he recalled it, she thought at the time. As she left, his handsome face was sideways on the desk. He was snoring.

Chapter 20
Doom & Disclosure

Sary stopped pacing. She hadn't told Tommy everything. She was picking and choosing. Now the thorny part. Tommy looked at her as if he had never seen her before.

The next dawn, Sary had awakened to foreboding.

The sky was the shade of the granite statues littering wet gardens outside her window. English rain slashed sideways. Inchoate clamor rattled the bones of the great mansion in which they "fortnighted," manifested by distant wails and curses echoing throughout.

Sound bouncing off marble walls and floors made it hard. A whisper was heard from the servant's quarters, while chat in the music salon was silenced by a pianoforte.

Sary scrambled from downy quilts, not donning a morning coat but riffling closets—no doubt her maid would be scandalized—buttoning a barely suitable uncomplicated dress.

Quickly she scooped abundant hair, winding it in an intricate-looking but simple series of French rolls. Let them wonder.

She bit her lips, added a slash of carmine, a slap dash of pearl powder, splash of antimony for the eyes, and she was girded for whatever calamity lay outside.

In English fashion, not to dismay her hostess's propriety, they did not share a bed. At least not all night. So as not to scandalize his valet, Tommy had returned feeling "feckin' foolish" to his room before daybreak.

She was happy for once not to have Tommy rolling over, all drowsy and beautiful with his tousled mop of crow-black curls and sleepy eyes, saying he loved her best, all soft and heated beneath the quilts. If he were there, they'd snuggle, burrow, and hide among pillows, tickle and tease and kiss and murmur gossip before the new dawn.

She could not say why, yet Sary fervently wished Tommy to not rouse early that morning and, God forbid, not Jude! with his demands for breakfast, his toy pony with the general riding lopsided off the saddle, a real puppy, and so on.

Easing out of her room, Sary peeked over the balustrade and down the many levels. It seemed from each some hysteria erupted.

As he listened to her tale, Tommy made a rolling gesture. *Go on.*

Sary said, "I wasn't concerned yet." She recalled she even smiled, denying her disquiet, thinking perhaps a guest had been caught with the kitchen help. *If so, it must be happening all over the house.*

Thunderous notes. A tray dropping. Something hurled. Glass, judging from the crash. Boots racing to the entrance.

Sary leant over the railing. She picked out the words "scoundrel" and "absconded."

Her heart lurched.

Alarm came from a suite down the hall, with sobs

and accusations. They'd waken Tommy! Already she sensed he must be kept in the dark until she identified the cause. It wasn't long.

A maidservant ran into her, eyes wide with the need to tell. Sary waved her close.

"Oh, madam!" The servant smacked her own mouth. "I daren't."

She'd get the truest tale from this slattern, as she finished the last buttons and slipped into shoes.

"Oh, *ma-dam*! The handsome gentlemun? He runned orf! Yes, ab—ab-sconded, he did! He took ever so much silver. An' all Duchess Marlborough's jew-ry! An' as much as he could carry from t'other gennulmens, sirs, and ladies, and—and even the Countess of York—"

Sary checked her jewel box. The gaudy pieces purchased when first arrived in England, then Paris, were still tossed on top.

Apparently, the wretch didn't bother with that. *He only wanted my fortune.*

The maid babbled on, seeing the story in her inner mind. Sary strove to concentrate.

"She's 'aving the vapors at the mo, but the countess vowed—oh, she's ever so het up—she'd set the dogs an 'ave their guts fer garters!"

Their? "Which gentleman? Be precise. What color hair?"

"Hair? Why, one uv um, sort of copper-warmin'-pan color."

Sary gripped her arms as if this fiasco were her fault. *The man who sold her the shares—red hair atop a towering frame, bright as a new copper.* The other man had straw-colored hair, the one who, she saw plainly now, had steered her.

The servant made to go. Sary grabbed the drab's shoulders, still clinging to a wisp of hope fragile as a poppy, praying the certificate was not a poppy-tissue of lies, and asked once more.

"Madam? The one with all the blarney," she whined.

Sary dropped her arms. So even this poor drab who could neither read nor write saw through his fairy tales. To mortify Sary further, the artless girl continued, breathless and giggly.

"When I 'ad me tussle wiv' him, I knowed I wasn't the fairest rose in the bush, li' genulmun sez...'e just wanted me bush!" She guffawed over her conquest.

"Still, he give me a foine toime." She looked away at Sary's stormy face. "Jes' wish he'd a nicked me outta this place too, along wi' the silver."

"Sounds as if he had a goodly portion of you already," Sary snapped waspish.

"Oh!" The maid wailed. "Beggin' your pardon. I'm all undone! I don't ken what I'm a-sayin' 'arf the toime."

"Or you were," Sary snarled, "undone. Let us hope it is not permanent, nine months down the road."

She halted lamely, patting the wretch's arm. Had not she been in the same position, no matter how it happened? The poor soul would be on the street without a penny and a babe to feed, if true.

"Wait," she demanded.

"Yes'm?" The girl sniffled. "Oh, don't tell no one."

"Not I." Sary pressed a fifty-pound note in her hands. *So I'm fifty pounds poorer. What is that to five hundred thousand?*

"If need be. Save it, now," she warned. "Do not show this to anyone. Trust no one."

Sary glanced over the rail. But the girl clung to her hand. "Don't ken why you are bein' so," she stumbled, "ben-i-fer-cent. Kin retire or even buy a shop, or…"

Sary sighed. "That's the general idea," she said kindly, considering the turmoil in her head. She must return to her one faint hope, shutting the door, leaving the girl still enthusing. "Far too costly a parchment to be fake. Of course it is real. I will catch him at breakfast."

Yet Sary knew, reading the parchment with fancy seals and engraved stamps she repeatedly smoothed her fingers over, that each embellishment was as worthless as paper one took to the water closet.

Sary skimmed the carpet to the dresser, lifted the lid, and held her breath. Yes, there it was. Unexpectedly lighthearted, she declared, "Not a figment." Sary lifted out the noisome map with rusty lines and squiggles. She made out a few words with the first niggle of renewed doubts, quickly quashing them.

She held the leather close.

"Oooph." Wrinkling her nose, Sary took the goatskin to tall windows, barely registering titled guests below gesticulating in irate huddles, summoning carriages, the ladies stiff-faced, occasionally touching throats at thought of a remembered choker or stroking an ear as though to find a lost dangle. Footmen and ladies' maids simmered with excitement.

Thank goodness I'm not one of them. Of course the certificates are real.

She held the leather to the light. It *had* been used to swipe mud, and some drink stained it, the eight-inch roughly triangular piece. She made out the magic word—*diamon-*.

A sharp knife had cut off the final "d."

She did not allow an *"and so?"* to creep in on sly cat feet, instead cramming the scrap to her bosom as if it were silk.

Her maid eventually arrived. Tommy poked his head in. "Tommy. I slept late. What is all the ruckus?"

He ruffled his black mane and sleepily kissed her. "Haven't a didgeridoo, love." Sinking into his new cockney slang.

"Didgeridoo? Clue?" He said to her clueless face. "No breakfasting in bed? Rather look forward to munching a morning crumpet, myself."

"And I fancied mingling. To see what the tempest is about."

She'd pull her own teeth before admitting unease.

Remaining titled guests cruised the sideboard as if it were laden with tidbits from an army's mess, stealing hopeful, morbidly interested glances at their host gracing the end, his face set in stone.

His countess had not joined them.

Sary reached for a boiled egg. She dropped it as they all jumped when the great man's fist hit the table. Hefty silver jounced—a peach rolled off. A servant upset a coffee urn.

"Damn him! No need you mincing about, all po' faced. I have been played, sirs and madams! Bamboozled! For all who bought into a spurious railroad—my apologies, but I say fie on a fool warned."

Sary sagged against the sideboard, but then she stiffened as if before a firing squad and set her face in pleasant curiosity as her host continued.

"I take responsibility for attracting that play-actor here, but I will have him hanged, drawn, and quartered if I catch *whoever* invited him." He subsided, muttering into kippers and kidneys.

Sary stared at her egg and piled on toast, grilled salmon, bacon, fresh oranges, blindly tossing on whatever she saw. She'd need the strength, though she could have been chewing a damask napkin.

The meal buzzed with whispers. Close heads, darting to see who nodded with fake sympathy, who had cream dripping from sly-cat faces, or who dared show their faces, and figuring who had already packed and stolen away chagrined.

Tommy joined Sary late. She smiled stiffly. She wanted to hear every scrap. He glanced up from eggs and kidneys. "Sary? Actors? Railroads? What's all this?"

She shrugged, painting a picture of "Oh, these eccentric titled inbreeds" on a face pale as cheese. "Who knows what tempest in a teaspoon?" She laughed lightly.

He waggled brows. "More like Shakespeare's *Tempest*, sweeting."

"He dropped so many names, surprised the ruddy floor didn't cave. In fact, not a soul clapped eyes on him before." This was said with supreme smugness, obviously not a victim.

"I must say, the scheme was tempting as a showgirl's bottom," Sary heard through an open door as they left. "Even servants below stairs put a few bob in."

Then, chuckles. "I was born in the morning, but not yesterday morning. Ha-ha-ha-hah."

Sary with her best "we are not amused" face, sailed

on. Tommy exclaimed, "Oh, that was good. I must place that bit in my latest play. Tempting as a showgirl's…"

Sary turned on him. "Oh! Do, but don't be awkward, Tommy!"

Tommy cocked his head. "I'm weary of that phrase, *sweeting!* We've stayed too long at this particular faire. All the elite's bad manners stick to you like hooves' glue."

Chapter 21
Confession

"So you see, Tommy, that is how it happened." She bit her lip to keep from saying, "It could happen to anyone." Sary held up a palm. "Don't. Just don't be nice."

Tommy was ominously quiet, hands folded on his head, back against the bulkhead. He spoke softly. "*All,* you said? All our money?"

"Yes, Tommy! I said that. Or near enough."

"How much is—near enough?"

"We have a few, as you say, a few bob. Enough for this trip and some extras. It was in a separate account," she added. *For Jude.*

"Perhaps he didn't…?"

"He cashed it. Must have ridden off in the night to the nearest bank. He and his—cohort. I must have been his last victim," she said bitterly.

He put his arms about her, while she clenched her jaw to hold back tears. "Sary. Love. We have enough."

"Don't say we *have enough*! That we have each other. I worked so hard!"

Tommy kissed the top of her head. "More than most poor souls."

Yes, at one time, I had plenty to eat, and the love of a strong man. Would that still satisfy me? I honestly don't know. Instead of being a farmer's wife, I live with an actor. I have borne a bastard child, killed a few men, and made a fortune…and lost it.

"Never. It can never be enough—now. Besides, we're not, as you say, exactly spoiled for choice."

Tommy looked cold and blank over her head.

His silence made her uneasy. "It's not riches. It's safety! It's never having to worry *ever* again."

But that wasn't the real reason.

She had a fever, not for wealth born in the dank pits of the gold mine but a ferocity to see, to do, to grasp the world in her arms and squeeze it dry.

Instead, she said, "Never having to darn my stockings when…when I can scarcely see the…"

"My heart bleeds for your poor fingers." Tommy narrowed his eyes. "You never lied before. Why now? There is a wicked wildness in you I never saw before. A recklessness!"

You didn't know me, then.

"*You* were the wandering *thespian.*" Sary twisted her face as if biting a sour plum. "Traipsing all over." It was said with the scathing tone as though meant for a murderer.

"A love of craft," Tommy protested.

"Craft, indeed. What bliss! Muddy roads and cheap taverns."

Tommy winced. "Where *we* met, I might add—a cheap tavern. Two of them, as I recall."

"I won't do that again!"

"*And* we weren't traipsing in brutal heat, with more promised in the heart of bloody Africa on the strength of a scrap of filthy goatskin with unintelligible hen scratches, if that's your desperate plan!"

Tommy yelled, paced, and made a mess of his hair.

"Sary, I could not write a *play* more inane. We'd be hooted offstage!"

They both stood, glaring, chests heaving, gathering their resources.

Sary's face crumpled; her mouth twitched. Then Tommy gave way, and they both hooted with laughter.

Sary sobered.

"Oh, Tommy. I am so—so sorry," she began. "Now, I must make it right. Don't you see? I would never be content if I didn't at least try."

Tommy held her as if she were an addled child, looking down at her with such condescending kindliness she wanted to kick or kiss him. Instead, she clenched her teeth, deciding it was useless to tell Tommy anything more. *He'll come around.*

"I'm certain there are hungry theatergoers starving for quality entertainment. Now forget about a fairytale map."

Sary smiled sweetly. "Yes, Tommy." *In a pig's eye.*

Sary stood before the mirror.

Green eyes assessed green eyes swimming in the cabin's looking glass.

"Port Elizabeth," she breathed.

Chapter 22
Captain Escapes Cape Town in a Hurry

"Tommy!" He sat up, banging his head on the top berth.

"What!" Tommy lurched, joining her, ducking from spray at the open porthole. The *Constanzia* was moving at a spanking pace before the wind.

Tommy ruffled his wild hair. "Thought we had three days?"

Sary breathed deep as if she were smelling fresh sea air.

Thank God she had found the duke on the second night. That must be a sign.

The captain paced before the helmsman at the wheel. "Bit of trouble back in Cape Town. We're outracing it." He looked shifty and away. "None a your concern." And busied himself staring up the mizzenmast. The helmsman looked grimly ahead.

Chapter 23
Portents

"What've you heard?" Sary hissed, though not a swabbie was in sight.

"Shorthanded. Half the crew. Gone." Tommy muttered, leaning forearms on the promenade gunnel. "No one cares unless the tea's cold."

Sary eyed the complacent missionaries, a middle-aged couple distracted by their brood, and one elderly couple pleased and jolly over any happenstance, strolling the aft deck.

"Me too. From Cook. The captain left his helper behind. Seems we left in rather a rush," Sary finished dryly.

"First Mate. They'd *never* just leave the First Mate, Sary. We have to prepare. Something on the serious side."

"Fiddlesticks. Could be nothing. Perhaps he was ill, or the cook's help didn't show. Shanghaied. I've heard that's quite common."

"Either way, the next stop's Port Elizabeth. Quite nice, I hear. Bound to find decent employment there."

The screams were familiar, heard only at the edge of distraction, yet no matter how far out in the ocean the boat was, gulls appeared at the first sign of Cook.

"Where do they come from, so many miles from shore, to scoop potato peelings in midair like circus acrobats?"

Sary looked out at the galloping sea, and her face turned to horror.

Gulls screaming—Cook reaching in the bucket of swill, tossing refuse… Her heart stilled.

"Tommy!" Her throat unfroze, and she pointed.

There was Jude, half over the rail, flinging scraps with abandon. It seemed Cook had found a new helper. With each toss, his little bottom slid further over the fulcrum of a taffrail slick from many hands. Swiftly, Tommy ran and snatched Jude, who flailed. "'et down, Mommy! He'ping Cook!" Jude bawled, indignant.

Once again they were family.

"Naptime, young swabbie."

Tommy toted Jude away, the boy still yelling he "was he'ping Cook!"

Sary watched them go. It wasn't naptime. Did Tommy wish to get away from her?

Chapter 24
Shroud

The sun unfurled a gilded ribbon across the flat blue cloth of sea, preparing to wrap up the day.

Sary and Tommy watched the glittering wake on the aft deck, until Tommy suddenly dragged Sary behind the main mast, putting finger to lips. All was quiet, the hour of the doldrums when most passengers napped until the captain's mess.

"What?" Sary blurted. Tommy's grip tightened.

She looked out.

Jumpy and furtive yeomen, along with the captain himself, tilted a sailor's naked body over the taffrail— the body plummeted beneath cold navy water with an apologetic ripple.

No winding cloth, no shroud. Even queerer, after hasty words and a sign of the cross, the sailors nervously dropped the board in after the corpse.

Then a curious-er thing.

The burial crew stripped, flinging clothes in after, and shivering as they scrubbed their flesh raw in cold salt water and put on fresh clothes already stacked on the deck. Further puzzling, the captain heaved the oak bucket over, too, and watched till it sank. He cast a warning finger at the sailors before hastening away.

The sailors shuffled uneasily, not looking at each other, and slunk off.

Tommy and Sary melted around behind the mast until the men had gone. "Can't wait until we drop anchor," Tommy muttered. "Still think this a magnificent idea?" He looked back at her. "Something wicked this way comes."

Chapter 25
Hasty Departure

That evening, the captain's table was feverish with forced gaiety. The captain gamely brought out "old saws." The boson played "Nearer My God to Thee" on his harmonica until the captain banged his fist, and then the boson ripped into a jolly jig called "Marry Me, Carry Me, Mollie."

"Next port o' call is Port Elizabeth," he announced afterwards, to the complacency of the missionaries. "*Thank the good Lord,*" one couple breathed, delighted, echoed by Sary's thoughts, though for differing reasons.

"Such a lovely name," she said innocently.

"We, ah, might, ah, *all...*" The captain coughed in answer to the elderly couple's questioning. "Debark there." His voice trailed off uneasily.

But Sary didn't notice.

Chapter 26
Port Elizabeth

A gale, in which Jude delighted and which Sary and Tommy endured, swept them far off the coast. Perhaps the storm, if it had mercy, would have blown them back to England, or even America.

But at last, the captain raised the top gallant. They were no farther from their port than a day or two's sail against a head wind.

"This is it, Swinford," Sary whispered to the mirror. "Return in poverty, ruin Jude's chance of any advantage, and suffer Tommy's tolerance?" *And the back roads of an itinerant theater troupe.*

"Or find a treasure in diamonds?"

The chance is slim.

Slim would be a fine chance!

She mugged ruefully at her reflection. Somehow, someway, she'd repeat her actions in Cape Town, slip off the ship, no matter how ignoble, and this time find that damnable tea trader.

Tommy needn't know until all was done and done.

Like finding both halves of the map?

Chapter 27
Lost In Port Elizabeth

The *Constanzia* nudged the wharf like a calf to a mother whale. The yeoman threw the hawsers. Tommy scanned the sun-drenched city.

Sary smiled sweetly. "Might as well make the most of it—see the sights." What had seemed a bold plan back in England was a quagmire of doubt in Africa, the same as Jude's game boards: *Go three steps, beware of quicksand, two steps back, be attacked by lions, lose a turn...*

Tommy laughed, complacent. "Sary, what did you think? An explorer would pop out of the bush and lead you off on the backs of elephants? I can see it now: This way to diamonds! Diamonds be here!"

Yes, exactly. A mustachioed male, square-jawed, experienced (yet humorous) eyes under the shade of a pith helmet or a dashing leather Akubra, with boots laced to the knees. His capable hands would grip a carbine, as if the polished mahogany were part of his burnished muscles. Flanked by respectful bearers, he would speak fluent native, no matter where...

Odd she didn't see Tommy in this scenario.

"Don't be fanciful, Tommy."

Again, Port Elizabeth was more modern than supposed. Telegraph poles strung the sidewalks and autos prowled the streets.

It was déjà vu. Here too, masses of natives were herded one way, then the other, like a flock of angry starlings. Sary faltered at the top of the gangplank. They both watched as soldiers in kepis and gators ran down a scrawny old woman. With fire in her eyes, she jabbered and shook her fist under a soldier's nose, stamping splayed bare feet in rage.

Sary winced, but he backed from the spray of spit. Another broke out of the herd, hauled back by the point of a spear. "Must be prisoners."

She looked where Tommy pointed. People ran from stores lugging food in their arms. "Look! They are stealing."

She scanned the rear guard. The soldiers were pressing forward. Hysteria intensified. Natives lay on the street, like in Cape Town. The mob spread, close-chased by soldiers firing randomly.

A bullet sang by Sary, thunking into a belaying pin. Sary flattened, holding Jude close. Tommy covered them both. "Nice. Very nice."

The captain studied Jude. "Best stay on board a few days again, madam—sir."

"Is it always like this?"

"These things die out. As I said…" The captain dipped his head, mumbling, "A touch of sickness—consumption among the natives. They resist quarantine."

"But *they* are leaving." Sary pointed. True enough; the missionaries hustled down the gangway, wading into the thick of it. "Tommy? What's worse than consumption?"

Chapter 28
Again the One-Eyed Man

He hated the open-air saloon, though a stray breeze escaped long enough to dry his sweat. His neck felt prickly, but not from heat. *Fuckin' hell.* He'd picked the closest thing to a corner, backed by scruffy banana palm.

Liked it dark. A smoky den pungent with whiskey fug.

He slammed his shot glass on the plank.

"Hey! Piss-ant! What's this rum crap? Whiskey— rye or corn. What a man drinks."

The only shit-heel in the place splashed more rum in his glass, rolled black eyes, and rushed off, looking wildly about. The barman snatched bottles, only to drop them.

"Hey, you. Piss-ant! Leave the bottle!"

"No, sar!"

"What dya mean, no? Said a drink! Gimme the bottle!"

"Leaving, sar! I go, sar!"

The native ran over broken glass with bare feet, cash box in hand, and immediately hit the post, swirling about, cash box flying.

He didn't stop.

Rope sandals, boots, and black and pink feet trampled coins, soon buried in slurry.

The man with the eye patch realized he was alone.

Hell's bells. Ten hours. Just waitin'. Slept most of six. He stretched and moseyed out. Seen bodies aplenty in his life, but this—layin' in the open or slumped against buildings or under scrub—was disgusting.

Probably a thing that happens in this godforsaken hole. Some heathen brawl or other.

Wasn't scared, more like superior. *Dang it. Wisht I knew a word of local lingo.*

He looked for a white person who might have sense about him and leaned—*not too far*—peering at a victim. The chest and neck were thick with lumps, angry purple, shining fit to bust.

He stepped involuntarily back.

"More'n wastin'-away disease. Kinda hellish place is this? Only that bitch Swinford would get me here," he answered himself.

He looked across, and there was the sorceress on horseback herself—Sary Swinford, at the top of a gangway.

Chapter 29
The Other Man With The Map

"But surely, if we're careful?" Sary attempted to ease past the captain.

"Stay aboard with your young scamp for the day or two."

Two burly yeomen lounged at the bottom, smoking and picking teeth, but with belaying pins in hand also. *Damnation.*

Tommy, furiously writing plays for the new touring company he'd conjured up, was content with scribbling on any foolscap he could scrounge. Jude was still a bane to the crew, but a pet too; at least, they kept him from falling overboard, while Sary restlessly paced the decks.

The flurry of soldiers and natives had died out. Why the fuss? *Drat.* A simple trip to the city. She peered up streets leading from the wharf. Telephone poles, motor cars, women with big hats and parasols. So *normal.*

She could say she was going for something mundane, like sewing thread. Even so, Tommy and Jude would develop a hidden yearning to see the inside of an embroidery shop.

At any rate, the enormous yeomen at the foot looked more like prison guards, and city patrols in scarlet and toupees blocked the wharf farther in.

Beyond a scowling contest, the yeomen's presence put paid to her nipping away. *At least in daylight.*

That night, when at last Tommy's eyelids drooped over *Ben Hur*, Sary removed his grog tumbler, tucked Jude with his three-legged wooden horse into his hammock, and softly closed the door, her face aglow.

****

Wearing her darkest clothes, a scarf hiding her pale hair, Sary was able to slip past the guards undetected. The first time, she had plied Tommy with spiced rum one drowsy afternoon, plus paying the cabin boy to keep Jude occupied, with promises of another shilling if upon return she found Jude unscathed. Sary had slipped unnoticed down the gangway while a lone boson reamed out his pipe and soldiers changed the guard. They caught Sary before she crossed the wharf.

This time, Sary slipped across the deserted quayside and managed to reach the town. All she had to go on was that the "fat man" was a gambler and drinker called Groot and owned or *did* own a teak shop, or possibly a tea shop.

Chapter 30
The Immensely Fat Man

The man lumbered patron to patron, cadging drinks, at the far end of the bar, as Sary parted the curtains separating the ladies' parlor from the bar proper. This was the fifth saloon, and she was despairing, her feet were sore from walking, and it was getting toward midnight.

But it could be no other. Even now, the fat man held grubby cards in one fleshy hand as thirst for drink interrupted his other vice.

He felt her, turning as far as his neck allowed, squinting with uncertainty, and abandoned his quest for free drink, changing from jovially conniving to stupidly calculating as he studied Sary.

He looked side to side and wobbled his head, indicating "outside." Sary looked behind to see if he meant someone else.

The man reached for his crotch, then turned to his unhelpful cronies, thumbing at the beer the bartender shoved over, whether out of pity or disgust. The fat man drained the glass, gave her a wink, and shambled out. *What was that little show all about?*

Perplexed, Sary watched the door. To go into the dark with a strange drunk? He couldn't think it was concerning the map, or did he suppose she was a bar girl? Nipping around the building, instead of threading

103

the bar, she figured she'd set that to rights soon enough.

She heard a pattering. There he was, indeed, relieving himself. She marched over. She'd seen how God formed the male of the species, this one apparently shortchanged. Why would he be so proudly nonchalant about his "*petit* gift"?

She stared boldly above his waist. He grinned like a schoolboy, but the grin faded to confusion, and he hastily fumbled trousers closed.

"When you are quite finished with your little business…" she said.

He pulled himself together.

"Are you Groot?" she demanded.

"I see the look," he interrupted, both petulant and triumphant. "Yer all after me!"

"I assure you—"

"You all want it! You all want my map!"

Sary let her breath out slowly. *Could it be this easy?* "The—ah—map?" Her breath stopped. "You said 'map.' Who else knows?"

"Chinwag." He babbled, "Yah, I got a map—a very *precious* map. A valuable map! I see the look. You all want it." He neared her with a face filled with greed.

Sary looked behind, tensed for the crackle of feet on palm fronds, feeling the cudgel on her head—her arms snatched behind and her purse taken.

"And if you had—and I did?" she said slowly.

The fat man looked shifty. "Wouldn't just *give* it away," he snickered, "even for a kiss." Sary caught the odor of beer and stale armpits. Saw his pursed fat lips. She stood her ground.

"Curious." Sary cocked her head. "If you had such a thing, why have you not sold it already?"

The fat man fiddled his drawstrings. "Only thing I got."

Sary saw the lonely man beneath the conniving.

"If I give it up…" He heaved plump shoulders and pushed out his lower lip.

"You will get no more attention." Sary finished the thought and bent as if to share a delightful secret.

"No one need know you exchanged it for say— monetary rewards. You could have your cake and eat it too!" she whispered triumphantly. "You see? You could pretend you still have it. Who would know?"

Light dawned. He was lost in Sary's lovely face so close to his, but a look spread across his face like butter on a lumpy biscuit.

"What do ya say?" She asked as waves of bad hygiene rolled from his beer-soaked body. "Are we agreed to put one over on all those greedy jackanapes?" It was spoken in a tone of "us against them" conspiracy.

She nodded to the bar. "In the meantime, you would have money for more beer." Sary waited a moment before she stuck out her hand as the con had done.

He looked at her outstretched hand as if it were a viper. "How much?" He licked his fat lips and rubbed forefinger and thumb.

"I might wish to actually *see* it." She could not believe her luck, her mind racing ahead. *Supplies, proper clothes, get bearers, and—*

He rubbed his mouth. "Naw." He was ready to lumber back to the bar.

"Wait!" She grabbed his soft arm. He looked down, stunned at the strength in her right hand.

Sary raised a brow. "I have *money*."

"Yah? Is it on yer?" His face crowded with greed, fear, sorrow, connivance. Glancing at the tavern, he snatched a guttering lantern, lumbering off with remarkable speed.

Sary stared at his back. *Does he expect me to follow? What time is it?*

He did not reappear. She rushed to the corner. He wasn't there. She approached the other corner; he damply grabbed her hand, dragging her through mildewed overgrowth, where the lantern made a green palm-roofed cave.

"You—actually have it on you? Here?" Sary looked behind her.

"Didn't s'pose a lady wanted ta conduct business in a saloon."

"You'd be surprised," she answered dryly. "I'm not showing you my great aunt's laundry receipt until you show me the other part of the map."

"And I'm not showin' bugger all, 'thout seeing the copper, yer gelt, silvery nugget, or ruby orf a tiary. Not fussy." He nodded to her large reticule.

"Good as. I have gold aplenty—in the bank." *Well, she amended to herself, there were a few nuggets left after the scoundrel cashed in.* "A note, drawn on any bank, made out in your name." *She'd make it up to him, somehow, in spades, she bargained. She would.*

He shuffled. "In my name?"

"It's how business is done, now." She gave her toff's voice another workout.

"Can't high-muckety-muck me. Want cash money!"

She waved a check. "I don't carry *large* sums."

"Uh, how large?"

She waved the buff paper. "All I need to do is sign. After I fill it in, of course. What figures were you thinking? My money is secured at the Transvaal—" *Well, it could be.*

He waved it away. "Maybe, m'be not," he said, mulish. Time seemed suspended in aspic while he dithered, the aspic melting fast.

"I don't believe you really have it," Sary challenged.

"Ya can't give it ta me tonight?" he whined. "An' no one'd ever know?"

"I'd never tell." She waggled her fingers. "Come. Paper for paper."

He sighed. "An' you won't be around tomorra ta go to the bank?" he asked plaintively.

She felt like Alice chatting with the mad hat maker. *What time was it?* She looked at his sly fat face, a Halloween pumpkin in lantern light.

"I am on the *Constanzia*. We may be leaving soon. Take it to the bank, first thing in the morning. Here." She withdrew a corked pot of India ink and a fountain pen from her bag. *This should be ending.* "What is your name, sir?"

"Shellie." He straightened. "*Sheldon* Pratt."

She wrote out, *Esquire Sheldon Pratt*, with great flourish. "The sum of…?" She raised her brows. "How much do I put down, fifty?"

"One hundred!" He watched her carefully. "Uh— five hundred pounds?"

"Of course," Sary said smoothly. *Why not a million? Might as well be the moon, for all he will get, at least for now.*

"The sum of five hundred pounds, to be drawn on

the Bank of the Transvaal." She signed it with an illegible scrawl.

"Whatcher name, this here?"

"That says, uh—Sara Bernhardt—my name!"

He ignored her as she still held on to it, devouring the paper. "What's this *extry* word here—these here letters? E-S-Q? Don't mean shoot on sight, do it?" He chuckled, "Har-har!"

"No. It means 'Esquire'—a grand title for mister."

"Oh, 'at's all right, then." He held out a grubby hand.

Sary held on to the note. "Then we're done here. The map!"

"The money."

Sary handed the check over, blocking his way if he bolted, though he could bowl her over like a medicine ball made of lard.

Instead he reached under his arm, withdrawing a pouch and tucking in the bank note. She saw a cord cross-braced around his body. He dug in his voluminous trousers and from them opened another pouch with great care, withdrawing a stiff, ragged skin, or vellum, with forefinger and thumb.

Sary's heart leapt.

Mottled and stained. A patch of fur in one spot making it infinitely more authentic.

He unfolded the last bit.

Reverently, Sary held it close to the lamp, now burning low.

The markings were poor, true: What seemed a wiggle of peaks, meaning mountains—dots for sand for desert, and so on, with some splotchy small writing. What alarmed her—one end seemed neatly sliced, yet another portion missing.

Sary flipped it over—bare but for raw cow or goat hide.

"You've cut this again," Sary said with a scream somewhere in her throat aching to release. "You will now sell me another part!"

He backed, looking beyond her. She whirled. No one. The lamp died.

"Chap's gotta think of 'imself."

His fat body thrashed though foliage and feet pattered off. Sary raced out. He was nowhere.

Heading for the ambient light leaking from the bar, she studied what she had. *Damage wasn't too bad.* It looked as if the tea or teak merchant had snipped off a bit where the roughly triangular shape tailed off. Surely, with logic, she could conjure up the rest, with what she already had.

She held it to her breast. She had most of the map. Just a tail end missing.

Sary hastened back to the wharf. Now to get to the *Constanzia*. Tommy and she—

Her steps faltered.

Chapter 31
The One-Eyed Man Again

He bit into what a toothless vender called an *im-be*, whatever the Hades that was. Not an orange, but it'd do. Until this trip, oranges were the most exotic fruit the one-eyed man had tasted. *God dang it, but orangey fruit is dirt in a pigpen here. Common, flyblown, but this side of heaven.*

For all his strengths and cruelty, the one-eyed man was a parochial soul at heart. Nothing like the cold dark arms of Big Bear Mountain to keep one safe. He despised these sunny, wide-open spaces.

He spat the huge seeds in Sary's direction like bullets. His wintery skin had browned to leather, face concealed behind a mustache, middling salt-and-pepper beard and long sideburns. A silver braid hung down his back, unusual for Africa. Less unusual, the black homemade leather eye patch. He was sinewy, with rangy shoulders and arms, and knuckle-y hands.

The man knew her.

He knew her by the gall in his spleen and cinders burning in his belly shrieking for fitting vengeance.

He winced, checking his leg. The violent foot-long scar was a long call from the broken end sticking through after his plummet through Delacorte's rafters back in Big Bear, when he almost had hell's bitch in his grasp for once and for all.

All Sary's fault.

He'd even broken the old bastard Delacorte's fall, in the cellar of that burning house. Still *he* survived and Delacorte met his reward.

He judged his leg had another week healing until the ugly scar closed completely. Over a year of festering vengeance, too. Didn't care, long as his legs carried him, iron brace or no.

The one-eyed man hawked Sary as if he were a starving mountain wolf and she a yearling fawn. Now what was she up to?

Chapter 32
Found Out

Tommy blocked the way, brows lowered, fists clenched. All rather dramatic.

"Thought I didn't know." He sniffed her hair as Sary tried to edge past. "A *saloon*? You love your whiskey, I do avow. But to steal off like some—"

"Sot?" she finished. "Harlot?"

"There is a devil in you I do not know, Sary." He turned as if he didn't trust himself.

Sary tagged at a safe distance.

She ran out of luck, time, or explanations, resenting she need explain at all.

"Tommy, I will explain!"

He rounded, his eyes cold as the bottom of the sea, and as black. "You always do. Too late, love. I no longer give a fiddler's fuck why you are sneaking off or where you go."

She attempted to pass. He caught her arm.

Sary slapped him.

"You could have trusted me!" She jerked loose, racing up the gangplank.

"Sary!" he roared. It was a command.

She turned, still blazing.

"I only wanted you safe."

Sary saw his pain. "I know. I won't do it again. *I won't have to.* Give me time. It—it is not what you think..." Sary finished lame.

"You act as if I care."

With that, Tommy stalked off.

Chapter 33
Deserted

The captain still held them under confinement. How appropriate that gesture, Sary would find to her regret. He avoided his passengers, other than mumbling that they were welcome to stay aboard till unknown troubles were settled. It was the unspoken words that were unsettling.

Routines fell apart, with meals not served, or else cold, with half-cooked beans or burnt oatmeal, and coffee or tea more like dishwater.

Little did the passengers understand that the captain, squeezed by rapacious merchants, ship owners wanting to keep on schedule, and town heads tamping a financial lid on Port Elizabeth, conspired to keep from them the horrific fact that the Black Death rampaged along the coast of Africa and through unknown interiors.

To give the captain credit, he thought it his Christian duty to keep the passengers onboard until the local bigwigs decided he could either sail or allow them off, with panic avoided at all costs.

If Sary considered it, his unease couldn't be over an outbreak of consumption. That was universal. However, she didn't.

Nor could she know the fat trader Groot caught the plague shortly after their meeting but survived.

Between Tommy's absorption over his latest farce, with his avoiding her otherwise, and Jude's deepening bond with the cook and his helper, Sary was consumed with her own plans and did not mind the quarantine, at least for the while.

In the mean salon, Sary laid the maps side by side, studying them among spilled tea, biscuit crumbs, and lingering fried fish and pipe tobacco smells. Few sought out the room, and the missionaries had not returned.

The map was near complete, with N/W/E/S directions and a squiggle she thought was a river labeled 'V' surely indicating the Vaal. Sary redrew the map on Tommy's foolscap, checking it with an ancient atlas in the ship's library, whose other volumes consisted of religious tracts, mysteries, and *Tess of the D'Urbervilles*.

Sary unstitched her stays, wrapped each scrap tightly around a whalebone stay slightly above the waist, and sewed them back in again.

She collared an Afrikaans planter, also fretting to go ashore, and learned the name of an outfitter. She chafed.

"Mainly soft city folk who fancy themselves great white hunters." He tapped his forehead. "Mostly, they don't return, at least not as their mothers made 'em."

He looked Sary up and down until Sary fixed him with a stare hard as malachite.

"And where would one find bearers?" She softened. "If, say, one were an explorer? I am ever so interested."

"Well, little lady, I'd say, drag a wild pig and beat the bushes." The plantation owner fixed her with his own hard stare, finally muttering, "Where angels fear to tread," and stalked out.

"How unpleasant," Sary grumbled to his back.

Chapter 34
Providence

A hot night with a full moon on a platinum sea decided Sary's fate.

Indeed all their fates.

Humidity was a second skin. With Port Elizabeth in her sights, Sary fanned and paced the promenade. Serene. Little traffic. What she did not know was that many inhabitants stayed behind doors or had already fled, either out of the city or by way of death.

Making certain Jude ate a nourishing supper— thick stew, for once, with goat cheese and Irish soda bread—the cook was generous where his new little mate was concerned—she made up her mind.

Tommy glanced up, vague from his scribbling, soon drawn back to his own wit, chortling at his cleverness.

Sary tucked Jude into his hammock, removing his thumb from his mouth, satisfied he slept the sleep of the innocent.

She could not.

Sary fanned herself at the porthole, watching oily swells. She glanced back. If anything, Tommy had grown more handsome with his darker face and body. Sary ran hands down her hips, sensing the fullness of her sex.

Yet her Tommy was still frosty as a fall morning.

I will not go to him.

Rashly, she dropped her chemise, her petticoat, then her long skirt, as if already sensing it might be for the last time.

Tommy's gaze traveled her bare gleaming legs, her body burnished with the feeble gold of a whale oil lamp.

"My maddening mad Ophelia, unchain thy hair from its bounds…" he gritted, backhanding his mouth.

She stretched her arms to reach the timbers of the tiny cabin, then folded them over her head, slowly revolved, and smiling a cat's smile, shook out her hair. Sary winced, slowly lowering her stiff arm.

Tommy put his lips on her shoulder, kissing the bullet scars as he always did.

"Does it ache?"

Sary revolved, lifted her lips with tears greening her eyes.

"Only my heart, because I am so *wicked*."

"It's been a while." His voice was thick with longing.

Sary bit her lip. Somehow, it felt like…farewell.

That's mad. Of course it isn't.

She sucked in as he sat on the berth pulling her down astride him. Tommy's urgent kisses consumed her. She wriggled and lifted slightly, and he entered— one second they were two, and now melded in the most blissful way as he moved harder, deeper.

Seconds later, he stayed her, gasping, "Not yet— not yet," as if he too wanted to make it last. Then he could wait no longer than she.

She laughed, joyful, wanton…and still connected, tumbled them off the berth; wedged between the door and the bunk, they made love with fierce abandon, as if each sought forgiveness for a sin not met, until she slumped, sweating and gasping, across his chest.

He drew her up, running lips over her slicked breasts, and once more desire grew like a jungle flower in heat and moisture.

Later, Sary waited.

Tommy slept the sleep of angels to the sound of Jude, gently blowing his tiny trumpet of a nose. She watched them until she knew she needed to leave.

Taking a substantial amount of the monies left, at least aboard ship, Sary slipped off after the nine bells. She knew in Africa shops opened late, some after dark, to escape the noonday heat.

At the head of the gangway, seeing the sentry sleeping and two soldiers smoking on the wharf, Sary slipped past and away. They had grown complacent, it seemed.

That was the last any aboard ship saw of her.

Chapter 35
Oblivion

Sary stepped off the *Constanzia* to enter hell. The figurehead's cracked image followed her with smooth indifference.

As hoped, there was still commerce, but more subdued than she supposed.

Sary asked for the outfitter's the planter had alluded to; after a short walk, she entered a large corner shop and, surveying the sturdy attire, nodded approval. *Tommy will be so surprised.*

Vests with pockets for ammunition, jodhpurs, canvas trousers, boots, broad hats, pith helmets. She'd wear men's gear too. No skirts this time, recalling sloshing Big Bear's icy streams, panning gold, in wet petticoats.

The proprietor looked harried.

"Excuse me, sir, I—"

Gathering ledgers and fiddling with a safe, he gave a distracted glance and didn't answer.

Good. I can poke about.

Sary selected canvas trousers, two shirts, one soft blue cambric and the other dun with lots of pockets. Lastly, boots, thick socks, and a broad canvas hat, plus bandannas. She placed them on the counter, all the while accompanied by the shopkeeper's distracted muttering as he dragged off ledgers and banged about the cash register.

Even then, she didn't wonder why she failed to select gear for Tommy and Jude.

Sary rapped a display of compasses, multipurpose knives, sulphur matches in a tin box, canteens—all survival paraphernalia.

It didn't matter. He frantically searched shelves, ignoring her. "Here, puss, puss." And dragged out an elderly cat.

"I'll need bearers, supplies. Perhaps you could tell me...?"

The shopkeeper gathered his cashbox. "City's full of them, all wanting to escape"—he chortled, near hysteria—"provided soldiers allow them." He hooted, *"Bearers!"*

The man bolted with the cat, ledgers, and a strongbox, leaving a scatter of coin, and was directly bowled over by a soldier, in fancy red uniform, chasing two natives. She heard his howl and the cat screeching.

She picked up the coins, dithered, and in the end tucked a few rands under his register before methodically selecting a jacket, with shoulder patches to brace a rifle, and a bedroll.

She eyed a nice shotgun.

"I'll pay him back." *How many do I owe now?* Sighing, she eyed the open door. "If I don't, someone else will." She wrapped the gun in butcher's paper, aware of voices raised and rushing feet—it was as if the sky had suddenly split open, raining dust and confusion.

She watched a moment, then ducked and ran, confused by the onslaught, swept into a mob rounding a corner, buffeted by elbows and shouts, chased by tomato-red coats and bayonet-shine.

The mob scattered around Sary, who was knocked violently aside, bundles ripped and trampled—a flash of knee, then face down in churned-up grit; bare pink feet and dirty sandals trod on her or raced around her.

From the ground, Sary eyed the shopkeeper sprawled on the crossroad, money flying about, yet no one picked it up. Sary struggled to the sidelines, hanging onto the bundles she had left and the long, wrapped package that was the rifle.

What have I done?

She dragged more packets to safety during a lull in the crowd. The last soldiers passed, picking up stragglers at bayonet length. Nipping between buildings, Sary ripped open her bundles, drawing on the trousers under her skirt, buttoning on the two shirts, then the jacket—ungainly, but she could manage the rest. The extra boots had vanished.

She tried for hansom cabs and the odd racing flivver.

Finally, a man in an open Ford stopped. Yes, he was going that very way. "I have a family…" he began.

"What's happening?"

"The sickness. The bloody sickness! Where've you been?" He ground gears, ready to leave.

"Please. To the ship!" she yelled.

"Probably brought it yourself," he said bitterly.

"None of us are ill."

"No matter. I must get to my wife. Go back. The plague makes monsters of us all, dead or alive." But then he sighed. "Hop aboard before I change my mind."

Sary scrambled on.

He clashed gears and sped to the wharf.

"The plague reached here? I think it was in Cape

Town…" Sary shouted above the rattle.

His laugh was crazy as he stomped the clutch and pulled the lever. "Get out."

"What?"

It was no use. She felt her long skirt ripping, but before her was the forest of masts.

A soldier running to nowhere barged into her. "What are you doing? Get to safety! It's an uprising! Bloody devils won't stay put."

Sary felt half demented, dragging ripped bundles, her skirt torn, hair askew. She tried a step or two, only to be immediately whirled about by a mixed mob pelting past her headlong to the ships and the harbor.

She lifted herself on her elbows—a gibbering monkey leapt over her, followed by a knee to the head as someone tripped over her.

Have to get up, or I never will.

Rolling aside, Sary sensed her first true panic, instantly bowled over again. She covered her head, suffering a trod to the kidneys. The crowd veered. Now only a few racing feet leaped around her toward the ships, where a wall of red coats awaited them.

Sary caught a glimpse of white—a sail unfurling, growing larger, and catching the wind.

"Noooooo!" she screamed.

She looked in horror at the earthquake of thudding feet.

A new mob, black, white, and in between, thundered from between buildings. Sary saw another wall of red, chasing them with rifles and bayonets.

Will they help? Will they see me?

The ragged wall of soldiers lined up before the ships of all sorts bobbing in the harbor—steam, sail, fishing craft—jabbing fixed bayonets at the throng frenziedly fighting to get aboard any floating sanctuary.

The soldiers were winning, trapping the mob between the advancing wall of rifles and bayonets.

Sary froze, caught between the mob and the new influx, when she felt her arm, the stiffened one, yanked nearly from its socket. Her feet dragged the cobbles until she was against a warehouse with a whisker of space between her and the two mobs.

"Oh, bless you! I must get to that ship." She pointed, breathless. Sary looked around, grateful, to her benefactor. Her veins stopped pumping, and she croaked, "You're *dead.*" She turned chill as an icehouse in December.

The man grinned a mean, one-eyed grin, touched his leg brace, and snorted. "Half dead. Ya *half*-finished me, Swinford. Too damned seasoned with gall and gunpowder ta *die.*"

Ratchet shoved her behind the telegraph office.

Ratchet.

He was a dark memory tucked in a moldering trunk relegated to a bloody corner of her mind.

Cannot be.

She had seen Ratchet sprawled four stories down in a boulder-strewn cellar with Julian Delacorte half-lying atop him back in Big Bear. *He cannot be alive.*

Sary registered the scar, the eye patch. *Neither one of us escaped unmarked.* She backed from long bony fingers.

"Yer in a tight corner, Swinford," the one-eyed man grated. "I'm all you got, or they'll herd you with those sick bastards out there. Think nancy-boy'll protect ya?" Ratchet spat, pointing to the dead, dying, the frantic being forced into a *kraal* for humans.

She stopped fighting him. "I don't know what you are doing here, but I have to get to that ship. Ratchet, you can come too."

He snorted. "'At's right, 'at's me old Sary. Calm as a plaster saint in a church hall."

Tommy doesn't know where I am.

Ratchet was knocked aside, cursing a blue storm. He clawed back, and for the first time she saw the cumbersome iron/leather brace and the slow stain below the knee.

"If we stay, we'll both be pushin' up daisies from the wrong side."

"I'm getting on board that ship," Sary gritted. "Leave be!"

Ratchet's laugh was gravel on rocks. He threw his head back, hooting. "What ship?" He waved a rangy arm.

She scanned the wharf.

The *Constanzia* was there. She had seen the cracked wooden figurehead when the motorist dropped her off...of course it was.

Sary scanned empty moorings.

Her heart stopped.

Only an empty space, awash with the *Constanzia*'s retreat.

Sary looked out to sea. Other boats dwindled.

The *Constanzia* drifted backwards five, ten, twenty feet, the distance widening, her sails luffing, halfway to the open seas, catching the wind as yeomen tugged the topgallant—the gap more impossible with her every racing, pounding step as Sary lifted skirts high and pelted, waving her arm.

She ran unheeding of shouting soldiers, crashing into people, using her bundles as a weapon, smashing the rifle butt—anything to get to the ship.

She overbalanced, skidding to the edge, teetering— only a buffet of wind shoved her back, toes dipping over the edge of gray splintery boards, or she'd have tipped headlong forty feet down, every cell of her wanting to jump.

I can swim, she thought inanely, straining to see, and there was Tommy on the aft deck, wild black hair whipping like a pirate flag—his arm raised.

He called, or she fancied she heard it in the scree of wind.

"*Sa—!*"

Waves swallowed the sound as they dashed up the stanchions, drenching her.

The white face with its cap of black hair was just a blotch. The main sail billowed taut.

Did the figure hold a child? Was it Tommy? Could he make her out?

Surely, they will come back.

The big square sails ballooned out. The ship turned broadside and shrank down to a windswept toy.

Sary stood, arms dropped to her side, hair undone and blowing wild.

"They sailed without me." She cried to no one.

Please come back…

She ran the curve of headland, keeping the *Constanzia* in sight as long as she could.

The soldiers ignored her as no threat.

She forgot Ratchet when finally she stumbled, aimless, back to the wharf.

Boots. She saw boots, one with a thick iron brace

that extended up the leg outside his breeches.

"Go away."

"Ya can wait till yer skinny arse is a bag a bones. Come on, make tracks."

"Tracks? Where?" Sary asked dully.

"Wanna die?"

"Maybe."

She stirred—an old, old woman.

"Inland," he barked. "Before they lock it down. I seen it. Typhoid in Saint Louis and…"

Sary glanced toward Port Elizabeth, disinterested. She still could not believe the *Constanzia*'s place at the wharf was now just an empty wash of dirty sea water.

Sary darted killing looks and stiffly rose. "And you take me—not out of Christian charity."

Chapter 36
Flight

Ratchet gathered bundles and the shotgun.

"Well—comin'?"

A soldier at last took interest. She would explain to him…

"Hie! Halt!"

Sary looked at the far end of the wharf and saw soldiers with bayonets rounding up strays, heard the crack of shots. *Maybe not.*

Ratchet slipped between buildings.

She followed without thinking. She had little money, no food or water, but she had her maps… The precious scraps burned against her ribs.

Ratchet peered out. "Rest easy on that score, sister. Don't want yer society. You're here for *some* reason. You're a walkin', talkin' treasure map, and believe me, you will sing a pretty song before I am done."

Map? Certainly he speaks metaphorically. There was no way he could have that intelligence. "Don't be idiotic."

"I tracked ya, didn't I? Just saved ya, didn't I?" Ratchet, stumping along on his ironclad leg, weaved between abandoned buildings, leaving chaos behind, until they wandered into quiet suburbs of elegant homes where the only movements now were heavy drapes and glimpses of worried faces.

Sary ran to the nearest and banged at the door. "Please, let me in!"

She saw a face at a window. The face vanished.

Sary waited, hopeful. The door remained shut. She ran to the second. A man watched from a half-open door and rushed out with a shotgun, yelling something in Dutch or Boer.

Ratchet smirked, watching her antics.

"Hold the horses. Looka there. Must be living right."

A skittish, bewildered horse moseyed down the road.

"Come on. Ain't no punkins turnin' inta carriages."

Ratchet, dyspeptic, vaulted onto the horse, then hauled her up and twitched the horse northwest.

"Didn' never think I'd see us ridin' off together."

He clamped a hand tight on her thigh.

She looked back the way they came. Each clop of the hooves took her farther from Tommy and Jude.

"How'd you find me?"

Ratchet ignored her. "Seen a map in the post office. Wilderness and farms up north—and a sorta mountain range called an es-carp-ment cuts east and west. We can make the rail line, somewheres northwest of here. It'd be going to the Kimberley Mines, or if not Kimberley, some other place not touched by this god-blasted pestilence."

Silence from Sary as she mulled this.

As they left chaos behind, Sary grew numb. *We make a lost pair, me with a gimpy arm, him with a patch and a damaged leg.*

But there were few to notice, and if they did, they were far too preoccupied to care. The two riders entered and passed other silent or abandoned neighborhoods. Here Sary saw the first dead, draped in unlikely poses over rustic porches. One was face down in a trough. A woman slumped in a rocker, with a pan of green beans to shell still in her lap. The illness raged through Port Elizabeth like a forest fire, leaving some parts undamaged and others scorched.

"Eggs for breakfast, death for supper." Ratchet's chuckle was a box of gravel.

As they clopped along, dark shapes skulked, barn to outhouse to shed, staring out with white, frightened eyes. Ratchet cocked his revolver.

Farther out, picket fences eddied with sand, surrounding neat farms with an oddly abandoned look—a window open, flapping curtains already tinged with dust. Creepers crawled crushed stone paths and dried fronds sagged untended.

"Why weren't we told?"

"Money." He snorted. "Always money."

Sary smiled at the irony.

Around dusk, the horse drooped. They stopped at a gentleman's farm, deserted. Dusty laundry flapped forlornly, waiting for a *hausefrau*'s attention. A few goats, a cow, and what caught Sary's interest—fat hens scratching up bugs. She realized, against all logic, her stomach growled like a bear.

"Ain't nobody home?" He grinned, lupine. "Now, ain't that a shame. A body might take advantage." And he was already disappearing inside the kitchen door.

"Hallloooo?" Sary surveyed a scrubbed wood table with a half bottle of clabbered milk, a tub of melted butter, also rancid, and a melting side of bacon, thick with flies. She looked away.

Ratchet sniffed it, commenting, "Not too off."

"Go ahead."

She opened pantries. Here was better fare. Canned jellies, chutneys, potted beef, piccalilli, a tin of fruitcake, and signs that either the departing family or pilferers had depleted the larder, evidenced by the spilt flour, oats, and salt. They ate where they stood.

Ratchet wandered off.

She heard him stomping through the house, randomly breaking things...a vase, a lamp overturned. He stumped upstairs, his bad leg thudding and hitching across floorboards, bedroom doors creaking open—a second later, Ratchet seemed to tumble down the stairs, bursting ashen into the kitchen.

Sary clamped her mouth and nose, and they tore out, leaving their bounty behind. Sary let loose the cow and goat, to Ratchet's rare approval.

"Never like ta see animals in pain."

Sary just stared at him.

More farmhouses squatted in the distance.

Chapter 37
Lost Hope

Toward dusk, the tired horse plodded to a poor farm. One barn, a few sheds. Chickens busily picking the last meal from the weeds by the light of a bloody sun.

Ratchet checked the house, returning with a shake of the head. The hens and one rooster led Sary and Ratchet in a futile chase, comical if they hadn't been so hungry. Sary regretted they'd been so persnickety at the first place.

A rooster sprang squawking and flapping from bushes straight at Ratchet. "Manna from hell." Ratchet began plucking while the creature was alive; feeling Sary's steely gaze, he gave the bird a quick wring of the neck.

"Not big enough," she commented.

"Warn't meanin' ta share it none."

Sary later stripped a bone clean, looking at the sliver, saying a brief prayer, wondering what Jude and Tommy were eating.

Was that Tommy on the aft rail? As hard as she wanted it, she'd seen no small face by the figure's side, or in his arms. Perhaps a woman with dark, undone hair. Were they still in Port Elizabeth? Were they—dead?

"Don't thank me none," Ratchet sneered.

Sary tossed the bone at him.

Rounding the coop, Sary wandered into an overlooked kitchen garden. She dropped to the ground, plucking withered tomatoes off the vine. Finding a burlap sack, Sary stuffed sweet corn, wilting cabbages, turnips, Brussels sprouts, green onions—*must not be a growing season in Africa as it was back home.* Wherever that was.

Ratchet climbed from a root cellar holding clay jars with snap lids. The first gave off a sour smell.

"Botulism," Sary warned.

Ratchet tossed it, smashing the jar. She sniffed a jar of green beans. "Good." They filched them straight.

"Too heavy to take. Eat what you can," she mumbled.

Ratchet tossed that jar, too, breaking it, and reached for another. Sary hoped the owner wouldn't grieve. Hoped she'd return.

Sary bundled what was left of the ravaged garden into her gunny sack. Ratchet raided the hen house, smashing eggs against his cheek and sucking out the inside. Sary wiped egg off her mouth. When she looked up, Ratchet stared steadily across the dying campfire where he had roasted the chicken.

She eyed the house, aware his gray eyes glittered red in the flame.

"Take your clobber off."

Ratchet nailed her, unblinking, with a wolf's eye—cold, flat, and yellow; also, a gleam of fire banked too long beginning to flare from embers of lust.

It took all of Sary's will not to tremble.

"What are you on about? Don't be preposterous." She reached behind for a broken fence post.

"Ya will, if I haveta rip 'em off."

Sary kept her green gaze hard. "First you need to catch me—*old man*."

She dropped her gaze purposefully to his shackled leg, traveling slowly to the eye patch on his wolf-like face, while her whole body shook.

Funny, he could have been fine-looking, with his stark features and deep widow's peak gone salt-and-pepper.

The flame shot higher in his one eye.

"You never seemed that way, Ratchet. *Bent.* Didn't think you *liked* women, except to hurt them."

Sary backed, aware she could outrun him to the horse. She was puzzled; she had never detected a spark of manly desire, only sadistic, cold, bloody-minded "play" back in Big Bear with the doxies.

He rose, unsteady, circling with grim implacability.

Sary thrust the picket into the fire; the dry wood flared, and she waved it while she backed to the horse. She saw the eye reflecting orange recalculate. The fire went out.

He snickered.

"Don't want your skinny ass. Wanna check if you got marks of the devil. Any—*plague boils*. Ugggh!" Involuntary shudders rippled his frame. "Ugly enough, already," he decided.

Sary dropped the picket. "What of you? You've been here longer. How do I know you haven't the 'mark of the devil'?"

"Well, now," he drawled, "ya don't, do ya." Rubbing his chin with his gun barrel, he reflected, "Naw. Checked meself out pretty good. Ain't itchin' nor scratchin' nowheres. No big lumps on my neck. Do

I?" He thrust out his neck with a look of secret fear.

Sary grudgingly shook her head as he holstered his gun.

"I'll let you know if things change," he grunted, deadpan, and watched her, lean and hungry again.

She looked again to the horse.

"Gal—gal, you sure are somethin'."

"Not anything to you."

"Oh, yeah, purely are. Intend to stick ta you like second skin. Not gettin' away from me this time, little girl." He strung out "little girl" in an obscene, breathy snarl. "If I havta strip your bones and cut every stitch off ta find that map."

He waved the knife Sary knew so well a lifetime ago.

She whipped her hair side to side in a blinding golden fury. "You don't know me, then." *Oh, Sary. You just verified a map's existence..* "What is all this crazy talk about a map?" Sary scorned.

"I have my ways." Ratchet cast a sly, maddening look and said no more.

Chapter 38
Where Angels Fear

Where am I? Sary started awake, cold and cramped, still dreaming of mahogany walls and Tommy jammed by her side in the ship's cozy cabin. Instead, a bed of chilly sand.

She raked clay pots, dead bulbs, musty loam. *A potting shed.* Must have crawled in during the night.

Ratchet. She peered out and jerked back. His hunched gray form lay curled around the fire pit. *Dangerous, mercurial Ratchet. Sadistic, homicidal Ratchet, whose moods changed on a dime.*

"Must go back, no matter how bad it is," Sary muttered.

Last evening, all was dusted with night. The sun now colored the brilliant flowerbeds, heavy-laden fruit trees. Figs, pomegranates, oranges, lemons, grapes, and fruit for which she had no name. So peaceful and normal.

Too late.

Ratchet rose, seemingly unaffected by the rampant splendor as he scratched his underarms and groin. He tied three squawking chickens to the horse's pommel. "Best git goin'." His pockets jingled with coins and filched jewelry.

Chapter 39
Ratchet Reminisces

Sary awoke, ravenous, four days later. All the fruit she'd picked and the vegetables and fowl were gone, mostly down Ratchet's gullet.

No Ratchet now. Only embers. *Good. He's gone. He's left me.*

Sary revolved, searching the vast night sky. *The moon's there. It sets where? Which way's north? That big star by the moon is the North Star. I think. Should I head south to Port Elizabeth or north to the Kimberley?*

A choice of two evils.

One closer, rife with pestilence, the other a no-man's land.

South to the ships. Perhaps the sickness would have passed. Jude and Tommy might be waiting there.

Sary jumped up, gathering her things. *It's not that far, if I go now.*

She crept south, past one of the tough little trees with yellow blossoms. Ducking. Oh, my lord! Ratchet! Stark naked, doing what nature urged him in the middle of the night. Even the brace was gone. She watched, morbidly curious.

His bad leg was a snarl of burn, the shank crooked as if badly set. His back was laced with scars too, some of which she herself had put there, in another lifetime.

Sary backed. Curious, though. *What is he doing?*

137

Checking himself. Feeling under his arms.

He's frightened.

She looked away. It would not do if he caught her.

"Get a good gander."

Sary cringed.

"Fine specimen of a man, now, ain't I?"

Ratchet turned, giving her full benefit of his manhood.

Sary refused to look below his neck.

"Impressive?" He held out his arms, revolving, favoring the damaged leg. His face turned cold. "Some of this *physique-ie* got your name on it."

"I thought…" She bit her lip.

"I left you on your stony lonesome? Hunh. You'd like that."

"Best get dressed; you'll catch your death."

Ratchet slowly hauled on his trousers.

"Got me all fired up, lookin' at me that way." She heard him snap the iron brace and his feet shush sand as he limped after her.

Their eyes locked on the pistol.

Sary made a dash but was clamped by Ratchet's gnarly hand. He bent on one leg, twisted it away, and slipped it home in his belt.

"Told ya. Not goin' nowheres."

"You shot me in Big Bear! I am riddled with scars I'll never be rid of. You tried to cut off my ear. You tried your *fiercest* to drown me! What do you want from me?" Sary screamed, at the end of her nerves.

"Well, look at me! Look at this iron bedframe I'm a-wearin' around my leg. Look at this eye patch. Seems like I recollect I had *two* eyes, before you come along."

Suddenly, Sary's mouth twitched.

He chuckled.

She gasped for breath. She couldn't be laughing with him. Could she? With Ratchet? As if they shared the biggest joke that only they two could understand?

"Yeah, yeah, we had some times." He bit his mustache. "Never liked women much."

"Surely, you jest." *Lord! That was Tommy speaking, through me.*

"No. S'truth. Never knew ma." He sucked a tooth, reflective. "Stepma. No better'n she should be. Pa beat the bejesus outta me. She never lifted a hand. But no never mind. Ever'body beats the crap outta ever' kid."

"Can't believe you were a child anyway."

"Got that. Been on my own since five."

"Five? You exaggerate."

"Wish't I were. Hooked up with this—gold miner. He was ah—was lookin' for a pretty young boy. Oh, don't laugh. Used to be quite a toothsome young lad. Least he presumed so."

Ratchet looked off for a long time.

Sary examined her toes, not quite sure what he was talking about but loathe to think on it.

"So now you hurt everyone."

"Now, that's a thoughty notion." He was silent. "May not appreciate it, but we belong like trees that stand together too long and twine."

Sary froze.

"Why not hook up together?" But he meant the wider scope, it seemed. "You and me. Hell's fire! Diamonds. I could help cover you up in them hard gaudy stones you womenfolk fancy. Could be rich— richer'n you are now," he said slyly.

Sary tensed.

He grinned his long, yellow, tobacco grin, checking her from the corner of his one eye. *"*Not that ya got much."

Sary ignored him.

"Wouldn't be scratchin' away, leaving yer loved ones, iffen ya still had scratch—the long green, the *gold*!"

"And you don't have tobacco," she shot back.

He winced. "Sure do have sand!" He stared into the night. "I know yer up to somethin', and I want part of it."

"You made your own hell. How did you follow me?"

"You women. Curious as cats." He rubbed his leg. "Don't mind. Word got around back in Big Bear. Someone heard tell you was yellin', 'There's diamonds in Africa,' like a fuckin' idjit, as you made your getaway."

Sary flinched. A random boast made true through fate.

"Anybody knows you knows full well it meant somethin'."

"But it didn't. A figure of speech. It meant nothing. Who heard me?"

"Didn't matter, did it? Goin' to track you to the fiery pits of hell anyways."

"Wait. It takes money to follow someone…" Sary began.

"Pearl showed me where old Julian's stash was." Ratchet showed yellow teeth. "I had plenty a scratch after that. Pearl thought I was gonna marry her." His laugh was rocks tumbling down a stream. "I just checked the rail station. From there, it was easy.

'Course, I went steerage, while you steamed first class."

"Pearl," Sary breathed, remembering the sad doxie back in Big Bear.

"Yep, been close to you as ticks on a dog. Funny how liquor loosens servant's tongues, even in grand houses. Sorry for your loss." He sniggered. "Never did think women could handle money."

Sary burned inside and out. *Just remember the map, remember the map.*

Every night before she lay down, Sary traced it in her head. *Even if it's worth nothing, while Ratchet thinks it exists, I am safe. He can't torture me any more than these blasted stays. A saint wearing a hair shirt could be no more miserable.* Yet, oddly, the stays helped her breath and braced her back, if she laced the bottom tight and kept the top open.

Tomorrow, tomorrow. Sleep, sleep, sleep.

What Ratchet revealed made a crazy sense because that was the only explanation left. Yet did he really guess about the map? Had he also heard her and the fat tea merchant? Or teak.

Chapter 40
Land Of The Lost

They rode through desolate scrub, the purple of red dirt and gray-green of tufts, fit for nothing. She hated Ratchet's bony back against her chest as the horse plodded on toward the distant green escarpments. Mainly she rode with her hands braced behind her.

On the fourth day, the horse gave out, stumbling to its knees.

"Reckon we oughta eat it. Make a fine roast, that haunch." He kicked it and took out his hated knife.

"That horse saved us." Sary picked up her belongings.

"Be sorry." Ratchet stretched his cramped leg, leaving the beast, and followed her, mumbling morbid predictions. He was right, as it happened, as they trekked into the vast Karroo desert.

Sary hardened her heart over Ratchet's intermittent grunts of pain.

Rarely, now, her interest quickened at the sight of habitation as they wandered through land dotted with crumbling huts and derelict kraals, heading roughly northwest. The places they passed seemed derelict from neglect and not, thankfully, because of the plague.

Either way, Sary's heart ached. With each beat, Jude and Tommy faded away.

Chapter 41
First Hovel

Roads had turned to footpaths, dwindling to little more than animal tracks. That was days ago. The travelers lost the tracks under blowing grit, then wandered into them once more.

They tangled in barbwire, one end fastened to a post, the other sunk in sand, as they saw the homestead with smoke rising, already dreaming of water, food, and —most of all—rest in the shade of the lone tree clustered with yellow blossoms. Children scuffled in the dust underneath.

Ratchet fingered his holster.

She ignored him. *Just his nature.*

The children stared, silent, as if weatherbeaten strangers showed up all the time.

"What? Imperiled by five-year-olds now?" she finally asked him, irritated, for none looked more than that.

Eyes staring back were palest blue, not the beautiful brown and black she'd seen in the ports. Each solemn face was stamped from the same cookie cutter.

At first, she didn't make out the hut as a house. Revolving, Sary shaded her eyes, expecting a face at a doorway, a hand lifting the cowhide flap. The yard was derelict. A broken, overturned bucket, dead nasturtiums, and bits of cloth littered the sandy enclosure. A kraal fence drooped. A single goat was tied to the tree. Surely, these children weren't alone.

"*Muttie*? Where is your Muttie?" Sary tried. *No, that's German. Here it would be* moeder *and* vader.

One toddler, about three, chattered a string of Dutch, pointing vaguely west. Sary saw no one. She studied the bare yard—no toys. No swings, balls, or spinning tops. Not even a jump rope, but the two oldest had gathered colored pebbles, playing a crude game of marbles using the largest as mibs.

A child with a tousled mop of dirty blond ringlets played a sort of tic-tac-toe in the dust, flinging handfuls of the stones at her older sibling when she lost. Her baby teeth showed. They all ignored the two odd strangers until the little girl dropped at Ratchet's feet and gazed gravely as he flipped his knife into the sand. She made to sit on his lap.

Sary raised her hand as if to ward off a blow. The sight was unnerving.

Ratchet stared the child down and moved irritably aside when she was unmoved. She hunkered over to him again. Finally Ratchet stood. She followed him like a forlorn ghost.

"Done sightseein'?" he grunted.

"Should at least say goodbye," Sary remarked. Besides, she was curious. She glanced at the hut, seeing movement, but it was only the cowhide flapping in the hot breeze. Wattle and daub, window flaps, and the door. Not to keep the rain out, certainly, but the beating sun.

Ratchet dipped a gourd into a bucket of water and drank, then dunked his head, wallowing in the sensation.

"They need that."

He shrugged, drank his fill, and poked his head past the flap and pulled it out again with a look of distaste. "Nothin' 'n' nobody."

She waved as they left. The children stared after, and Ratchet's conquest shyly waved back. Sary looked once more for a parent. Perhaps they—*she,* hid. Seeing Ratchet, she couldn't blame her.

Chapter 42
Hunter

It was hot, frying her feet through the soles, when at last sun pouring across endless scrub bled mercy, healing the wound of heat. Sary dropped as the blood-red sky turned thick with purple haze. She wished they traveled by night, but stumbling in the dark had a ghostly, lost feel.

She turned to breeze ruffling her hair with the faint chill foretelling night, but always, this brief temperance. It had rained two days before, another blessed event, topping canteens and cleansing their bodies.

Sary tensed, flattening at a *shush-shush-scrape-scrape* and a harsh rasping like heavy breathing from an invisible presence.

Ratchet, whose hearing wasn't as sharp, noticed and crouched, hand on his holster.

A man-shape about five feet away moved awkwardly about, apparently digging. Burly, wide-shouldered. If it weren't for the *shush-shush* of the shovel, a short folding thing used in the Boer War, they would have run into him.

Sary nodded her chin, gasping. Seven grave-like mounds surrounded him.

The man looked up.

Ratchet clamped his hand over her mouth.

She spat it off.

Swiveling, the shadowy man held the shovel like a weapon, showing his teeth in a snarl. He laid his shovel close by and stole for a pistol. He listened, then renewed grunting and digging. A foot deep in the hole, he tossed the spade and staggered out, briefly scanning the other graves. "Damn me. Puts paid to ya filthy buggers." He laughed harshly. "Me too, old chaps."

He dragged over a native, a boy lying in a tangle of limbs, booted the body into the hole, and scuffed sand over it until there was a last mound.

Beyond, she spotted the campfire. Blankets and supplies were messily scattered as if by animals.

Wearily, the man selected items from among the scattered junk, rolling his choices in a messy bedroll; he checked and shouldered two shotguns, searched the mess for ammunition, tucked a pistol into his belt, and dug a box of bullets from the dirt.

Suddenly she could see him better as he turned toward a rise. She saw the bloodstains, and the fact he was devilishly handsome beneath the weariness and strain. *Go, go!* she urged silently.

Maddeningly, he shook a canteen and slowly scanned the night as if sensing their presence. He finally clapped on a large hat and slogged off, bent like an old man.

After he disappeared, Sary ventured to the mounds, grave to grave. A brown hand stuck out of the last as if clawing for help. She turned. "Ratchet?"

"What?" He poked about the graves, not much interested.

"Why bury them? All of them? If he were dangerous, why not just leave them?"

Ratchet scratched his jaw where the scar ran.

"Maybe plague?"

Sary stepped back.

"But he took time. If he killed them, he wouldn't bother. Or if they had the plague."

Ratchet gave her a sour look.

"Let's follow him. Whoever he is, he looks like he knows where he's going."

"Looked sickly ta me."

"Just bone weary. Wouldn't you be, after eight graves?" *I'm not saying he resembles the great white hunter of my imagination, but...*

Ratchet, scratching under his eye patch, finally nodded. "Just tracks," he warned. "Looked sick ta me."

They followed the footprints, already filling in, watching him vanish over another dune.

Chapter 43
Curious Stranger

For hours, they played fox-and-hounds, ducking as he changed directions or checked behind. By late afternoon of the next day, as the stranger jogged in and out of view, using his rifle now as a staff, Sary's mind was focused on her empty belly, sunburnt skin, and sand fleas, in the endless slog under scorching sun.

It happened that fast. The stranger's tracks changed to formless holes, and, as the sun sank in the west, one second Sary dragged wearily around an island of scrub tossed up on a sea of desert, the next her foot trod *something*...spongy, alien, giving...

Down she went. The sand was still warmed by sun as the first nip foretold the arctic chill of endless night skies, when heat rushed to the stars and she shivered in a cold bed.

She closed her eyes. *Just lie here a while.*

Drowsily opened them.

Ratchet—far ahead. A pin dot now, blindly plodding. I could cover him with my thumb.

Her lids fluttered—then sprang open, when she saw the hand.

A hand just lying there, palm up.

A hand she must have *stepped* on.

The hand twitched, cupping itself, as if beckoning.

"Rat—chet!" she yelled.

149

Then Ratchet stumped beside her, breathing ragged.

"Leave 'im," he rasped. "Dead, ain't he?"

"Who? Dammit! Leave who?"

"Don't get yer knickers in a twist. It's yer gravedigger."

Ratchet quickly rifled pouches and thrust knuckled hands in the man's shirt as the man made feeble protest.

The sun sank like a stone, as it usually did.

Sary shuddered. "At least build a fire."

Ratchet snarled, tapping his own neck. "Look for boils."

Sary studied the stranger's arresting face, the strong column of neck showing a faint pulse.

"He doesn't have any. Light a fire."

"Get on."

"Light one, or I stay."

Ratchet bent in answer, bad leg stuck out, and wrapped his long hands about the man's neck, thumbs deep in his Adam's apple.

The man choked and struggled feebly, grabbing Ratchet's wrists.

"I'll give you reason ta leave," Ratchet gritted out.

"Ratchet!" Sary yelled.

Ratchet thudded beside her like a dead tree. Night was a velvet glove pressing her face, and then she saw the gleam of teeth in midair and the-man-who-buried tottered in view, holding a gun.

"Didn't turn me enough," he grated. "Forgot old Vickie here." He was leading-man handsome, square-jawed, widow-peaked hair flopping carelessly over a broad forehead.

He gazed fondly at the short ugly revolver in his

hand. "Named her 'Good Queen Victoria.' Ugly, fat, and graceless." He chuckled through blistered lips. "Short, stout, but always does her duty for England." His laugh choked with sand, and he crumpled without warning, with a face pale as cheese.

Ratchet got up, holding his head. "Fuckin' killer."

And you are not? Sary snatched Vickie, holding it steady.

"Aren't I dead enough?" the man slurred.

"All those men," Sary snapped. "You buried them. We saw you."

"Dead, weren't they?"

Sary jumped. Undetected, his hand had crept up and cupped her neck. His eyes fixed on her face.

"You are an angel in hell," he whispered. "How d'ya manage? My sister needs a regiment of maids to muster up a single spit curl…" His voice faded; he closed his eyes.

"Never mind your sister," Sary said. To Ratchet, she advised, "He's no danger. Can't you see?" Then, "Oh!" Sary's hand came away bloody from the ugly glistening black patch under the man's vest.

Ratchet rolled his one eye. *See what we get?*

Chapter 44
Raving

Lending her body's shade, Sary waited for his chest to rise and fall.

"Sorry. Couldn' dress f' dinner," the stranger suddenly called out, thrashing.

Sary shook his jaw.

He started awake.

Her fingers burned where they touched.

He stared with intense blue eyes. Though unfocused and bloodshot now, in days to come they'd be changeable as the Thames, gray one second, blue-green like iridescent glass the next. Any other time, with groomed hair the shade of old mahogany, trimmed beard, a square jaw, and strong nose called noble, he would be extremely masculine and fine-looking.

"Ain't that touchin'? Clara Barton now, are ya?"

Sary was only surprised Ratchet ever heard of the Civil War nurse. She didn't rise to his bait.

Ratchet snorted, reaching for the water.

"Don't drink much."

Ratchet took a long gulp. "Why? Savin' it for dandiprat there?" Ratchet smacked the canteen, sending it tumbling. His hostility went so deep he didn't care if it was stoppered or not.

"Defensive cuts on his arms," she finally said.

Ratchet chewed a twig, shrugging.

He's hotter than the sun. If he doesn't die of thirst, fever, or blood loss, infection will carry him off, but not on wings of angels. She looked at the sun. How long must they wait? Alternatively, how long would Ratchet stand for the delay?

He made it through the night.

The man groaned and slid up, more focused. "Dashed embarrassing. Allow me to properly introduce m'self after popping up so unexpectedly. Harry Swallow. Anthropologist, paleontologist, archeologist, and damned fool, at your service."

Though weak, his voice was plummy and cultured.

Ratchet tossed a rock. "Screw the horse you rode in on." He kicked him with his bad leg. The man cried out.

"Ratchet!"

"Do what I said, Sary. Leave him, the great carcass." Ratchet stumped off, disowning them.

"Ratchet. Damn it!"

"Ain't sharin' water. You can."

Sary leaned close to listen to her patient.

"Soldiers rounded the natives. There were heaps, literally mounds of the dead. Quarantined or worse. We left, but my bearers were havin' none of it—slipping off God knows where."

"Port Elizabeth. You were in Port Elizabeth?" She shook him. "Tell me."

"Yes."

"It was better? The sickness died down? When did you leave? Were there ships?" Her words tumbled out.

"Week ago," the man breathed.

Sary drooped. "Least there's shade." She nodded at the now-familiar yellow-blossomed trees with wicked thorns like fangs of a snake.

"Come, help."

Ratchet stumped over. "Jes' prolong the dyin'." But he helped tug him under the tree, taking time to dig his pockets again.

Without opening his eyes, the man gripped his wrist.

Ratchet sat back as if Lazarus rose from a winding cloth.

Sary gave Ratchet a look that would fry bacon and turned the man over. The bullet or knife had exited by a scabbed hole. God knew what it hit on the way. He wasn't bleeding—much. "Clean. Looks as if a bullet went straight though. Seems not to have damaged anything important."

"Ain't that a blessin'."

"Maybe he can help us."

"Put a bullet though his head. That 'ud be a big help."

"He might know the area." She discerned Ratchet's peevishness was merely habit now.

"Dig." The man scrabbled sand with disembodied fingers, muttering, "Tree. Water. Dig. Close to tree."

They studied hot dry sand that seemed damp as a crust of zwieback.

"Should bash both your brains in," Ratchet pronounced.

She bent over the man, feeling the imagined *thunk* of Ratchet's tree branch-crutch on her head, hearing the potential crack of cheekbone.

The moment passed.

"Under the damned acacia!" The man snarled in pain.

Ratchet was a broken cog. When the wheel

snagged, he was not in control, but then the wheel caught again. Ratchet dropped uncomfortably close, gouging his crutch into the sand as if stabbing her, to dig.

A foot down, grit changed from dun to dark gray, and a teaspoon of moisture seeped up. In ten minutes, a half cup of water filled the bottom.

Ratchet put his face in the tiny well, sucking it dry, announcing, "Not bad. If ya don't mind grit in yer craw."

He handed her the branch.

Another ten minutes and Sary knelt to gulp sandy water—a blessing, thanks to this stranger. These yellow-blossomed trees were ubiquitous. They would not die of thirst.

"Sweat off more'n we git." Ratchet sneered as Sary spooned water into her canteen.

Harry Swallow muttered, "You have all the cheerful aspect of a hanging judge."

Sary dug the branch extra hard. Like the little pot that didn't stop boiling, in the fairytale, more water oozed up.

She dipped a scrap of shirt tail into the small pool and dabbed his wound. Where she touched, he still burned. She squinted up. The sun was a white explosion hurling shards of heat. Perhaps it was sun—not fever.

The man stared. Had Sary known, it was as if an angel hung over him, golden hair blowing like wings about her shoulders and a corona of sun gilding her head.

Sary studied the stranger, feeling an odd stirring. He was so virile and fine-looking under the bruising beneath his eyes.

Sary suddenly had a picture of herself—burnt nose, grimy face, ripped clothes, wild hair—and unconsciously pinched the top of her dress, looking to see if Ratchet noticed, for Ratchet was a jealous dark god.

And why do I care how I look?

"Luck lives on your shoulder, sir," she said briskly. "No bullet to find."

"I presume you've had experience with such." His polished voice overlaid a sneer for the working class.

Sary smiled, cold at the implied insult that nurses were akin to prostitutes and actresses. "I have."

Ratchet hooted.

She accidently brushed the man's wound.

"Sorry."

"Anytime." He revealed white teeth with a lazy, knowing look.

"I doubt you will die," Sary snapped.

She ripped another scrap, sticking it to the wound. "It'll keep sand flies out."

"I hate to presume, yet I am famished—very. And I apologize for being so horribly curt."

"Don't have much, but we can share."

Ratchet's lips curved downward, thin as a scythe.

"Perhaps, first"—Sary gazed levelly—"you should tell us what that burying ritual was all about." *As if I haven't buried bodies in the dark of night...*

Chapter 45
Plague Bearers

"One or two bearers started out sick," the stranger said. "Soon they dropped like flies, with as much notice, two days out. We had made surprisingly good time. The healthy bearers all wanted to bolt. I told them, 'Nothing's back there but horror.' That we brought it *with* us…" Harry looked off for a moment before he continued, "They had none of it." He barked a laugh. "They decided, rather pointedly,"—touching his wound—"they didn't need *me* to plan their future. What there was left of it." He laughed. "Scarpered with my provisions, tremendous lot of good it did 'em. Burying the last when you—"

"Why didn't you…"

"Die?" He grinned, spreading hands wide. "I'm an English toff. Didn't you realize?"

Ratchet wandered off, cursing. Probably to a call of nature, though he had no such compunction around her.

Sary leaned close.

"Watch Ratchet. He's not *anyone's* friend," she whispered. "Watch him at all times. He's like a scorpion in your boot."

"I gathered that. And you, sunburnt angel of the desert—my Salome, my Sheba, my Nefertiti…"

"Don't know who those ladies are. Maybe Salome or Bathsheba, like in the Bible, and somehow you don't

157

seem a 'Harry.' I'll call you…Hunter."

"You have my express permission to call me anything you wish, madam." He looked up under his lashes. "Or anytime."

"Mercy. We are getting better, aren't we?" Sary flushed.

The clefts in his jaws deepened.

Chapter 46
Lizards

"I was anticipating the lost tomb of a Hittite princess rumored to be this far south." Hunter flung sand hand to hand. "Would have made my name. Like bloody Heinrich Schliemann! I had maps, even!"

Was it paranoia, or did Hunter seem to study her as he mentioned maps?

Hungry, parched, lost with a lunatic and a sick man, with plague nipping at my heels, and still I think on diamonds?

"I'll be back." Wincing, Hunter heaved himself up, swayed, and plucked his hat off a thorn.

"Yeah, we'll wait right here." Ratchet cleaned his nails and flung his knife. It quivered in the acacia where Hunter's head had been.

The man Sary would think of only as Hunter threw Ratchet an unreadable look, barking a laugh. "Suit yourself."

A blast—and another. Hunter strolled back as if in a Sunday park, swinging two large lizards by the tails, items soon to be high on the list of menu favorites.

Happy and filled for once, Sary watched a sun scarlet as poppies shed petals across the Karroo. Even Ratchet searched the sky as colors deepened to a dark turquoise, with a moon so brilliant it cut her eyes; the third act was an ebon cape sequined with stars.

Sary mellowed under Africa's dark magic, meeting Hunter's gaze across the campfire. She looked away.

"I don't have the pleasure. Did you tell me?"

"It's Sary—Sarabande. Sarabande Swinford." She lifted her arms, pinning hair off her neck. She knew Hunter noticed the rise and fall of her breasts, the sweat stain; blushing, she vanished as if for a call of nature.

She needed to be alone. Hunter flustered her.

Watching her back, Ratchet leaned close to the man. "Sary may look like sunshine and crocheted doilies, but watch her. Tried to kill me more'n once."

"And that's why you are together, no doubt?"

"Not your concern, now, is it, Sir Muckety-Muck?"

Hunter shrugged.

"Ask her. As soon put a bullet in yer head as breathe."

"Again, sir, may I point out, if so, why did she attempt to save me so assiduously?"

Ratchet spat. "Look here. I was deputized in Big Bear to bring her back as a runaway murderess. Been chasing her ever since. She kilt two men and buried 'em in Big Bear Mountain back in the U.S. of A. They don't know what all she did to her brother, what took care of her and—hell, won't trouble you with the rest of her heinous crimes!"

"Sound as if you rehearsed that."

Ratchet's eye turned flat gray. "Suit yerself." He spat venomously and rolled a twig between his teeth as if longing for a cigarette.

Hunter stared long into the night.

Chapter 47
Boer Woman

Goats nibbled skimpy pasture, accompanied by a black cow and a red one. A small holding. Sary's stride quickened.

Closer, a woman hastened indoors.

Sary gratefully ducked from the scalding day to a hot fusty dimness—then Hunter, then Ratchet. The wide-hipped female, her faded dress held across her ample bosom by one enormous safety pin, eyed them sullenly.

Sary's eyes adjusted. It was a squalid hovel, roughly partitioned to form a bedroom and kitchen lighted by two small windows. Dirty calico tacked on rafters made a ceiling. The earthen floor was oddly shiny.

"Cow dung," was Hunter's cryptic comment.

"What?"

"The servant polishes it with a paste of cow dung and water—weekly. It's quite hard," Hunter whispered.

Sary shook her head. "Servants?"

Sary checked a pot of something simmering on a crude stove; the air was redolent of gamey mutton. That and the heat were overwhelming. Sary swallowed hard. Flies thick on the table investigated splotches of dried food. Hunter checked the room as if it were an archeological find. Perhaps it was.

A scrawny, dark-skinned woman ducked inside past Ratchet, toting water.

Hunter looked amused. "They all do,"—he nodded at the older woman—"no matter how poor. The Boer do not *do* menial work."

"But what does she do all day?" Sary whispered as she assessed the room. "We can't ask for help."

"It's tradition," Hunter said. "She expects it, no matter what she thinks."

"We mustn't." Sary looked about, impatient.

A rope frame laced with rawhide made a bed. There was a chest of drawers and a cracked mirror, with a grimy rag hanging beside it. No wash bowl or pitcher. Rawhide seats—a slab table with a crusted bowl of cornmeal porridge and a half-eaten meal of gray mutton boiled with rice.

The woman reappeared—alone. Somehow, she had neatened herself—stringy hair tied with a bedraggled red ribbon. A different but no fresher apron. Sary raised a brow. "Aren't there any men in this country? Only women alone?"

"That's how I like 'em. Alone." Ratchet showed yellow teeth.

"Goeie dag, vrou!" Hunter strode across with a dazzling grin and a hand out. He gave a short bow.

"My naam is Harry." The *vrou* glanced sideways at Sary, muttering words that sounded like, *"Hoe's dit vir 'n ding!"*

Sary looked at Hunter, uncertain.

Hunter looked at his boots, flashing the cleft in his cheek, and the woman plastered on a smile smooth and polished as her cow-dung floor, Sary thought sourly.

"It—it means, '*Oh, look who we have here,*' " he

explained.

Somehow, she didn't think so. "Tell her we need help," Sary said.

The disdain in the *vrou's* ageless eyes was plain, despite her years of shielding them from a harsh African sun and treeless desert. Plain also was the scorn in her voice as she replied in a flurry of guttural speak.

"She said," Hunter translated, coughing, "With two men in tow?"

The woman's eyes fixed on Ratchet's rangy, bony figure. Perhaps it was the eye patch.

"Go on," Sary said.

"She said, 'Should hardly think you need help, or maybe' "—Hunter hesitated—" 'you, ah, help us.' "

Ratchet snorted, hands resting on his gun belt. "Ha! Miss Bible Thumper?"

"Ask her—You speak her language—where are we?"

"Her man is at the Vaal, diamond panning, most likely…" He stopped.

Sary's heart lurched. A tiny drum of hope, thrill of the chase, beat.

"How close?" Sary nagged.

Hunter tried a brief guttural exchange. He shrugged. "Not very helpful, I'm afraid. She's not dimwitted, just dull. I wager she hasn't been far from here for a decade."

Sary sighed. "I'm still hungry."

Hunter spoke a few words.

The woman showed yellow teeth, wriggling herself in between the two men, scowling at Sary. She shouted something. The elderly African drudge brought a wood plank with four mismatched, cracked cups, plunking down coarse wheat bread to soak in a gritty black coffee-syrup.

She motioned.

"Brood? Botter? Kaas? Koffie?"

"Goat cheese and butter," Hunter muttered. Ratchet immediately scooped up a half loaf of bread, slathered it with butter, heaped on goat curd, and gulped a cup of scalding black *koffie.*

"Ratchet!" Hunter grabbed his wrist as he poured the second.

Ratchet shrugged. "I left some." He grinned evilly at the woman, looking like a wolf with a mouth full of teeth.

The woman fluttered, simpered, and pushed the goat curd closer. *There is no man at all. Perhaps we might leave Ratchet as payment or punishment. I can dream.* How little she knew.

The butter had turned, but Sary supposed it would take a miracle to keep it fresh. Somehow, it was gone, and she chased the few crumbs left.

"We are so grateful. Thank you for your…" She spoke loudly, but the woman was smiling and nodding broadly at the two men, saying, *"Goed? Ja?"* and ignoring her.

Hunter spoke gracious nothings in Boer or Dutch or Hindustan, for all she knew, holding the woman's reddened hands—reddened from what? Sary wondered, looking around. The slattern did all the work. The woman blushed, bridled, and did an awkward barefoot curtsy.

He tipped his hat. "Ma'am."

Sary stepped outside, breathing the hot spicy air, hearing the *vrou* talk excitedly in guttural chatter behind her.

Hunter studied the distance.

"She says stay the night, or as long as we want. Us—not you." He grinned. "Though I don't think I could stand another of her buffets."

"I wouldn't mind bathing."

Hunter translated.

The woman thumbed a direction and gave Sary a pail, indicating she fill the barrel, too. It took five trips. Why the Hades did they not build the hut next to the bloody well?

She refused Hunter's help.

Ratchet flirted with the woman.

Sary scrubbed the scummy basin with sand. Bent over a crazed enamel bowl of rapidly graying water, she rubbed *seep* foam through long tangled hair, pouring a gourd of clean rinse water. She felt eyes and heard a body brushing a wall, and looked up sourly at Ratchet, who leaned, picking his teeth, seeing what he could see.

She gave a blank stare.

Ratchet heehawed, moving off.

Quickly finishing before she entertained Hunter with her striptease, she washed underarms and "druthers" before flinging water on the wilting geraniums.

"Frankly, I could use a night of rest *not* under the stars. Might be decent food in the morning. I saw eggs."

"Of course." She put on a good face. She would sleep by the door.

Chapter 48
Ratchet Finds Love

She heard the sounds and squeezed her eyes tight, yearning for sleep's escape. She knew what it was without opening her eyes. In the far corner, the woman slithered up. Ratchet lazily watched her approach.

Sary could see how comely the *vrou* had been at one time, in a Dutch-doll way, flaxen hair almost white in the moon shining through a gap, big blue eyes a bit bulging now, a tip-tilted nose broadening over the years, the once-plump rosy cheeks now jowly.

That wasn't kind. Her life must be agonizingly lonely. Sary saw the need to be comforted, saved, loved, and held. But that she failed to see what Ratchet was? That was repellent.

Through lashes, Sary searched for Hunter.

Although unschooled in such matters, she sensed that was Ratchet's appeal. The *danger.* The eye patch. The woman saw his cruelty as strength, as she leant for a kiss.

But Ratchet locked elbows, holding her up under her arms, studying her as if she were a piece of hanging meat.

Longing to be anywhere but here, Sary eyed the oblong of dark beyond the flap.

Still she watched.

The woman sat on her knees, striving for seduction

in the awkward way she clutched her hem, slowly dragging it up, spoiling the effect by catching it on her knees.

Hitching it free, the woman raised it over her head, a faded thing with flower sprigs, until her face was covered.

She kept raising it, revealing grubby, threadbare underthings, a shapeless shift held with safety pins.

So hot in these blasted places, why underthings at all?

The Boer woman's breasts were large and pale, with huge pink aureoles. She tugged a string holding her knickers. Ratchet flung himself on top of her, rolling her under, grinding her into the dirt floor. The woman gave a yip of surprise and pain.

Sary flinched and looked away. No welcome from this woman if she interfered. Now the woman was on top, growling something guttural. And so they tussled and thrashed, grunting, moaning.

Sary reached up, wrapping her fingers around a knife's cracked horn handle from the woman's rough table. She hoped it wasn't her only one. She felt bad, but without it, Sary would feel even worse. She tucked it in her pack. There. Somehow, she felt safer, vindicated. Ready for anything.

What happened next left Sary trembling in the oppressiveness of the hut. Not the coupling itself. Ratchet suddenly took the woman—rolled her over, even as she dragged him down to her, where they gouged, dug, grunted, and struggled—animals fighting for supremacy. It was brief, and left the woman gasping and unsatisfied, for she pawed Ratchet further.

Sary wanted nothing more than to leave. *Please let*

me go.

Ratchet shoved the poor woman off, growling unintelligibly.

Sary scarce let her chest rise and fall in the silence, frozen in place, embarrassed if Hunter were awake. *Why didn't I leave!*

Heretofore, Sary had supposed Ratchet a sexless man deriving erotic pleasures from the pain, ugliness, and distress of others, that he ferreted the weak.

A slice of moon showed half of Hunter's face, and that half mirrored Sary's thoughts.

When the woman began anew, making small whimpers, meant to be murmurs of passion or even love, Hunter moved, and Sary felt herself lightly touched.

Neither spoke of what went on behind them as they stole into the clean, crisp night, leaving the goatish hut behind.

They tracked stars blooming like silver flowers on a black bed, the sweet, balmy air lightly fingering their faces. Her newly washed hair blew errant in the breeze.

Then she felt his breath brushing the words, "Don't stay so near. I'm dangerous, too. Very."

Then, in a moment, "This is how it is done," Hunter said.

Though she resisted, still awash with the scene inside, Hunter cupped her face with rough calloused hands and gently but thoroughly kissed her.

"Who are you—really?" she whispered, breathless, when he finally released her. *Why am I reacting?*

His eyes seemed colorless, black, and impassive. "Why—a pedantic. A boring scholar grubbing about the desert." His voice hoarsened. "But tonight, I'm a man holding the most tempting creature. A sorceress with tousled hair. If your aim is to tempt me beyond reason, I would not go that route, unless one wants the tables turned. I will turn them, believe me."

Then Hunter nuzzled words against her hair. "I am not him."

Unseemly, for him to whisper these sentiments after the sordid acts they had just witnessed.

"And I am not like that! Sir."

Suddenly repulsed and embarrassed, Sary swung her hand, connecting with his jaw.

He stood like a stone. "Don't fear me, Sary. I am a man like any other. Things…stir me, which would not a lady. I am not like *him*."

She almost softened, but then he uttered, "I *could* tease you to death, however."

Sary stiffened.

Then she felt her feet lifted from the scrub. She was a thistledown light as dandelion fluff. If he'd let her go, she'd have sailed off.

Sary did not realize her fair hair blazed a waving corona in the night desert breeze.

He looked up at her. "Ah, Sary, Sary, you seem a wanton madonna."

She slipped down his arms and back to ground.

"The only way to erase that ugliness is to replace it with an act that is clean and real and pure."

Oh, he is clever, very clever. It took every effort to shove away.

He was right, though. She knew they would fit together like two spoons, two halves of a walnut shell, reacting and acting in perfect rhythm. She felt the flow of heat leaving her like a river to the stars as they parted, wanting nothing more than to burrow back, nestle in his warmth.

Forget.

Her feet moved away. *Stop! Call me back. Come after me.*

Sary, thrashing and turning, huddled in exhausted sleep close to the doorway, willing the morning to come.

****

Hunter stared down at her, almost touching an errant curl pale as wood shavings.

Conflicting passions crowded. She was a beauty. Unique in that. Even with her sunburnt nose and eyes that fought heaven or hell, she was matchless.

Even that stiff arm she hides is touching. Wonder what story's there. And those bullet scars? Now, that's an intriguing wonder. What dark tale do they tell? Did the detestable Ratchet tell it true? My, I'm waxing poetic this night.

Sary was a wanton saint, a lusty gamin with womanly attributes, a choir-singing temptress, one as dangerous as any Circe luring him to perilous shoals of…*feelings.* He could not pin her on a board or put her under a bell jar in pride of place until he figured out what in the hell to do with her.

Chapter 49
Lust

Out of the woman's hovel into first light. A quick gourd of water, scrubbing all over again—Lord knew when she'd next have this luxury—Sary felt ready to face the devil or the day, let alone Ratchet—or Hunter.

Sluicing, she dragged fingers, untangling a mare's nest of sun-bleached hair, quickly braiding a side plait.

Behind her, the Boer *vrou* hung over Ratchet, roguishly offering sips from her cracked mug of ersatz coffee. *Ugggh! What is the attraction? Does she suppose Ratchet would stay?*

As much as she might want that, with images of Hunter and herself, alone last night, coming unbidden, Sary kenned well Ratchet would never linger unless there was something in it other than a lumpy, faded wife whose husband might or might not return.

Hunter locked eyes with Sary. They communicated briefly. Ratchet threw the woman back against the doorframe.

What else? Sary strode resolutely on. "What should we do now, Hunter? Did you learn anything?"

"From what I made out, there is no sickness up this far. That's the good news. The bad is she hasn't a clue how far to the rail line."

"Our canteens are topped, and she did give us some bread…"

Chapter 50
Fury

They didn't get far. All three plodded off lighthearted and refreshed, with Ratchet cracking tasteless jokes at the woman's expense, but then the wind picked up, and the sky cracked open with a mighty peal, spilling out rain.

Sary looked back. The woman still watched them.

Behind the hut, a front, dark and deep as a coal mine, tracked them in an enormous U.

The woman closed the flap as the sky marched, a malevolent army thrusting lightning spears between shields of iron-gray cloud; the crack and boom were not unlike cannon fire.

"Go back!" He didn't need to tell Ratchet and Sary. Hunter and Sary sprinted, Ratchet hitching and cursing behind, back to the mean shelter, before hail big as hens' eggs thudded the ground.

Later, Sary stared at the hut's raw ceiling, so generously porous that morning, now a conduit for lashes of rain dripping cold on her head. Nowhere was safe and warm. Turbulence sent vicious waves of drenching cold though the cowhide flap.

The woman didn't bother placing pans to catch fresh water, just a moldy rain barrel outside, there since Moses. She took the room's one chair, knitting a gray knotted thing, more a long dish rag than anything useful, with the only blanket about her shoulders.

Sary crouched by the doorway, watching the storm. Ratchet flipped his knife, taciturn. The woman read him, staying away. Grudgingly, toward noon, the *vrou* brought out coarse bread and more rancid butter, and for ceremony—celebrating what, Sary had yet to discover—a pot of crusted jam.

"*Gietende reën*," she muttered, as if the rain was all Sary's fault.

Sary ate the bread, sluicing it down with cold rainwater. The sooty skies melded into true night; still the rain pounded. Sary curled in a ball away from the wet, hoping there wasn't a reoccurrence of last night's passion play.

Chapter 51
Obsession

Odors of stringy hair reeking with mutton fat, an unwashed body, stale armpits, sweat-stained clothes dried in the Great Karroo heat assailed Sary as she jerked awake. *The woman.* Sensing warmth against her face, Sary lashed out to ward off—a kindness? A blow? A dark-time confidence?

The woman's shielded candle lent her an evil nimbus, keeping her face, hair hanging down, in shadow. Sary saw the gleam of blocky teeth and the whites of her eyes.

She wants to kill us as we sleep. Or—just me?

The woman raised a hand holding something sharp and glittering. The bone-handled knife Sary had returned. "You wanted my knife?" She muttered in Boer, but Sary translated just fine.

Sary yelled, kicking out, catching the woman's stomach. The knife flew. Hunter awkwardly grabbed the woman by the waist, hauling her back as she struggled and screeched.

Ratchet's guffaws filled the hut. Then, grunting, he turned over, the entertainment done.

Hunter threw the *vrou* into the chair, and still the woman protested. Sary directed anger toward Ratchet, not this sad woman, as she crawled to the furthest corner, glaring, miserable, and sad.

"Voetsek! Voetsek! Jou verdomde! Damn you! You ruined everything! I had me a man here! *Vies vark!"* the woman growled.

"Let's go. Rain will be refreshing after this."

"Coulda buried you out there! Under the sand—and no one the wiser—after taking off those fancy *klere!"* Her spit flew.

'*Klere?*" Sary looked puzzled at Hunter.

"She wants your clothes."

The woman stabbed toward Sary's feet, beginning to crawl with a sly look. "*Kaalgat! Kaalgat!*" She hissed. "Myn!"

Kaalgat?

Drawing her feet up, Sary looked at Hunter.

"Boots, too," he muttered, looking off, biting his cheek as the *vrou* kept up a string of spit-laced oaths.

Sary backed to the door.

"She wants to leave you, uh, with your fanny showing."

Sary frowned.

"Bare-ass neked," Ratchet growled.

Sary's face crumpled into laughter; she hadn't laughed for so long, her throat caught.

"No more. Please."

"Yes. Methinks we overstayed our welcome, unless…?" He tipped his head at Ratchet. "Perhaps I presume overmuch?"

"Hunter. Don't." She wouldn't wish Ratchet on any lonely member of her sex.

"All in agreement, then." Hunter tipped his hat, leaving the woman screeching and running after them.

"Vat jou goed en trek! More is nog 'n dag…!"

Hunter glanced back, not with unkindness.

"Yes, madam. We *are* taking our things, and perhaps your morrow *will* be another better day."

Sary glanced back at the sullen, stringy-haired female with her dumpling face that used to be rosy as an apple, now sagging like unbaked dough. Sary's mouth twitched a sympathetic smile.

The woman slumped at the doorway as if holding it up, forlorn and bitter. "*Vies vark! Vies vark!*" was her hurled farewell.

Hunter shook his head. "Scarce think we're filthy pigs!"

Sary looked back. The woman had vanished into her lonely sanctuary.

Hunter put his arm about her shoulders. Sary felt his hard, protective length with a ripple of desire that had her instantly tugging away.

As the three plodded over the drying earth, they little heeded the mud-washed stones of bright colors trampled underfoot.

Chapter 52
Ants

"Why not rest the day and walk now?" It seemed logical as the sky deepened from peach to purple.

"'From ghoulies and ghosties and long-leggedy beasties and things that go bump in the night, Good Lord, deliver us.' Hard slog in the dark, Sary. Might fall down some varmint hole."

Sary gasped and halted. "Hunter!"

For an instant, she spied four—no, five—strangers looming in wait. But the tall lumpy shapes stayed still as Lot's wife, like pillars of salt, soon receding in the night as Sary and her companions plodded on.

She blew out and stopped again when they had passed. *"Can't go farther now anyway."*

Groaning, Ratchet too fell flat, weakly clawing his brace. "Wouldn't say no ta that."

Ratchet had gamely limped without protest, even though Sary noted stains each day blackening his legs from the knee down. A wonder the wound didn't turn septic, but Ratchet's blood was already bad. Nothing could harm him, it seemed. She held a grudging respect for Ratchet. He could give pain, but also take it.

Hunter seemed entitled to perfection, with grace under pressure by birthright.

Ratchet hobbled for scrub to burn, mumbling something probably scathing. Hunter slipped his pack and helped. For once, Sary was not compelled. She knew nothing after that but the cold kiss of sand on her cheek.

On her cheek!

"OW! OW—OW!"

Sary jumped up, clawing frantically through her clothes. Her face was on fire. Her clothes crawled with *things.* Biting *black* things.

"Hell's fire!" Ratchet joined in yelping, digging frenziedly through his shirt and swatting his body.

Under the moon, Sary saw a black, undulating tide rushing toward her. She shrank as the erratic flood raced closer around her—millions of evil, winking carapaces swarmed in a swift, glittering river.

She backpedaled, too shocked to scream, and then the skittering hoard was on her, racing up her legs as she slapped, brushed, twirled, stamped. Her legs turned black as if painted—the things gained her body, swiftly crawling over her neck and face, where they clung, bit blistered lips, forcing between for moisture.

They crawled up her nose, invaded her ears, scuttling through her hair. Sary tripped, falling in the middle of a black fury rapidly covering her in a moving, stinging blanket.

Hunter, with his jodhpurs tucked tight in his boots, rolled to her side. Yanking her upright, he harshly brushed and slapped her body, yelling above her wails, "Off! Take them off!"

Sary danced unhearing.

The black biting things wriggled under her clothes, poured over breasts spilling above the hated corset. Sharp nips traversed ankle to calf to thigh as Sary stamped and turned, madly swatting Hunter's hands, shouting, "They burn! Stop them!" *I'll go mad.*

Hunter, dragging large hands heavily down her body, roared, "Hold still!" He dragged her away from the worst and gripped her shirt, buttons popping, sailing white in the dark. He yanked at her corset.

Sary stayed his hands.

He backed off, exasperated. "Keep the bloody thing on, but they are crawling under it!"

Ratchet howled in the dark, "I could use some help here!"

Through her confusion, Ratchet was a writhing shape black with insects. She instantly forgot him as fresh bites seared her flesh. She couldn't brush her face, screaming as another horde invaded her mouth.

Hunter hooked his fingers, clawing out a mass of wiggling things. She choked, biting down on the last few, crunching the black, sour, oily taste, and spitting them out.

She saw one on the back of her hand. Huge. A goliath of an ant. Big, fat, shining, with long pincers.

Swatting the ants from his own hands and arms, Hunter lifted Sary, racing her away from the main tributary. There he ripped the remaining shreds of her shirt, again unlacing the bodice, with her clinging to it.

"Don't be childish."

"No! It—it's keeping them out!"

But they were under it. She watched one and then two insert between the tight confines of her corselet.

Giving a mighty tug, Hunter snapped the last laces. The corselet dropped, spraying ants and releasing her body. Her poor tired corset lay like gray wings of an angel at her feet. And she had red stings on her bosom.

It hardly mattered.

The tenacious ants clung, biting and skittering down her belly. Hunter brushed her breasts, meeting Sary's eyes. They both looked away at the same time, yet Sary saw a flicker of desire and something enigmatic, even amidst the havoc.

The ants for some insect reason swarmed around instead of over Ratchet, making him an island as they continued their race across the Karroo. When they abruptly changed back to a six-foot-wide army, and Ratchet was again in their path, he bellowed like a wounded bull as he stumped to their place of safety.

Ratchet, his face swollen with bites, brushing at some that tried to crawl under his eye patch, plucked the last of them. "Oooh! Ugggh!"

They ignored him as Hunter fumbled Sary's waist, thick-fingered in his haste, and Sary's dancing about did not help as she whirled and plucked at her hair.

"*Owwwwoooh*," she continued wailing. "Please! Get 'em off! Get them *off!*"

Hunter placed hands on her hips, forcing her still. In agony, she stood. *Oh, but she wanted to leap about— to run!*

At last, both their hands were tearing at the strings of her pantaloons. *Only two pair left—don't tear them.*

Hunter had ants swarming his arms now; ignoring them, he snapped the frayed cord barely holding her knickers on narrower hips, flinging them in what seemed a shower of soot.

Sary stood naked in the moonlight, welcoming Hunter's rasping palms soothing the itch, the red welts; she didn't mind she was naked as he cupped her narrow waist, scraping the last ants off her slender hips; each hand spanned her thighs and calves, crushing and dragging the remaining insects clean away.

Ratchet was down to his grubby long johns, moaning and grumbling.

Sary felt stung by a thousand tiny deaths, but she was free of the ants—and her clothing—beneath the un-judgmental moon, while the army of ants swarmed on their mindless journey across the desert floor.

Chapter 53
Marble Venus

Sary remained still, shocked, little caring she shimmered blue-white as a marble Venus, her breasts gleaming and pale beneath the vee shape of her sunburn and all the bullet scars and wounds from her past revealed.

Hunter and Ratchet fell back nonplused, each in his own way, Ratchet with awe and Hunter with admiration, although Ratchet made a great show of stomping on the remaining insects.

Frozen under Hunter's stare and Ratchet's frequent glances, Sary stood iconic as any marble Athena or Diana. She would not hide or act a virginal bride, gazing coolly for what seemed a levitation of time, floating, feet above the sand, feeling the chill healing her skin, glorying in it.

Placing her hands at her waist in an attitude of "Seen enough?" she stared them down. "You, Ratchet. Why are *you* gawping?"

Ratchet didn't budge. He scratched his jaw, wiped his mouth, his one eye never wavering. Finally, he looked away.

Not knowing what else to do, he swerved on Hunter.

"Hie, ya. Ya dragged us in the middle of a confounded plague! We're damn well eaten alive, and

I'm so damn dry, I'm turnin' inside out, Mr. High in the Saddle! Thought you knew so much!" He spat. "Yer all guns and no bullets! With all your palaver, ya don't know beans about where in this godforsaken hellhole we're at."

He ground to a stop, cramming on his hat, and stomped off.

"We fled the Black Death, or have you forgotten? Without me, you'd be bones scattered across the Karroo or a nameless corpse in a trench doused with lime."

Not quite true. Sary closed her mind. She'd had these same thoughts, shameful as they were. *The plague would be better.* Crossing her breasts with one hand and cupping her sex with the other, she sought out her scattered clothes.

Yet, where were they going? She shook her head. She must trust him, because that was all there was. That and her own tenacity.

Sary caught Ratchet's eye. *Time to stop the show.*

The peculiar spell was broken. They still hawked her, but not openly. *How to make a dignified end to this?*

Sary shook out her garments, poor as they were, fastening the corselet first, oddly more naked with her sex and bosom exposed and the rest covered, swiftly stepping slim, bitten legs into her torn pantalets, knotting the drawstring, and dragging on the ripped shirt, buttoning the one button.

"I appreciate your help," she said stiffly.

Hunter doffed an imaginary cap, giving a last linger at her bosom above the famous dirty corselet.

"My pleasure."

She felt a strong grip on her elbow.

A thousand thoughts swam behind Hunter's eyes, like a flickering lantern show. His voice was thick. "Beware a patient man, Sary; he could become enflamed beyond reason."

They locked eyes.

"You two havin' a private party over there? Or can anyone join?" Ratchet called, peevish, from a distance.

They moved off.

A movement broke the spell with the sound of many feet scuffling sand. Sary started. *What, on God's green earth, now?* Laughing, Sary saw a pride of lumpy, ungainly creatures with long snouts, funny ears, and bristly bodies scurrying, not at them but chasing the ants.

The moon slid beyond a cloud curtain, highlighting tributaries of crazed, disoriented ants streaming toward the tall mounds.

Silent Towers of Babel... The brooding sentinels they had seen earlier towered manikin-like several feet over even Ratchet's head, the tallest of them.

"The demon ant-slayers!" Hunter roared as the unwieldy animals lurched among the ant heaps, licking up insects with long, gray, prehensile tongues as the ants scattered to the tall mud towers.

Ratchet predictably bellowed, "Kin ya eat them fellers?"

"Aardvarks. Means earth pig." One nearly knocked Hunter over in its zeal to get to the ants.

The pig-like animal had pointed ears, and the closest was at least seven feet long, including a muscular tail, a narrow head with a blunt snout, and bristles all over. Sary nipped behind Hunter, watching their lethal claws rip into the dirt mounds. Their teeth were like long, round, shoe pegs.

"In answer to your query, Ratchet, one can eat them. Considered quite good."

Chapter 54
Earth Pigs

The aardvarks scattered under the force of the blast. Ratchet aimed his long revolver again. Hunter shunted him aside, toeing the giant felled aardvark. "Why waste bullets? Can't eat more than one."

Ratchet blinked. "Uh. I just kill varmints. Never skinned one." And, incongruously, "I'm a city fella."

You only skin humans.

Hunter turned to Sary. "Scarcely my thing, either, old girl." *It must have taken ages of inbreeding and money to hone that look.* "Not much good in the scullery. We always had…"

"Servants for that sort of thing, *old bean,*" Sary snapped. "Give it!" She snatched Ratchet's knife.

"Farm girls are not fainting violets, nor are we particularly safe to be around!" She included both of them in her glare and turned to the giant beast. The skin was thick with bristly, brownish hairs.

Hunter and Ratchet gathered scrub. After Sary butchered the choice bits, they held chunks on a knife tip over flames in good humor, though Hunter shot enigmatic looks at her. Soon the aroma, very like roasted pork, filled the night.

Sary groaned, rubbing her belly. The meat was sweet, tender, satisfying, and like the aroma, very like roasted pork.

Ratchet grinned. "Ya wield a wicked knife, Faintin' Violet, give ya that. I'll have me another little taste."

For once, the three of them were in rare harmony.

Sharon Shipley

Chapter 55
Ancient Bones

Strips of aardvark spiked on acacia thorns dried in the fierce sun. Ratchet dug water, and Hunter scraped strips of hide, tying them around Sary's boots.

"Might soften the heat."

Later Sary discarded them because of insects.

The trio wove their way past the brooding mounds. They never mentioned her nakedness, yet she caught Ratchet's gaze wandering her body in its tattered trousers and shred of a shirt held closed.

Eventually she didn't bother.

Her hat had vanished somewhere. Sary bitterly wished she'd plucked up enough energy to chase after it as it skittered hither and thither across dunes, snagged on scrub, and then disappeared.

Sary tied a rag over her brow. It shaded her eyes. Tough aardvark meat made her parched, and she ate little, though Ratchet and Hunter relished the gritty strips.

Another man thing.

Sary squinted up. A soaring vulture rested on ragged, outspread wings. She wished she could see what it saw up there. How close were they to any civilization, or was the world this endless desert?

Hunter seemed bent on further educating them. Sary was already prickly. Underneath, she discerned

188

Hunter kept them occupied.

How little he knows how irritating that is.

She studied the endless sandscape for life and found only the ever-looming green escarpment as they headed northwest. It was ten days since the last hut, the one with the amorous widow.

"The great Karroo—an inland basin formed, oh, two hundred fifty million years ago..." Hunter was saying.

"That's nice," Sary murmured. "Will we be part of it? Bleached bones unearthed two hundred fifty million years from now?" She heard the snap in her voice.

"Ya dig up lotta old bones and sift dirt and think yer godallmighty."

"...great inland deltas, seas, swamps. Ancient reptiles, amphibians of immense size thrived in wetness." Hunter flung his arms. "Bones all over."

"Wish they were yours," Ratchet rumbled predictably.

"Forgive me. Karroo's the Eiffel Tower, the Great Pyramid, the whole bloody Nile, to us paleontologists."

Thought you were an archeologist?

"...Mesosaurus Aquatic Dwyka. An early carnivore."

"Wish I had one a them carny-vores," Ratchet grumbled. "I'd show it who et who."

"....Bradisaurus, Dictodon, Lystrosaurus, Thrinaxodon, Eupakeriaa, Massospondylitis, Megazostradon..." Rolling off in his agreeable baritone, the names brought magic—*cool wet green jungles.*

His magic did not work.

"Except in a fickle seasonal rainfall, the Great

Karroo is shunned by almost every living creature. Save us."

"Even lions are scared to venture from a favorite water hole. Won't see many, or rhinos—nothing to tempt the rhino from his muddy bed and lush thickets. Only mad Englishmen…"

"Enough racket, *perfessor!*" Ratchet glared under his deep hat.

Hunter ignored him. "The springbok still haunts the Great Karroo…"

"Why great? Always spouting 'great.' What's so fucking *great* about the great *Karroo*? Like walkin' on hot sandpaper, ya fuckin' idjit!"

Ratchet had an unholy gleam of homicidal rage. His leg must drag him down with pain. He constantly blinked the one eye.

He's on the edge of breaking. Shut up, Hunter. If he kills Hunter? It doesn't bear scrutiny. To be alone with Ratchet in this endless waste? No. No!

"Any notion how vast—"

"If you tell me, so help me, I *will* gut you." Ratchet picked up a stone.

Hunter looked back. Ratchet dropped the stone.

Hunter seemed to taunt Ratchet with words.

"Bigger game—blessbok, hartebeest, kudu, and wildebeest that used to feed…"

Ratchet's kettle of bile was ready to boil over.

"Be quiet, Hunter." Sary spoke low but firm.

She looked back. Ratchet seemed in a sullen stupor.

"Not surprising diamond seekers rarely saw any mark for their rifles when they journeyed these deserts," Hunter continued, oblivious.

He mentioned diamonds—again. First maps, then diamonds.

Sary glimpsed Ratchet creeping behind, a rock raised and madness in his eye.

"Hunt—!" Sary managed. Ratchet swung wildly, with maniacal force, sheering Hunter's ear, the rock thunking off his collarbone, going down with the swing.

The two wrestled, kicking up gritty flour.

"Stop it!" She waded in, snatching anything she could. "Aren't we dying fast enough?"

She sat hard. "Oh, go ahead. Kill yourselves! Least I won't be bothered by either of you." She tasted salt and despair as tears trickled dusty trails down her face.

Ratchet still gripped the rock, slowly rising, focused on Sary with a gaze more silver and dead than usual, his screeching oddly high-pitched as he limped toward her. "All your fault, crazy bitch! Ya goddamn whore! Don't belong here! Ya bring us all down! I'll put an end to—"

He darted a mad gaze at Hunter.

"Just the *two* of us." He thunked his chest.

"Shut up, Ratchet."

"She's got something. A secret. Probably keeps it up here!" Ratchet thunked his own head, then squatted, muttering.

Sary made out, "All gonna die here…"

"It's true, Sary," Hunter said, low.

"You think we'll die too? I've had sorrier odds," she bit off.

He looked away.

"Look, Sary. I've only a vague notion where the hell we are, since the bastards took my compass, and all my maps. Been near a month—"

"Three weeks."

"Right. Three weeks since the last house." He looked off a long time, studying the distance they had traveled and then where they headed.

"I'm half in love with you, you know. I wouldn't tell you all this lightly." He barked a laugh. "Maybe it's the heat. Englishmen in the noonday sun."

Only half?

"And he"—he jabbed a thumb at Ratchet—"he's unquestionably in love, if one could call it love, in his black heart."

We are all going mad.

Chapter 56
Unbridled Passion

A squall heartened them; they drank their fill, topping canteens, but Sary was restless, too indifferent to gather damp scrub for a fire. She didn't know what she wanted.

The touch was gentle—a stray breeze or flap of clothing.

Hunter.

Ratchet snored, on his back with his mouth open.

Sary laughed and without thinking scrambled up.

Hunter carried her over a rise, dropped down on the other side, and they were the only people on earth under a sparkling blanket, with the whole vast desert as a bed.

Sary wondered what hot purple magic coursed her body with a life overwhelmingly its own when Hunter pulled her to him like a man starving and kissed her before breathing hotly in her ear, "Wanted to ravish you since I first saw you."

Ravish away, one part of her said.

No! another part wailed, but it was all in her head. Her hips and mouth pulled involuntarily to Hunter, grinding herself into him as Hunter bent his head to hers and searched her lips.

"Married," she finally gasped between Hunter's near-brutal kisses.

With his lips on her neck, her breast, her mouth, he growled, "Not true."

How does he know? As good as. Better even, Sary wanted to whisper.

She made it hard, pushing his shoulders, ramming his chest, jerking from his mouth.

Hunter nipped her chin with his teeth, gained her lips, slid her down his length, arched her waist, kissed her fully and long, until she finally clutched his neck as if chained to him, kissing him back as if she were starving. Her tongue searched his. Her mouth felt bruised. Her feet dangled. His breath was harsh and rapid as he carried her down, pulling her, crushing her body into his so hard her ribs ached. Still she pushed into him even harder, as if she wanted to be on the other side.

Sary greedily drank him in, thrusting her tongue with a *yes* on the tip, writing *yes—yes—yes* with each thrust and exploration, ripping his shirt, frantic to be naked and free. She was out of her trousers. He gripped her corset. Sary snapped awake, clenching his wrists.

He gritted, "Bloody hell, Sary!"

Sanity fled. Hunter could not wait for the corset to be free but reached below, sliding hands between her thighs, drawing down her pantalets, cupping her sex once more. He thrust inside with the lust and passion of a first time, groaning her name—"Sary, Sary, Sary"— over and over with each plunge as her body relished his weight. He stopped, allowing her to catch up. She caught his rhythm and stilled, only her pulse throbbing.

They lay a moment, savoring unexplored electricity and passion-spawned heat, Sary groaning halfway between a moan and a whimper.

Sand was damp with dew, cooling her flaming body. Sary opened her eyes wide, sensing a further swelling while still connected. Again swimming the warm seas of desire, she gripped her strong slim legs tight around his brawny thighs, feverishly kissing his throat, his chest—all she could reach, as he cupped one great hand around her breast and then did something even Tommy or Jonathon had never dared.

He ran his tongue around her nipples, hard as young raspberries, and vigorously sucked. *Sary was on fire!* A flame shot to her epicenter. Once more hard and harder, he was kissing her with renewed passion—she yielded her body the third time, sparked with thrilling need.

The delicious action continued, slowly, softly, gently, and then Hunter changed rhythms, thrusting manically, with her meeting him when she could match his chaotic cadence, until she had no strength and let go, allowing him to gallop ahead, both awash in humming emotion until he dropped, exhausted, on her steaming body.

Sary and Hunter lay there stroking, savoring the heady afterglow, until they cooled off and relative sanity returned.

"You made love..." She hesitated. "You made love as if there were no tomorrows. Is this the end?"

"Forgive the unforgivable, Sary. I was weak. I did not mean to harm you in any way..."

Sary giggled.

"You've been reading women's novels."

He stiffened, then chuckled.

"Was I that bad? That transparent? But I do mean it, Sary—most of it. You drive me insane with a need I have never known."

"Shhhh. Stop while you are ahead in my esteem." She laughed. At this moment, Sary cared for nothing, drifting in blissful peace like a satiated angel. She ached pleasurably. Her sex felt full and bruised and delightfully used. Sary brushed hair off his face. Tenderly they stroked each other more, murmuring, kissing as if familiar. Then they lay on their backs, holding hands, and watched the stars.

Sary pointed out, with her toe, the constellations she knew, amazed they were still visible on this side of the equator. Hunter pointed out others, including a large cloud he called.*al-Bakr*. A smaller cloud was near it.

"They look like the Milky Way," Sary commented, "But we can't see that."

"No, but these are related. You can't see them north of the equator. Some people call them Magellanic Clouds, maybe because Magellan made note of them on his voyage around the world. I prefer the Arabic name, *al-Bakr*, which means "the sheep.""

A small silence ensued before Hunter again spoke. "You appreciate we are up to our necks."

Sary turned onto her elbow. "Hunter, what are you saying—really?"

"God! One forgets how vast Africa is, once one leaves Cape Town or Johannesburg. We should've crossed the tracks to Kimberley by now, love. I figure we made fifteen miles on a good day, five on a bad. That makes three hundred fifty miles, more or less. Sand could have drifted over the tracks just as we trod our merry way across. We could be anywhere! I won't lie to you. Ratchet's weaker and crazier by the hour. I'm flagging, and you—you, my beauty, are a marvel."

"Don't be so hard, Hunter. I've been honed by fire."

"And bullets?"

"Yes," she said shortly, "that too."

"Ah, Sary. In our old age, what tales we shall tell."

That jolted her. *But I already have a man I love, whom I feel wedded to.*

Hunter began kissing her again.

She turned her face. "No more, Hunter." He stopped, leaving her breathless. *Why did Jonathon and then Tommy intrude? Where were they when I needed them?* Her thoughts were unfair, she knew.

Chapter 57
Naked Lust

Sary luxuriated in the night breeze playing light sandy fingers over her naked flesh, brushing her cheeks…

Shivering as her body cooled, she knew reality must flood in.

She missed Hunter's body heat. She looked over. In the moonlight, Hunter hunched over a pile of something.

Her clothes.

Rooting. Rummaging.

She sat, unconsciously crossing arms over her chest, letting her hair clothe her. "What are you doing?" she hissed.

He didn't flinch. Instead of chagrin, Hunter displayed a lopsided grin.

"Oops. Caught me."

"Caught you…what?"

"I noticed"—he waved her corset in awkward fashion—"it seemed to chafe, as if something pinched. Several times I've seen you rubbing your ribs—right here."

Hunter rubbed his own finely muscled chest. She couldn't help but notice how broad the shoulders, hugely defined, arms strong and sculpted. She recalled the way they held her… She shook her hair to clear the image, still perturbed for a reason she could not pin down.

She sat up. "Please give it to me. Please." She smiled and waved her hand prettily.

Instead, he rubbed the lump in her stays. "This must be the varmint."

"No, silly. That is the way it's made! For comfort and support. I did not know you had a fancy for women's corsets." She laughed, curling her fingers. "Perhaps I will lend you my apron, too."

He couldn't see the green chill in Sary's eyes.

He gave the lump a last thumb-rub and tossed it to her, shrugging. "Must be painful, even so."

"I'll manage," she said brightly. *Strange. How odd and disappointing the night is turning.*

He looked down at her. "We must enjoy each other again"—he gave a careless, crooked grin—"soon."

Sary smiled falsely up at him. She didn't see his frowning glance at her corset.

Chapter 58
Ravenous

Starving again. The last of the aardvark strips turned, despite the drying. Even Ratchet was afraid of the aftereffects and reluctantly tossed them to ever-present carrion birds.

Each dawn, Sary strained to see another small holding, even though they were in the middle of nowhere, as far as she could see. *Anything* in the endless scrub, dotted with occasional acacia, would be reason for rejoicing. Sary checked Ratchet. Lagging, he never complained, she'd give him that. She couldn't go much farther herself. Now Ratchet had halted but was gazing up to where sound rushed them like a runaway horse. Sary was conscious of the buzz for a while before she realized…

"Hunter!" Sary screamed involuntarily. *As one Biblical plague ended, another began. What is happening?*

In a gale of black snow, swooping as a single dark, flapping wing, then a dense question mark rising in a column, broadening to a swarming, rasping…

No, not birds…

The waving black cape separated into a darting, hissing, susurrating, deafening roar, enveloping them with sound and fury. Just as abruptly, the winging mass separated into a rotten pattern, kaleidoscoping into new shapes…and coming for her!

Sary ran.

Hunter too raced without dignity.

Ratchet hobbled gamely—too late.

"Useless. Dive!" Hunter's voice.

The swarm dashed back, dropping a dense cloud over them. Instantly, the air sizzled and crackled, thick with frantic cicadas flinging into each other, colliding hard shells midair, dropping like dark green rain on her head.

The mass of shape-shifting, clicking, angry hornet-buzzes flicked and nicked, bit and gouged. Saw-legged bodies caromed off her flesh—her face took a hundred tiny cuts.

She screamed. She couldn't help it.

When she did, frantic insects flew into her mouth. The suicidal swarm tangled her hair and eyelashes.

Ratchet dove, swatting sand over his body like a badger as the incessant horde reached a frightening crescendo of maddening, whirring, darting, inexorable, stinging enemy, descending in waves of aggressive clouds.

As Sary, blinded and deafened, flailed—flung them away, swatted them away—one hundred and two hundred took their place, striking her like bullets.

"Drop!"

Sary twirled about, blind.

Hunter flung himself at her, slamming her to the sand.

She tucked her head into his neck, shutting her eyes tight.

"Wait it out!" he yelled in her ear over the buzzing roar.

Sary suffocated under his weight, feeling the urge to face him, pressing against his chest instead of the unforgiving sand. Sary felt the warm throb of his jugular and had an irresistible urge to press her lips to his skin as she burrowed, his whisper felt more than heard: "Shhhh-shhhh. Over soon."

"What have we done, Hunter?" she wailed.

"This isn't biblical. It's plagued locusts!"

For an endless hour, the swarm was both impenetrable and repellant as insects raced over them on their way to nowhere.

When Sary thought she could bear no more of either Hunter or the fury above, she felt a lifting.

The blanket became a lacy swarm, the swarm a whisper of frantically fluttering, beating wings colliding, crowding for space—and then there were none, just a black haze covering the west and getting lighter, with a few laggards, and acres of greenish bodies, kicking and making the sand heave as a living blanket.

Ratchet dug out, spitting grit, grunting as he said, "Thought I had me a game of numbers-up, there."

She pulled from Hunter, plucking still-wriggling insects from her hair, shaking her clothes, and surveying the landscape, feeling Ratchet's mocking eyes.

"Mercy Maude! I've never seen the like." She kicked her way through the casualties, some still alive with death torques and twitching saw-toothed legs.

"Mercy *Maude*?" Hunter teased, when her Indiana country speech broke through. "Gather 'em." He yanked his shirt off.

"These?" Sary plucked another one from her hair,

studying its plump green body and razor-thin, raspy legs below a meaty thigh-part—and the black bulbous eyes. "We can't eat these. Might be poisonous."

"You can't?" Hunter chuckled. "More for me." And in manly unity, Ratchet popped one in his mouth, crunching, reflective, pulling one of the thin legs out. "Not much thigh-meat, though."

Sary looked sourly at both of them. "You're grinning like hyenas."

They grinned wider—Ratchet's long yellow fangs and Hunter's perfect white teeth.

She felt an unreasoning jealousy—how quickly bonds formed between men, herself shut out.

"Oh, I think there is enough even for you gluttons—and I've had worse." Sand crunched as she walked through the heaving carpet of dying 'hoppers.

****

Sary sighed, rubbed her flat belly, and reached for another morsel. Hunter had organized a flat rock on top of four small ones, with a fire beneath.

"A bit of all right?"

"Mmmm." Sary cracked the one she'd just taken. "Can't eat another one."

"Could use salt," Ratchet grumbled, spitting out bits.

"Doesn't seem to slow you any."

Ratchet was unaware he had an insect leg sticking to the corner of his mouth.

Hunter and Sary laughed. Then Ratchet. Hadn't felt this lightheaded in…? She could not recall. She raked another of the crispy insects from the hot rock. They had a nutty flavor, with only a slightly bitter aftertaste. And crunched delightfully.

They were all convivial with the extra nourishment and spent the evening telling funny stories from their childhoods. Even Ratchet, though his had a hard edge.

Sary tossed another handful onto the hot rock. The insects popped and browned.

"No more, please," Hunter begged, rubbing his midriff.

"What we don't eat, we bundle up," Sary said practically.

****

For the first time in days, Sary felt hopeful.

It didn't last.

"This is where I think we are." Hunter scratched a crude map in the sand.

"Here's the tracks from Port Elizabeth to Middelburg I think we missed." He dragged a line and drew a rough triangle. "This track hails from a place called Mosselbaii, half way between Cape Town and Port Elizabeth."

He dug a spot on the coast.

"It heads to Middelburg, Bloemfontein, then the Kimberley, God willing. If we head west/northwest, we can't miss it."

"Like the last one?" Ratchet the crepehanger.

"Not if I can help it," Hunter snapped. "We all need to look sharp. You too, Ratchet!"

With full canteens, sacks bulging with crisp cicadas—or grasshoppers, as they called them back home in Indiana—Sary was buoyant.

If Hunter was right, they'd soon be on a train heading north to civilization.

Hunter droned on—a sop to the endless slog. Sary stopped listening.

"Karoo, also spelled K-a-r-r-o-o, is arid to semiarid..."

"No shit," Ratchet growled.

He nodded to Sary. "Shall I continue?"

Sary hid a grin. "Oh, please do…"

"This region is devoid of surface water…"

"Ya mean it's so dry, I'm spittin' dust?"

"Yes, very clever. The name 'Karoo' is derived from the Khoisan word meaning 'land of thirst.' "

"Ya mean one big hellhole."

"In some—"

"In all ways, ya fuckin' idjit!"

"I disagree. This place is rather majestic—"

"And I say it's fuckin' ugly, hot as a biscuit, and you're a crackbrain."

"I'm afraid you're still not seeing…" Of a sudden, Ratchet launched sinewy muscle against Hunter's bulk. Their sweat-stained shirts soon gathered sand.

"Stop! It's too hot!" Sary paced on. *Idiot men.*

She looked back at the meaty sound of a punch, hoping it was Hunter's.

"Fight, damn you!" Ratchet kicked out with his braced leg. The metal screw hinge caught Hunter's thigh. Hunter's face darkened.

For an instant Sary saw a far different man, like an ugly bruise fading away. Not *urbane* Hunter, but feral, detached, merciless Hunter.

The face smoothed. "I do not fight invalids—*sir*."

If Ratchet's glare could melt lead, Hunter would be molten slag. Stumping up, Ratchet backhanded him. "Gutless coxcomb!"

Hunter wiped his lip. "Now, there you stepped over the line, boyo. A peacock maybe, but not gutless." He hooked Ratchet's gimpy leg. Ratchet went down hard in a spray of sand.

Sary was troubled at his action, even though Ratchet stuck his jaw out. *Hunter has made an enemy. He will never sleep easy.*

To prove it, Ratchet fisted a knife, hurling himself at Hunter.

Hunter gracefully sidestepped.

Ratchet went sprawling.

"Do stop now, old man. This is tedious."

Hunter slid back into his lecture. "Now, the Acacia Karroo, also known as the Sweet Thorn shrub, grows to a height of—"

"Oh do be quiet, Hunter!" She smiled, taking off the edge. "Or I swear I will hit you." She glanced back at Ratchet assembling his pride.

"Common names include Karroo Thorn, Cape Gum, Cassie, *Piquants Blancs,* Cockspur Thorn, Doorn Boom…"

Hunter plucked a yellow blossom, holding it to her pale braids.

Sary scowled, tossing the flower away.

"A tad pedantic back there, but the acacia is the only source we have. One can make rope from the inside bark," he said seriously. "Tougher than steel."

"If we ever need a steel rope," Sary muttered.

"Gum, bark, and leaves are soothing and astringent for colds, bleeding…"

Sary looked back at Ratchet.

Chapter 59
Undercurrents

Affairs changed between Sary and Hunter. Jonathon, her dead husband, had been her due and duty—her intended, their love pleasant and not frightening, a reason to rest on hot Sunday afternoons after church and a week's toil.

Tommy was, well—*Tommy*. Exciting, adventurous, dictatorial at times—his head in the clouds. They shared their bodies but always seemed to be at war.

She and Hunter forged an unbidden alliance under the poisonous sun. Sary was in another world. Little by little, the lack of food and attrition of her body caused her past to seem as hazy as the new moving pictures so popular now, shown through gauze. Ignoring Ratchet's scorn, their unions were a sweetness at the end of grueling days where tomorrows had yet to be written…if at all.

One last pleasure. One last Eden. No more plagues, no more mishaps. No rivers of blood like in the Bible…Please.

Yet their river of blood rushed to them, like a scarlet sun casting long fingers and writing their future over the dunes.

Glancing at Hunter, Sary longed for the sky to drag over them its inky robe emblazoned with stars. She wanted to wrap herself in that dark cloak. That was what she and Hunter waited for.

Ratchet was already curled by a fire lit with his tinderbox. Earlier they had scrambled for tiny lizards scampering, for no reason she could see, across their path, tearing into scores of them roasted on a knife tip. The flesh, white, tender, tasteless, no more than a mouthful, was still a change from cicadas.

"Could use a bit of chutney or good Coleman's mustard," Hunter joked.

The moon shone in Hunter's eyes. He nodded at a higher dune. Ratchet eyed them, smug and knowing. Sary found she didn't care.

Hand in hand, they walked into a world of silver sand and moonshine. He scooped a still-warm depression and spread his coat. "Willst thou lie with me, my lady?"

Sary glided into him.

Hunter. It suited him, she the huntress, side by side.

Tommy and Jonathon—Neither belonged here.

Only Hunter suited the desert and her own wild imaginings.

"Hunter…" she breathed, anticipating his mouth on hers, a hard, demanding mouth conquering her with ease—forcing lips and legs apart, thrusting tongues, another new sensation, scraping with his coarse beard. She relished it all.

He could be gentle, too, lightly brushing fingers deliciously across her back, stroking her hair in feathery touches until she wafted on the wings of pleasure, teasing her to death.

Sary lazed in a delicious half-sleep from which she wanted never to awake, just drift on the warm soft carpet and not recall a world forever lost.

None foresaw their fate, at that instant. Not Ratchet, sleeping fretful through constant pain from his brace, or Hunter, fulfilled and powerful, or Sary, deep in her own reveries.

Chapter 60
Abducted

Animal pong, the punch of unwashed bodies, oil, sweat, sun-heated flesh.

Sary awoke with a sharp point piercing her chin.

Freeze!

Every urge shouted, *Roll—roll away—run!*

She opened her eyes a lash at a time, staring up— *up* at a long pole, the sharp metal point pricking her neck, piercing and rusty, affixed to the pole with leather thongs dwindling up into darkness.

"Don't move."

Hunter.

She wasn't about to. Only her eyes. The same spears pinned down both Hunter and Ratchet.

Her eyes adjusted. At the other end of the pole, a grimacing All-Hallows'-Eve face grinned down at her. Small teeth. Diminutive hands gripping the pole. A honey-colored face like a malevolent child's. Eyes glittering black…and quite mad.

Sary lay very still, panicked at the pierce-point at her throat, feeling warm blood trickling to the hollow of her neck.

The head, a dark blot against the stars, shifted, leaving an afterglow of teeth.

"Friends a yours?" Ratchet flailed, cursing, kicking, scooping sand into their pixie faces as he scrambled away.

The queer little men grinned, watching him flounder as Ratchet hobbled off. One of the diminutive figures reached back, plucked a polished stick, hurled it.

Ratchet went down; clawing his way back up, he swung like a blind bear, snarling, grabbing at spears. *Entertainment.*

"Ratchet. Not smart."

"Who are these runty little bastards!" Blood flew while the odd small men pranced, jabbing, renewing his bluster.

Hunter rose, hands up, armed with a mild expression. He uttered harsh gibberish, to Sary's ear, with high clicks and guttural grunts.

One of the small men with the big spears jabbered back. Grimacing, he ran up, whacked Hunter with the spear, and darted away, excitedly striking again and again, making more of the curious sharp clicking sounds.

Ratchet had no choice, held by long spears, one at his neck, one jabbing his belly. Sary saw red blossom on his shirt.

Hunter spoke low. "Watch the *ipapa*—the spear. Some of these fellas tip spears and arrows with rotted meat and…"

"Now ya tell me!"

Sary felt her own neck. Felt the blood. Felt sick.

Hunter, lifting palms, renewed his sharp clicks and clucks. The odd men chittered and clicked between themselves but seemed meditative. Several snickered.

If she had thought they were safe, Sary was disillusioned.

Sharon Shipley

First ants, then locusts, now this. Dear God!

Sary was a giantess amid the men coming up to her shoulder. They goaded with spears as they surrounded them, muscular and perfect in proportion, with tight, childlike ringlets, like snug caps. Yet they all carried very un-childlike bows, with long lethal arrows, along with the spears.

She smelt them. Felt heat. A mixture of animals. Goats came to mind. Leather, tobacco, and an odd sour tang.

Evidently, Ratchet was a subject of merriment now. Pinned, he stumbled about, howling outrage as they darted, pinched, and rapped his head, like bear-baiting.

Sary looked for a weapon. *Anything*. Hunter's rifle leaned against an acacia. *Too far.*

They were outnumbered, and destitute from hunger and weakness.

"Ratchet's changing the game," Hunter muttered. "They will tire. But he can't push too far."

"Game? What game? Who are they?"

"End this, Ratchet." Hunter's quiet order carried weight for both the attackers and Ratchet. "They might stick those pig-stickers in you by accident."

"These puny piss-ants?" Ratchet was only partly subdued.

"Dammit, Ratchet. You'll kill us all."

Kill. The unspoken fear.

"Sary?" he questioned.

She lifted her chin. "I've been in worse pickles."

Hunter, still watching the antics, with Ratchet floundering like a circus bear, murmured, "I doubt it."

"That's soothing."

"Not usually like this. A peaceable tribe. Something riled or scared them—out of the ordinary."

"What can they want? We *have* nothing." Afraid he'd answer.

"Not your body, never fear."

Sary stiffened.

"They think us ugly—revolting. Skin like maggots, I overheard one once say. Yellow hair's repulsive and sickly to them, like dead grass."

"Then what? They can't just—kill us." Just then, Ratchet toppled like a stack of bones.

"Ratchet. Up."

"Damned if I'll make it easy."

What is that old saw? Where there is life there's hope? Well, I am bloody well alive! "Any brilliant ideas?"

"Fresh out. Not exactly invited for tea, old girl."

"As long as we're alive—"

"Trite but true. Keep watching. Mayhap, Ratchet can distract with his clown act, till I think of something."

The small deadly warriors moved among them, yanking Sary's pack as if they goaded her—children playing "catch me if you can." Dangerous naughty children.

Hunter handed over his revolver with mock grace. "Certainly," he said smoothly. "Allow me."

"They don't have guns," Hunter whispered. "Just *ipapas*—spears. That's what this is about—guns, I think, very expensive—but stay away from the spear points."

"Why not just take them? What do they want with us? You say that to make me feel better? Well, don't,"

Sary snapped.

"No worries—yet."

"Too late," she hissed. "And how do you know what their spears are called?"

Hunter clenched his jaw. "Dead keen hunters. Like I said, watch the tip. Take days to kill."

Sary backed into an elderly man, laden with beads and a much more intricate headdress, as he stepped through a respectful mob. He took a dislike to Ratchet, barking explosive clicks, grunts, and clacks, jabbing him repeatedly.

Ratchet kicked out with his brace. The outraged elder's cadre hefted spears until he raised a withered hand and stayed them with more high, rapid clicks.

Ratchet, explosive as ever, hung on to his weapons; baring long teeth, growled at the small chieftain. "I bait with fishin' worms bigger'n you."

Slight but volatile, they herded the captives, who stumbled over scrub for what seemed an hour, dragging Sary, already depleted by hunger and thirst, seething on the end of a rope leash she chafed against until climbing a hillock, beyond which a fierce glow ebbed and flowed to the stars.

The pinpoint of light grew into a bonfire where twenty or more males, akin to their captors in size and features, commenting excitedly, judged their arrival. They clustered around Sary, lifting her hair, pinching her white skin, peering into her eyes.

Like children seeing presents for the first time around the tree. Sary, though grim, saw she was a novelty.

From twenty paces off, heat from the huge bonfire scorched her face, painting all of them orange, the warm light both welcoming and terrifying after their walk in the cold dark.

Hunter nudged her. Behind the males, petite females with childlike buds or large-breasted with suckling babies, a few wizened, but all with the same pug features and corkscrew hair, strolled after the males, feigning disinterest.

The mood changed. Two raced up, prodding inquisitive fingers at Sary's face, her hair, her corset. That gave other women permission to swarm, pawing and tugging her pale hair. One yanked strands out, turning it to the light.

"Oh!" Sary turned, swatting.

The woman danced away with silk in her fist and a baby bobbing on her back.

Sary swiveled, trying to keep all of them in sight, but was soon surrounded by more females of all ages, festive with their glittering teeth, beaded headbands, dangling pendants clacking as they walked, and wearing little else.

"The older ones are like the dried apple dolls my mom used to carve."

"Fascinating," Hunter bit off, more worried than she had ever seen him.

They were very pretty, in their doll-like way. Most were slender as fairies, with almond eyes and perfectly spaced black buttons across their skulls, though one had intricate braids in squares, like a lady's cap. Some wore short tops tied at a shoulder, with bare bellies. Some had animal-hide skirts with dangling paws and tails in the shape of the animal they came from, same as the men. Pixy children gamboled or hung on chests. Fat babies rolled in the chill sand—*How can they stand it?*—or dozed on their backs like naked puppies.

Sary eyed the fire. A branch of hefty size, with a blazing end, lay athwart coals. Hunter was tongue-clicking at the wizened chief. She was alone for the moment.

If she could…just…

The old man saw her eyeing the fire, kicked the branch aside, and motioned. Another gave it to him. He put it close to Sary's face, perusing her, clucking distastefully, lifting eyelids. The other held her. The old one blew on her pale hair so it fanned, pinched her cheek, spat with revulsion, and turned on a calloused heel, as if to say she was loathsome to his sight.

The chief seemed more intrigued by Ratchet's iron contraption, tugging it, laughing as if it were a game. Fortunately, they could not figure out how to unfasten the thing. In the end, Ratchet flung his pack at them. They subsided, squabbling.

The chief motioned.

"Hunter," Sary whispered and nodded. Five petite men approached, businesslike, with twisted leather thongs.

Rubbing his leg, Ratchet scowled. "Ain't trussing me like a damned hog!"

"Those little *piss-ants* have poisoned spears *and* our guns. Don't be an ass," Hunter snapped.

It took five of them to tie his hands. Sary almost admired his bluster against Hunter's distracted assurance. He politely turned hands behind him. Natives tied him more respectfully, roughly grabbing Sary's wrists and binding them in leather braid so tough it would scarcely knot. *Perhaps Hunter's pacifism has something there.*

"Why did you say you don't know, *now?*" Sary said out loud. They were back to back in a rough triangle.

"Called the 'San.' Close to the Bushman or the Bantu, related somehow but more primitive. The Bantu are a later offshoot." Hunter squinted. "Hardly ever see this lot."

"What's all that tongue-clackin' gibberish?" Ratchet broke in. "Ya cotton much?"

"Word here and there. *Sickness*—or maybe—*bad*."

Quick to interpret, Sary anxiously watched his face. "The plague? Here?"

"Could be influenza. Maybe consumption. Just as deadly. They've no history of it." He listened again. "They think we brought bad times. They've suffered. Looks like spears aren't our only concern."

Elders argued with the chief, stabbing at them. The crowd grumbled, darting fearful, angry looks at the trio.

Ratchet mocked their clucking. "Like a bunch a banty hens." He sneered. "Ain't no *roosters,* ya stunted, runty little bastards!"

"Stifle it, Ratchet."

Ratchet subsided, muttering.

Between the natives, Sary fixated on one odd lone foot outstretched by the fire, vanishing behind the shifting throng.

Hunter tried more words. Most stared as if he were a talking dog. One cocked his head and uttered soft clucks.

Hunter replied. The youth grinned, strutting off. The rest prodded Hunter with sticks to make him speak.

"Guess I'm the dancing bear now. See if you can make friends. That one."

A girl of about fifteen dimpled at Sary, giggled, and snatched her locket, dancing away with her prize.

"Hey!" Sary tried to jump up but found it hard to do with her hands tied. It was the locket with Jude and Tommy's portrait, made in England.

The girl laughed to a young man, pantomiming Sary's anguish.

"Friends?" she snarled. "I think not." She had been aware for some time of a heavy beat thrumming the air.

Around the bonfire, men squatted, slapping drum heads. The beat slowed her blood. Her heart stilled. The blaze blinded, dancing men blurred, and she nodded off to the incessant beat.

Tired. Fading. No food. Water, I need water…

Hunter elbowed her. She blinked awake. He looked grim, and even Ratchet seemed subdued. The cadence and mood had changed.

Women formed a ragged circle, wailing to the pulse. Men's ankle beads clashed in cadence as they twirled and leapt.

"Sary!" She heard the sharp command, raised her head again. Hunter came into focus. "Stay here."

"Did they forget us?" she mumbled.

"Not likely."

Hunger fled but thirst raged. Her head dropped, and she bit her inner cheek. "What's all this?" she mumbled, testy. *Afraid to know.*

"New to me."

"We're safe, surely, with children about?"

The chief pinned them with hatred. Frenzied dancers spun and leapt, eyeing them malevolently and thrusting spears. Ratchet cursed a youth dancing too close. "Get away, filthy varmint!" He kicked out at the prodding spear.

Keep still, she prayed.

"Sary." Hunter's voice was flat with intent. "Sary!" He commanded. She blinked up. "If you get a chance, any chance, run like the devil—*just run*. Keep that star in sight." He nodded, not to the brightest but one smaller, duller.

"Hunter, don't," Sary croaked. "We fight together. If anyone, it's you. You could help from the outside. Ratchet? His leg?" She was babbling. She heard herself.

Ratchet broke in. "What you two hatchin', by god?"

"How to get out of this. Suggestions?"

"Workin' on it," Ratchet grumbled.

"May resemble children, but their arrows are dipped in poison. Mamba venom, some poisonous plants, and crushed bugs in the mess. Work on your damned shackles."

Ratchet twisted his neck where the spear had pricked it, uneasy. He subsided, grousing, "Don't call the *federales* out."

Chapter 61
Fire, Fire Burning Bright

As Sary watched the frenzied rampage, she felt Hunter worrying her wrist-cords. She tried, too, but had no advantage. They remained unyielding. Then she tried Hunter's, until her nails scrabbled and broke against the tough rawhide.

She was a woman of five-and-twenty, squatting in dirt, starved, watching half-naked people go choleric, deeply keening over a vanished bright world of promise.

Nevertheless—Sary's eyes gleamed. She was savagely excited, too. *There must be a way.*

The cadence deepened. Women clapped, stamped, beads swayed, teeth glittering. Crazed dancers scuffed sand through a night febrile with drums and orange-tinted dust, while elders excitedly examined their guns, ejecting precious bullets.

Two young men grabbed at the bright things, tossing them hand to hand, laughing and chasing each other.

Several plunked near Hunter, and he stealthily palmed two.

The chief stroked the weapons with keen satisfaction. Cocked and uncocked. Checked barrels.

"Hope he shoots his damn fool head off," Ratchet snorted.

The chief divined Ratchet's words, pointed with a face like a hanging judge, and jerked his chin to the fire pit, where enormous flames shot steadily to a navy blue sky.

"Hunter, I, I just want to say…"

"I know. I do too."

I do what? She had not finished her thought.

"Hope they ain't extra hungry. Hear tell once where these fellers…"

"That's New Guinea," Hunter snarled, risking a glance at Sary. 'Not cannibals, either." However, he didn't look so certain.

Sary eyed a large pot, not big enough for her, but perhaps *pieces* of her…

"Hunter—*think* of something."

"Quiet!"

The chief walked over, almost grandfatherly, showing a brown-toothed grin, yet Sary saw the hidden slyness.

"Something's about to blow." Hunter shot a sad look. "Brace yourself, girl." He was already stiffening his back.

Sary nodded. "I always have."

The chief turned his glittering eyes on her, eyes that sparked orange from the flames.

Dancers stopped mid-twirl. Women ceased their chatter as the chief perused her from between crinkles of flesh.

She traded stare for stare until he cocked his elfin head and clicked. His aides chuckled like bootlickers anywhere. Then the wizened chief went into a rage like a freak thunderstorm, chattering long and piercingly. She felt spit on her face.

Hunter strained, rapidly translating. "Something about killing herds. Killing all that flies and runs…poisoned water. You"—he hesitated—"are a witch or an evil spirit."

"A witch?" *Doesn't sound good.*

"Sounds fuckin' biblical."

"Hardly," Hunter bit off.

"Could they mean…the plague? Way out here?"

"Pray not. Some white man's disease, you can rest on it…"

What he said next was lost. Two warriors hustled over with short knives. Sary felt hands, smelled heat and must as they bent close, felt a cold blade kissing her wrists, a knife sawing rawhide knots.

She rubbed her wrists. They had hauled her to her feet before it registered. Her legs stiff from squatting, her hands numb, they half dragged her to the conflagration as she dug her toes in.

Straining to see Hunter, Sary was passed overhead as many hands held her aloft. She licked lips with a dry tongue to summon spit to scream for him. The fire and the crush of people blurred. Haloes of orange-misted dust flew. Dancers pranced and leapt. Sound muffled. She was deaf.

Ratchet and Hunter? Where are you? No tall figure of Hunter. No limping Ratchet.

The crowd plunked her down close to the bonfire, and then men prodded Hunter beside her. He stumbled awkwardly, his hands still bound, sprawling almost in the flames.

Ratchet sniggered. They came for him next. Sary didn't laugh when they shoved him forward.

Five tongue-clicking youths watching with slanted

eyes glittered wetly to see her reaction as they dragged Sary even closer to the fire pit. In panic, she saw females look away or cover their children's eyes.

Sary looked wildly about. The festive throng rushing her the last two feet to the inferno blazing to the sky swallowed Hunter and Ratchet.

Is this the end? She looked everywhere for signs of torture.

They thrust Sary headlong through the parting mob and the final ring of people, the fire unbearably hotter and brighter. Sary felt her hair singe and her face blister.

"Sary!"

It was Hunter. Ratchet, somewhere, was cursing a blue streak.

"Hunter!" she screamed. "*Find my son! Tell my...*"

She didn't get to scream out her last plea, despairing, in those last seconds before they sacrificed her, that even Hunter or Ratchet would escape their obvious end.

She saw the heart of the flames, white hot, quavering with hellish heat.

They are going to throw me in! I'm a sacrifice...I—

"Fight!" Hunter's voice. With what? Her struggles—her protestations? Sary chuckled, hysteria bubbling up inside. The chief glared, furious over her laughter.

The mob prodded, teasing, playing with her. Her cheek blistered, her clothes singed. Sparks spat out. She whirled, snarling, "Stop that!" with teeth bared. She sounded hooting and eerie, as from inside a bottle.

The chief blocked her, his face twisted in a mask of wrinkles, arms outspread. They dropped back.

223

He was saving her!

Then he rigidly pointed to the fire. Flames leaped with a whipping roar. Men tossed in new logs. Sparks exploded. The last few women left. As she wriggled and fought, Sary twisted her head, seeking Hunter. They hadn't brought the men to the fire, only her. Through fear and confusion, Sary saw the chief point downward.

She looked, bewildered, focusing first on a lone foot, then the entire body—a boy, she thought, so close to the fire that any closer and he'd be part of the blaze. Unnaturally still, he held a ghastly look. A dead look. Then his chest slowly heaved, as if an ox cart sat on it.

The chief grabbed her by the scruff, bending her close. Flames licked her shins, her hair caught—she heard the crisping. "*Noooooooo*! Hunter!"

They are making me a sacrifice because of this boy. Please, no, it can't end like this. "Hunter! Ratchet!" She wasn't brave any more.

The chief lost his grip.

Sary tried to thrust back through the mob, aware Hunter rapidly fired clicks behind her.

She didn't get far—many hands forced her back as the chief, furiously clicking, pressed her nose to nose with the terribly ill boy.

Sary stared, both repulsed and concerned, momentarily stilled.

The poor boy's face was hideous with suppurating lesions. His flesh was studded with purple lumps the size of oranges erupting though his skin. Black bile trickled from cracked, puffy lips.

She tried to struggle up, but the chief, spitting a string of oaths, still clamped an iron grip on her neck, pushing her down. His bony fingers burned.

The mob stilled, expectant.

They leaned close, some impatient, shuffling bare feet.

Then she heard Hunter, as clear as if the earth stilled.

"The chief says to heal him, Sary. Cure him, or we all die."

Sary whipped her head to the chief. *"What!"*

The chief nodded, implacable, his face set in stone.

"Try somethin', Sary!" Ratchet sounded less than brave.

"Buy time. Our last hope," Hunter called once more, ending in a cough or groan as if someone punched him in the stomach.

Sary studied the gruesome boy an inch from her nose.

"But I can't touch him!"

Sary felt something give way in her head. Faint with hunger, she lost her will, staring into the fire, white hot now. It would be quick.

"Try—magic," Hunter yelled.

Magic!

Sary's eyes closed. She winged back to Tommy and the traveling troupe. She could hear Tommy: *All the art of illusion!*

Sary swatted the chief's hands away, warning him with a fierce look. Peremptory. Haughty. Bared teeth. Hands in claws.

He looked for once unnerved.

She turned to the boy, throwing her shoulders back. She heard feet shuffle as if giving her space.

Sary showily waved her hands, circling the poor

boy's body, feeling heat radiate, not touching but crooning, deepening her voice, flinging exhortations to the sky in a high-pitched banshee wail. Closing her eyes as if in a swoon, she let her head loll and shot both arms to the moon.

The mob fell back another foot. She heard confused murmurs.

"Four score and seven years ago…" Sary bellowed.

"Alice in wonderland," Hunter yelled.

The Jabberwocky. Yes!

Immediately the nonsense *Jabberwocky Song,* learned in her schoolroom, flooded back. Loudly and with great drama, Sary intoned, alternately moaning and shrieking, *"'*Twas brillig, and the slithy toves!" she yelled.

The crowd scrambled back.

Feeling damned foolish, Sary lowered her voice to a hollow, frightening, keening as she continued. "Did gyre and *gimble* in the *wabe:* all mimsy were the *borogoves,* and the mome raths *outgrabe!*" She screeched to the sky.

She glowered, forking her fingers, stabbing at several men, scowling and showing teeth, casting as much craziness as she could muster.

They shuddered and tried to hide behind their brethren.

She peered at them from the corner of her eye, mumbling in a low growl. *In for a penny in for a pound, as Tommy would say.* Sary made figure eights above the boy's head, chanting the only song remembered, beyond hymns—"Beautiful Dreamer." It had never been sung with such fervor, partly because she was sad she could not really heal the boy.

Sary finally gasped, running out of steam, desperately trying to recall *The Rime of the Ancient Mariner*, but her reason faded. Sweat dripped in her eyes.

Chapter 62
Bondage

Sary snapped awake. She had swooned for real, head lolling, mouth open, panting. *How long have I been gone?*

The boy's eyes were open, looking at her—or at nothing at all, but the crowd murmured, awed. She still swayed them—held them in thrall.

Impressed? She could not tell. *What more can I do? He will die, and then will we.*

She searched for Hunter—Ratchet. She was alone. Was she the last?

The chief peered at the boy, unreadable, but cast suspicious eyes on Sary, then the boy, who, Sary was heartened to see, yet had his eyes fixed on her.

Sary backed. The chief followed her with his eyes. *Now or never, for something—anything to happen.*

They wrestled Hunter and Ratchet beside her. *So they were the second act.*

Hunter locked eyes with her. His look said it all.

Sary nodded, numb. Gathering herself, she grinned cheekily. He smiled in a jaunty manner and turned his head, wetness in his eyes.

"This ain't good," Ratchet growled. He backed even as they shoved him closer.

"'Fraid not," Hunter whispered. "Be brave."

"Fuck that!"

Sary knew in her bones what the chief intended, made true by his next act. Clamping his bony hand about her neck again, he forced her back to the fire.

It took two men, in the end. The boy looked gray and dead and very, very still. Sary heard wailing and anger.

They wrestled Hunter closer, then Ratchet, turning the air blue with imprecations.

Hunter struggled to his knees. "Dignity, Ratchet, dignity."

"Fuck dignity and the horse you rode in on! Fight! You fuckin' gelding!"

Ratchet rammed his head at the closest natives.

Hunter gave a dismissive shrug.

No use. What is wrong with Hunter, even so? Defenseless and outnumbered by far. Little to hope for? Still... Sary looked askance...and then Hunter winked...

The chief had a triumphant, mad look painted on his face, sputtering a series of sharp clacks, twisting his mouth as if tasting bitter fruit, words running like juice down his chin, until the spew was uncontrolled gibberish.

His fired-up subjects rhythmically jabbed the tainted spears.

Females lifted feet, pounding sand, moaning chants.

Sary twisted to Hunter and even Ratchet in goodbye—offering courage, or just comfort, as the last human thing she could do on earth.

Hunter's regard held a lifetime of meaning. Regrets. Even fear. She shivered in the heat as the chief tunked his staff like a Roman emperor giving the thumbs-down signal to kill.

The boy closed and again opened bloodshot eyes.

The crowd drew back amid murmurs.

Then the boy gave a rattling sigh, and his head flopped back. The chief exploded, exciting the others. The crowd grew close, with blood in their eyes. This was the end. An appeasement by fire.

"Wait and watch," Hunter gritted. Sary saw a wink of orange light bounce off brass casings as Hunter awkwardly rolled two bullets her way.

"Toss them and flatten!"

Sary didn't think. She flung the cartridges into the fire, burrowing her heels and fanny into the sand as sharpness skinned by her eye and the bonfire…*exploded!*

Flaming logs—fiery missiles—soared to the sky, spat sideways, spraying the crowd. Sary fiercely rejoiced. *We weren't helpless.*

A second blast. Women fled, shrieking, deeper beyond the ring of death into the dark, taking up children in their arms. The chief was down, with a red splotch on his withered cheek. His aides stared in shock and awe.

"Get outta here! Run! Won't last long."

Sary made out creepers. Men proving themselves.

"What about me?" Ratchet snarled, kicking out at a crawler. A man readied a spear, another a throwing club.

"Give me another," Sary yelled.

Hunter clumsily rolled a cartridge from his bound hands.

She flung it. It landed at the edge; she waited, thrilling in its detonation, shooting faggots. Sary grabbed Ratchet's knife from his boot and cut Hunter's thongs.

A spear sailed between them, landing between Ratchet's legs, but she ran out of time as enraged warriors and a few women stormed the three. Ratchet sliced his own bindings.

Hunter snatched bullets in a running stoop, hurling them over his shoulder.

Another hot blast.

Sary grabbed dropped rifles, while Ratchet gathered bullets, cartridges, and a native knife. Hunter spied his water bottle. Spears thudded all around, jailing them—*no time.*

"Sary, go—GO!"

Hunter didn't need to tell her—an arrow whistled where she was an instant before bending for a stray bullet. It would've nailed her through the back. She ran, pumping legs high, scooping more precious winking ammo, then elongated her stride into a lope leaving all behind. Hunter jammed a bullet into the carbine and fired into the pack.

Ratchet clobbered one chaser in the jaw with his big-boned fist. Sary felt like cheering, if only she'd had the energy.

A saving grace was that most of the tribe had scattered or fled the other way and had not regrouped.

Sary ran on, head back to get every gasp of air, legs pumping, arms waving. Wind scorched her throat. Her legs turned to pudding; she collapsed hearing the inexorable pound of feet. A disembodied flare flickered as it bounced along with its bearer. Hunter dove beside her. Ratchet stumped gamely enough behind.

"Quiet!"

"Warn't thinkin' on givin' the Gettysburg

Address," Ratchet snarled as he hit the ground.

"Best trackers in the world."

"Who?" she asked faint.

"Bloody San. I told you," he said, bitter. "Descended from the oldest known man since Biblical times. Intimately acquainted with every grain of sand and star in the sky."

The three ran north instead of west.

Sary figured they'd zigzagged a half mile by the time, one by one, the torches miraculously gave out, leaving the moon a thin slice of light. She had no idea where her strength came from.

Ratchet's breath was a steam engine. They were all on their last legs. No food. Almost no water. They were dying. Moreover, they must keep running.

Sary's mind faded. She looked down. Stared at strange feet whisking below her. A lone light flared behind them. Wishful thought: was it farther away?

Sary didn't know how long they ran, shin-deep in sand or on tooth-jarring rocks rattling her spine, until finally dropping behind a mountainous dune.

The lone tracker slogged by.

They couldn't lift another foot.

She tried to raise her arm, and a hundred-pound weight was tied to it. The figure trudged back, every now and then stopping to listen, peering in the dark. Sary held her breath till he vanished eastward.

"How much left?" *Ratchet.*

"Water? One canteen," Hunter gasped. "Half full."

"One?"

Sary shrugged weakly.

Ratchet reached. "Could use some a that."

Hunter stared him down. "Couldn't we all? Save

your spit. One swallow in morning, one at night. I'll keep it."

Ratchet burned a hole in Hunter with his one eye.

"I got five bullets, two cartridges, if we got a rifle."

"Good man, Ratchet."

Sary held out two more.

Ratchet gruffed, "I scratched me up a knife and a broke spear."

"A little water. Ammo for a broken carbine. Anyone found a pistol?" The bullets matched a pistol; the rifle stock was damaged though still usable.

Sleep. She wanted sleep, but hunger kept even that at bay.

Ratchet winced. He held his knee. A shiny black patch glistened in the moon. Bleeding again. Pain must be fierce.

Hunter looked off, bouncing a bullet in his hand.

"Right. We've stayed too long at the faire. Be after us by morning." Hunter made no move to go.

Chapter 63
Fiery hell

Fourth day, by the sun's merciless calculation, after escaping the San. The three plodded roughly west/northwest, as before the attack.

Sary rose to another scorching dawn broiling away the dew. Usually they licked acacia leaves and dug a cupful of water. All three were more leathery. Hot breeze was like food. Solid and warm. She licked her lips, groping for her canteen, knowing it was dry, wishing she could eat and drink sunshine.

No. Mine is lost.

She eyed the one Hunter protected—he seemed asleep. Sary wept with frustration and looked up at the sun. The sudden movement made her dizzy, sprawling face down, aware Hunter carried her a piece and then collapsed himself. Somehow, Ratchet plodded stoically on.

"Won't go on in the daytime. Go to Hades, Hunter."

"I vote fer that," Ratchet grumbled. "If there's a damned railroad, how much farther, ya reckon? I'm fryin' like a damn pork chop anyways, if we keep goin' like this."

"We'll rest easier, Hunter. Besides, the tracks will shine in the moonlight as well as the sun." *Will they?*

Hunter hated being bested, on the verge of saying

he'd keep on. In the end, he relented.

They traveled mostly by night now, shivering, but it was better than the sun beating them into dazed submission. Something told them to keep moving or it would be their last day under an acacia, never to waken, with the tree as their tombstone, in time their bones turning brittle.

Day six after the attack. Somehow, they had made it this far, thanks to morning dew and the unlucky lizard or two. The acacias had dwindled out a day or so ago.

Sary plodded on without turning. The sun was just showing in a peach glow to the east. Soon it would scorch the blue from the sky.

She heard the sound of metal on metal. Clicking. Tinkling… She knew what it was. If she did not look, it was not happening.

She spun with sudden fear.

Her head kept on spinning before focusing. Black dots swirled in the predawn light. Her tongue was leather and her lips so swollen her lip touched her nose. She tried speaking. *No, Hunter*.

Hunter was clicking—rolling bullets in his palm. He was trying to fit the bullets into the pistol's chamber. One they'd found when they ran.

He felt her giving him a speculative, red-eyed look. His handsome face was blistered above the beard. Even their hats were lost along the way. Sary recalled one of the San men dancing with one on his head. She kept a twisted rag over her brows and nose. Only her eyes showed defiance. He looked away.

"What you doing?" Sary croaked.

He looked ahead.

"Aren't we dying fast enough?" Her words cracked

like parched earth. "Stop, Hunter. I know what you're planning."

Hunter stared at Sary with pity, sadness, and anger. He swayed closer, placing hard-calloused hands about her sunburnt cheeks, as if he needed to brace himself or he would fall. He bent and searched Sary's sea-green eyes, memorizing them.

"We are down to bare bones, Sary. Our clothes scarcely cover our asses. We fight for water. Even the damned lizards mock us."

He was near the edge. His jaws were gaunt and grizzled, his eyes sunken, as were hers, had she known.

He brushed her cracked, chapped lips with his own—the dry brush of a butterfly wing, but one that burned. She wiped her mouth, scorning his compassion.

"Save one for yourself, not me," Sary rasped, thumping her thin chest. "I'm not ready. Don't make up my mind for me!"

He cast an eye at Ratchet gamely digging his crutch in the sand. "Look at him. Have pity. How far do you think Ratchet can go? Do we stay and die too? He can't keep up. Sary, it's over. We could wander the wrong direction and miss the tracks altogether." Hunter looked away. "Him or us, if he doesn't expire on his own."

"It's all of us. We've come so far, Hunter. Besides, he is keeping up." *What do you really have in mind? Eliminate us one by one? To what end? Oh, I am not thinking straight.*

"That could come. Face it, Sary." Hunter's voice was harsh as the sandscape.

Sary staggered ahead, defiant. *Let him shoot her in the back!* Ratchet somehow caught up, using the rifle as a crutch, limping, grim, red-eyed, and determined too.

Hunter covertly pocketed the bullets.

"Hunter plannin' somethin', huh?" Ratchet leaned to whisper.

Sary nodded. Improbably, in that instance, she and Ratchet were a team.

They didn't know until later about Ratchet…and then, of course, fate tossed the dice and it wouldn't have mattered.

Chapter 64
A Starched Blue Shirt

Day seven. The sky was without blemish of cloud, as faded blue as the rag of denim shirt barely protecting Sary.

When she remembered to think of days at all, it was another hell without food and little water.

Last night Sary had caught Ratchet carving his name in a dead acacia. Somehow, they slept the day and night away, and it was morning again, or maybe two days had worn away.

The sun etched their faces with bloody light, luring them as it sank. *Their lodestar.* They walked like the living dead, not thinking, plodding one foot before the other.

Sary bent, clutching her stomach. Her tongue cleaved to the roof of her mouth, her lips so cracked that if she stretched them, blood leaked. Her nose was a raw blister. She saw her boots—the sand below, hot wind whipping tangled sandy hair over her eyes.

Her world: *One foot, two foot. Slog—slog. One more step,* one more…*one more…*

Hunter's urgings blended with the hissing sand and soughing wind, the shush of footsteps.

Shorter, dragging steps turned to wobbly shuffles. More often than not, she was face down in the scorching sand. Sary became an automaton, barely conscious for formless periods.

Only will kept her going, that and pictures of Jude and Tommy, as much as she could remember, frightening as she cudgeled her brain to recall Tommy's face, the feel of Jude's body in her arms…

Chapter 65
Mirage

Sary's shirt was stiff with salt. She barely registered the map chafing her ribs and, if asked, would not have been able to explain why she still suffered it. She would've tossed the corset long ago, but it braced her back and kept her rib cage lifted.

It took a time, as she slogged along, before the image registered.

Sary stared though scratchy, half-opened lids and a wilderness of tangled hair.

A blight, blots, or smudge, outlandish in the dun sandscape. Not drab acacia green but brilliant!

Sary squinted as the sun hit the mirage, the green-and-red sparkle so alien it hurt her eyes.

She swayed, croaking a laugh, falling to her knees. "Hunter!" she rasped. It sounded like the caw of a crow.

Hunter raised up, sunblind; Ratchet peered blearily where she pointed, through his one matted eye, before he too dropped in awe or disbelief.

Hunter crawled, digging toes in, desperately striving to rise, to walk—to run!

Is it real! *Is it real?"* she called, struggling after. Tears sprang thick and salty. *I can't bear it if it's a chimera…floating trees or shimmering sands…*

Lifting leaden feet barely above the ground, breaking away, she passed them.

"Hurry!" Her dry throat was the rasp of a file. "It might leave!" *Unthinkably cruel.*

But the vision waited like a patient animal. *Too silent.*

In her muddled head, Sary expected the hiss of steam, the mighty grind of pistons as the locomotive relentlessly started before they could reach it.

Sanctuary. Life. Safety. Water!

She feared it would gather speed until they couldn't catch it, no matter how fast they raced. So close. *It can't leave.* "Help!" Sary yelled, waving.

Ratchet limped faster.

Hunter yelled, "Hie, there!" He kept up a ragged pace ahead of them, waving, hollering, *"Hallllooooo!"* His voice turned to dust blown in the wind, yet still he croaked, "We're here! Hallooooo!"

Sary bent, breathless, sucking in oven-heated air; her chest was burning. *Saved. Just get on that shining beast, with its long tail of beautiful red cars with the brilliant green engine and glittering brass! All we need do is get on!*

Something made her look back.

Ratchet stumbled to his knees, then thrust his crutch futilely in soft sand. Sary struggled back, risking glances at the soundless locomotive for fear it was a fantasy.

Ahead, Hunter stopped calling. He reached out as if he could grab the train.

Sary shouldered Ratchet. Together they hobbled, until he used her as a fulcrum, thrusting her back in his determination to get there first.

"Ratchet! Damn you!" Anger fueled her body, and Sary passed him again without looking back.

Chapter 66
Green Monster

The glittering locomotive with the flared stacks was agonizingly close, mere yards now—so close she saw the engineer in the window. Sary called, "Hie! Wait!" Staggering on her last legs, still yards short, heart in her mouth, she fancied she saw the train move ever so slowly, building up speed.

Hunter too slowed, warily eyeing the ghostly quiet train.

The truly odd thing: black silhouettes of hundreds of birds sat atop the cars, lined against a bloody setting sun. The closer the wanderers got, the birds lazily flapped off, or resettled, coldly eyeing them.

"Odd. Vultures, just sitting there." Hunter echoed Sary's thoughts.

"Damn well wait for my carcass."

"Wouldn't have you, Ratchet," Sary said.

"But why are they *here*—not doing what they usually do?" Hunter wondered.

Ratchet studied the line of motionless cars. "Not stayin' up nights a-worryin' about it."

No more than feet away, in reach now, the train waited for them. Perhaps the engineer or one of the passengers had spotted them.

People lay on top, some sleeping alongside it, others waved from windows. The red took on an orange gleam as the sun descended behind it, and night crashed to earth as it usually did.

Twin rails glowed dull under a rising moon by the time they were under the shadow of the great machine.

The only movement now was the ghostly waving of bright cloth, a headscarf here, a shirt-tail there. Men, women, children sprawled on the sand like dolls left out at the end of play.

All wrong.

Now, she smelt something too ripe. An odd perfume wafted with the fragrant oils Africans put on hair and bodies, and something dreadful—coal, old engine grease baking in the sun, ripening fruit. Insects ominously buzzed.

Still the birds sat.

The locomotive waited like a patient horse—its flared smokestack smokeless, the traditional red open-windowed cars trailing behind, soundless, great wheels and pistons frozen in place.

Sary discerned what they all did, what they all *knew.* Her legs faltered.

Those people were not getting off. They were *falling off.* Dead.

Nevertheless, why weren't the birds attacking?

That man draped over the windowsill, not waving. A woman's sari rippled in slight breeze.

Sary held up her hand. "Hear that?"

It was only the wind soughing through windows.

They crept closer. Sary could move no faster anyway; her limbs were by turn leaden or soft as India rubber as they skirted victims, sprawled on the sand, to steep iron steps to the engineer's cabin, where the fireman had fallen backward, staring up at them.

Hunter held her back.

Her head creaked toward him. "Boilers. Water. What do we have to lose?"

Hunter gazed with odd respect. "Whyn't I think of that? It'll be clean."

Her emotions a crumbling dam, Sary was close to letting go.

"Like I said, all hat, no horse, Hunter," Ratchet grated behind them.

Hunter took hold of the fireman's cuff. "Care to help beyond working your mouth?"

Ratchet reluctantly hobbled over and grabbed the other cuff. Together they dragged the poor fireman off.

"Nothing for it, Sary girl. Up to this?"

She nodded.

"Right."

"Could we get a move on, yer lordship?"

Sary reached the cabin, but not before she wished she hadn't. Hunter quickly stepped in front of the engineer's body, half out the window, and they all crammed beside the fireman's perch in a cabin jammed with dials and levers. Two narrow windows beside a central console looked ahead onto the tracks.

Behind them, Sary saw a large round boiler, firebox, and coal supply in the tender. The fireman's shovel lay on the iron floor where he'd left it.

Sary placed her hand on the boiler that made the steam—cold halfway up; her hand looked frail against the old metal.

"It must be pure. Maybe boil rice or grain, if we can find it." She motioned to the cars. "Some of the passengers must have brought foodstuffs."

"At first light. We sleep outside again. We don't

know what we are getting into."

The wait was interminable. Next dawn, Hunter tied a kerchief over his nose. "Let me have a first go."

"As I said, I've seen worse. We *all* go." Sary slipped the rag over her nose.

Ratchet was in no shape to manage narrow aisles with his bad leg, but he did, though not well. He even dragged the engineer's body to the steps, booted him off with his crutch, and slumped on his seat.

"Little housekeepin'." He grinned lupinely. "Don't touch nothing, now."

This helpful advice from Ratchet, no less.

Together, Hunter and Sary crawled over the coal tender and down the ladder. Hunter easily hopped couplings, holding his hand out. She ignored it, stepping over and down to First Class rather than go past the dead engineer and his fireman at the bottom. For now, they had no strength to bury them.

As they stepped through, no particular atmosphere beyond a certain heaviness to the air, plus patchouli, or sandalwood, old wood, and dusty upholstery. The sills were gritty with soot. The cars were open-windowed.

"Must've died within the day's journey," Hunter commented.

"Right before we found them," Sary finished.

They discovered the passenger cars were uneven not just by class. Some were near empty, others crammed with people, who were some in nightclothes, others in various dress or undress. A few appeared to have died with little distress; others had old stains and seemed to have been closer to heaven or hell's doorstep earlier.

The first victim was a fashionable European lady,

clutching her jewel box, lying aslant in her First Class seat. Thankfully, a fallen-away hat obscured her face, but her clothing appeared undone and soiled. Hasty suitcases and a trunk blocked the aisle. Bundles littered the car as if their owners had fled a warring army.

Hunter stood at the end of the car looking back. "This line runs to the Kimberley and Vaal River from Cape Town. Guess it tells us about the coast. They ran fast but not far enough."

Sary nodded, numb. *Oh, please, Jude and Tommy, be on the ship—be back in England. Be safe.*

Sary and Hunter turned at a jingling noise. Ratchet, behind them, was riffling the woman's jewels and stuffing his pockets. He didn't bother looking shamed. "Won't be wearin' fancy gewgaws to a fancy dress ball anytime soon, I reckon." He snickered.

Hunter dismissed him, steering Sary onward. Whatever Ratchet did held no surprises for her.

Hunter snatched a canteen like a hot coal from the seat beside a man in tweed, sloshing it. Sary and Hunter locked eyes. Sary gave a faint nod.

"Boil it."

He began to fling it outside for later, but Ratchet grabbed it, unscrewed the cap and gulped it down, smiling craftily as he wiped his mustache.

"Jes' water. Won't hurt me none."

Sary licked her lips again. *Could it possibly be true? Are we too careful?* Then she scanned the bodies.

Two more Caucasian women—one just a girl— wearing all their finery, slumped against each other, the girl's head in the other's lap. Hunter, with rags on his hands, gingerly probed an overhead rack, prying open a bright cookie tin with painted roses. The rich pungent aroma of rum-soaked cake wafted out. A treasure of fruitcake, studded with jewels of fruit, wrapped in cheesecloth and smelling of heaven.

Sary looked hopeful.

They both nodded at once. Shakily, Sary broke off two chunks, giving one to Hunter, cramming her mouth with gooey cake, candied fruit, raisins, walnuts, and Brazil nuts, attempting to choke it down. She needed water. Already the sweet made her giddy.

"Careful," Hunter warned.

A veiny, knuckled hand came from nowhere to snatch a wad.

"Greedy guts. Thievin' hogs. Gobble that all on yer stony lonesome." Ratchet stuffed his mouth. "An' leave me ta die!"

"Exactly what you'd do," Sary replied evenly. Hunter held the tin off. "We are civilized, Ratchet. We share."

Ratchet didn't look far from death; his face was gray beneath his burn, the red-rimmed feral eye sunk in purple shadow. He stared like a lunatic.

She handed the tin over. "Here, take it." Already queasy after the unfamiliar richness, she needed water with every fiber. *How ludicrous! Standing among the dead, squabbling over Christmas fruitcake.*

"Guess we kick our heels a day longer 'fore we meet Old Smokey," Ratchet chortled, spraying cake.

"We're alive, and there's water," Sary said.

"And a helluva lot of dead folk." Ratchet sniggered.

Hunter was already on to the next car.

Chapter 67
Feast for Gluttons

They all saw the oranges. "Don't touch those," Hunter growled at Ratchet.

"If we scrub them with sand," Sary ventured, "the inside should be safe."

Hunter divided them, eyeing Ratchet. "Four each."

Sary savored one—large, sweet, juicy—and sucked it dry. Smirking, Ratchet gobbled his four in a row. Below his pallor, he still looked ghastly.

Hunter critically eyed the Second Class car with the open windows. "Still no vultures."

"They have no taste for death."

"This sort, at any rate."

They searched it, avoiding its three victims, coming up with a cloth sack of raisins, a bag of African fruit Hunter named gingerbread plums, a tin of rancid butter, and a packet of dry biscuits.

Sary nodded at a Caucasian girl huddled on a wood bench, wondering if she and Hunter and Ratchet were the vultures, putting the notion aside. This was survival. The girl's mother slumped on the opposite side with a kerchief covering her face.

She died first.

Ratchet busied himself riffling pockets of trinkets and watches, unpinning jewelry, stuffing them in his shirt.

Sary, using her shirt-tail, plucked corked wine, a wired bottle of lemonade, a flask of spirits, and spotted bananas. A melted cheese sandwich in wax paper. A box of taffy. She looked at Hunter. He nodded and shrugged. These they tossed out for gleaning later.

Ratchet was already tearing into a leg of chicken. *The devil protects its own.* "You will pay, you know," Hunter said.

Ratchet looked at the leg and tossed it as if it were on fire, wiping hands on his trousers. "Can't eat no more anyhow." He did look rather green.

Passing through the last three cars, they descended to Third Class. Open bench seats, hanging straps, overhead rack. These victims, not assuming anything in life, had been better prepared. The trio salvaged several tins.

****

Hunter and Sary leaned against the caboose's tiny balcony, peering south, where tracks dwindled toward Cape Town.

Ratchet was still riffling behind them. Sary gave up warning him of the Black Death; she didn't know of what to admonish him. Bad vapors, filth, or did tainted water caused this morbid disease? Some even said rats. But how to account for the wealthy being victims also? Beyond the sneer, he looked ghastly.

"Hunter…" She nodded and spoke quietly as both warning and concern.

"Bored robbing dead people, Ratchet?"

Ratchet gave Sary an unreadable look. Longing, pain, jealousy—*fear*? Perhaps a hunger very close to *not* wanting to be alone.

"What now, Hunter?"

"Tomorrow. Best sleep outside again."

Brisk. Authoritarian. "Ratchet, you can stay. Seem comfortable enough, and it's close to your—proclivities."

Ratchet chose to ignore his irony and was already slouched on the caboose's narrow bunk.

She looked back. Ratchet glared a hole through her. There was another layer. Loneliness, regret—*good-bye?* She must be imagining it.

Ratchet hadn't a human bone in his body and owned nine lives.

Outside, Sary and Hunter curled around a pile of passengers' suitcases and boxes, burning them. No one needed them on this earth any longer.

Chapter 68
Uneasy Salvation

Dawn. Ratchet was where they'd left him.

Hunter listened to his breathing.

"Like he's pulling a cart," Sary noted, feeling disquiet. Ratchet had been a cloud hanging over her for so long he seemed a necessary fixture—a punishment for sins known and unknown.

Hunter motioned. "I'll check later. Leave him. Let him rest." There was no need to say what they both thought.

They threaded back through the cars.

She averted her face from the dead; she could not come through here again. The birds were still present, but even such as they would have nothing to do with this cargo. Sary focused on Hunter's broad shoulders, avoiding view of those she passed. Pausing at a little boy, she tenderly covered him and swiped her eyes. Already the bodies took on a new cast.

"Hurry, Sary!" Sharpish.

They reached the engine. Hunter held her sunburnt face between two calloused palms, crushing her wilderness of pale tangled hair. "Let me forget all that"—he nodded—"in you." He spoke with the awkwardness of a shy suitor unacquainted with sentiment. "Sary, my darling dearest girl, I have much to say. For now, we need to make plans."

Sary remained mute. She would see if his everlasting affection saw the light of day once in civilization. Her vanity gave her that. *If we return.*

Slamming the throttle, Hunter thrust hands through his bronzed hair. "Pity we can't get this monster restarted. I'd wager Cape Town is in no position to look for it."

"But of course we can! Start it, I mean."

He cocked an eye. Even Sary could see the coal tender was only half full. "They apparently left in haste, barely enough, I dare say, to make any destination, let alone stir up a cold boiler, and if we stay, draining it for drink, we might last a…"

"But we won't have to!"

Hunter shook his head, his face saying it all: *Leave it to a female. All pie in the sky and Pollyanna.*

He sighed. "Sary. Love. Allow me to explain. First—"

Sary rushed on. "We uncouple the passenger cars. Leaving us the engine and coal car or—tender. Is that the word? Tender? Never mind. Aren't there water stations along the way?"

He nodded, amused. Slowly awareness dawned.

"We fire the rest. It's, it's *fitting.*" She was impatient to begin.

Hunter studied the tracks arrowing north to the mythical Vaal River and Kimberley mines, deciding how to reply, no doubt, with dignity.

"Actually, my love, I was about to suggest that very thing. Brilliant!"

Sary hid her grin. Hunter lifted her up, gave her a quick kiss, and let her slip lingeringly down his length. "One more accolade for my princess—my fairy queen."

If he says "queen of hearts," I will hit him.

She pointed to an odd tool. "That looks helpful."

Hunter studied the hefty three-foot bar propped in a corner of the engineer's compartment, picked it up, swinging it, and put it down again. "This, if I recall our old retainer, is a common spanner. Let's take a gander, shall we?" He took charge.

Fortunately for Hunter, he did not see Sary grip the spanner, slowly settling it to the floor again as he leaned over between the cars.

Sary joined him, studying the coupler between the coal tender and First Class. "A simple turn-screw affair. That's where the spanner comes to play. You almost had it."

Once again, Sary gritted her jaw.

"You'll make the most stunning fireman in all of Africa."

"Oh. I supposed I was engineer."

"Of course. You may sit your lovely derriere on my lap and pretend to steer."

Before Sary could shove Hunter off the train, he continued, "First, Ratchet. Don't fancy he'd wish to be a part of this particular ritual. Too much like a Viking funeral."

Poor Ratchet. Sary prepared to follow, but found herself looking down at his hand on her chest.

"No need for both of us to go, love. Back in a tick."

Sary shuddered, glad Hunter had stopped her.

"Be careful." *Of Ratchet.*

Chapter 69
Viking Funeral

Hunter walked the length of the train.

They were leaving none too soon. The buzz of insects had changed to a small roar. Besides, Ratchet had not allowed one valuable to escape his larcenous attentions. Hunter could relieve Ratchet of his spurious gains at any time.

Hunter footed the first metal rung leading up and over the caboose's small balcony. He studied Ratchet…

****

At the same time, Sary checked and poked around the massive locomotive's plethora of dials, brass levers, and round glass gauges to divine some meaning in them.

She tapped twin brass gauges with red-and-black dials and a scale of zero pressure to danger warnings.

Touching a lever, Sary muttered, "This has to do with the boiler. This, a brake of some kind." *Have I not driven a Mercedes up a mountain after fifteen seconds of instruction? This beast looks to be a dumb simple brute…* She spun as she heard Hunter drop into the coal car, with no second thump of feet.

She stopped at Hunter's face.

"Left him. He's dead, Sary. I hope you were not—extra close." Hunter seemed preoccupied and didn't sympathize further.

"Dead? Are your certain?" she asked foolishly.

It couldn't be. Her nemesis was as much a part of her as her bullet scars or withered arm. She was already backing, with one foot on the first step rather than wend through the cars.

"I wouldn't, love. Not a pretty sight—for a woman."

"Oh, let me go!"

Hunter's face gave an odd turn. "Don't you believe me?"

Sary slowly climbed back up. What motive would Hunter have? Except for his one odd turn in the desert, when all seemed lost, hadn't he been on their side all the way? Ratchet was dead. There was no good reason not to believe Hunter. Still…

He saw the troubled look. She couldn't smooth it away in time.

"He passed away. Peaceful, it looked." Hunter hesitated. "I think it was that iron contraption, in the end. It infected his leg. His blood was *sick*. What they call septicemia." He stopped. "Besides, he wasn't particularly careful with what he consumed."

He has over-explained. Sary sank to the fireman's perch. Yet he was correct. Dead is dead. Her eyes stung.

"Funny," she murmured almost to herself, "Ratchet was sly, and the only reliability he owned was that one could *never* count on him, and he'd cheat or hurt you just because it made him feel *something*."

"What an epitaph!"

"I never even knew his name. Not really."

An odd loss descended. Perhaps the lonely passing of any soul so far from home would feel the same. How could such an evil force be dead, though?

"I'd really best make sure."

"Please don't risk it, sweetheart. Please. For *my* sanity!"

Sary pulled away. "I have to." She stared green bullets and hopped down, shouting back, "Don't leave without me." She was only half jesting.

Sary ran along the tracks and clambered over the caboose's balconette, calling, "Ratchet?" She almost expected him to jump up hurling curses.

Silence. She stepped over the railing into the interior.

"Ratchet?"

Ratchet was sprawled half out of the bunk. She searched for mayhem and of course found none. "What did you think?" she muttered.

"What happened, Ratchet?" He did not answer. She gingerly tugged him back onto the bunk, placing her hand on his chest. It remained still. Warm, because the day was already hot.

His mouth was open, showing his lupine teeth in a last grimace; the beard concealed half his face, the eye patch the other. His features seemed twisted, and his long gray hands were clenched. He looked troubled. Probably because he had been in pain.

Her eyes shot to his brace. Indeed, the pant leg was stiff and black. "May you rest, finally, in peace. God take you, Ratchet." *No one else will.* Was it a curse or a blessing?

She swayed, off balanced, catching herself before she toppled into him.

Of a sudden, the train had rippled. The snake of cars had jolted sharply back.

The caboose lurched with a tremendous *schreeeechellll!* The line of cars jerked and screamed back along the tracks.

The floor tipped, looking ready to buckle as the cars slammed into the caboose.

Ratchet slid off, rolling into her, his arm pointing upward as if attempting to say something.

She backed from the accusing hand, screaming, "Hunter!" Leaving Ratchet on the floor and vaulting over the balcony, Sary pelted back up the line. *Don't leave me!*

She made the green engine—in passing, she eyed the gap between the coal car and First Class car, noting the decoupled tender and the long wrench abandoned by the rails.

The detached passenger cars had slid back ten feet, causing the massive jolt, and even as she watched, the cars rolled torturously another five or more feet, with a grinding screech.

Hunter was grim when Sary climbed hastily aboard. "Thought you started without me," she said, biting back more. Sary felt herself flush with mortification, anger, and fear. "Damn you, Hunter!"

"If you are certain now," he said with stuffy formality.

"Of course." She longed for the Hunter of before, the adoring companion. *Would he have left me?* She shuddered. *As before, trust only oneself.* Suddenly she was fearful of being alone with Hunter, without Ratchet's ruinous presence.

"Ready?" he asked grudgingly. Holding her by the arms, he kissed the top of her head.

Sary nodded, eager to be gone.

Chapter 70
Bring Out Your Dead

Hunter, wearing the fireman's gloves, dragged the few scattered bodies back into the cars—lastly the engineer and fireman—before setting the cars alight.

He wrapped discarded clothing around a branch, daubed it thoroughly with piston grease, and fired the torch with his novelty cigar lighter that created a cunning spark and flame from a tiny metal reservoir of fuel. He'd used it sparingly.

As they went car to car, his torch caught alight some article of clothing or package as Sary uttered silent prayers for the dead, especially the little boy huddled against his mother, in what seemed an eccentric funeral procession.

At the caboose, Hunter flung the entire guttering grease and rag bundle in. She looked off as black smoke rose to join the other sooty farewells to the skies. Sary bent her head, disregarding Hunter's impatience.

Farewell, Ratchet, gone for good. What peculiar trails you will follow now. She uttered a silent prayer for all the rest.

"Come, Sary!" Hunter stood impatiently waiting.

She jumped down as the car bloomed red out the windows and ran after Hunter without looking back.

****

Darkness fell. The necklace of cars was an inferno,

exploding with hellish light, heat, and greasy smoke in sequence, all belching out windows—an amazing sight. It seemed fitting and magnificent.

Chapter 71
Fiery Dragon

Smoke and shooting flames still blotted the stars for a good two hours, until leaving behind a seething line of smoking cars like a dragon's blackened bones.

"You look like a Blackamoor. Look at your funny face! Either the most cheeky chimney sweep or—"

"And you, sir, must be my bootblack."

Hunter checked his charcoaled arms and threw his head back, laughing. Both were lightheaded with relief.

With the dawn, Sary and Hunter eyed the snarl of cables, pipes, brass levers, dials, a turn wheel with a steering knob, throttles, brakes, pull cords, and bells smacking them in the face like the wet flounder of reality.

"Phew!"

"You first," Sary said, blank-faced, waving at the controls.

"But I am a gentleman. Ladies first. Now, I wonder what this is for." He reached to pull an innocent yellowed cord.

"Don't!"

"Right. Somehow, we must divine how this monster works, my girl. Have you any knowledge of the inner workings of a steam engine? A favorite uncle who was an engineer? I believe this was your idea."

"I thought you might." She played the queen of

hearts. "You *are* a man."

"Mmmm? Last I looked." Then seriously, "Not in this life, love."

"I've driven an automobile—a Mercedes," she answered with some pride.

"*Reallllly*?" he drawled. "Meant to get a motor car, but…" He shrugged.

"I suggest logic," Sary answered with her "we are not amused" face.

By trial and error, with Sary or Hunter alternately flat on their backsides, acquiring skinned elbows, sprained wrists, and smashed thumbs, they figured out the rudiments of firing the boiler and building a head of steam.

Late that day, in place of resting after a false start, they dove back in again. Hands on the throttle, with a firebox filled with coal, the boiler rattling and gauges in the safety position, Hunter and Sary locked eyes and sucked in deep.

Hunter eased up on the throttle. The engine went through internal confabulations, the boiler hissed—with Sary anxiously eyeing the gauge—the flared stack spewed smoke, their locomotive jerked alive, and the great pistons sluggishly began grinding, building speed until the engine and coal car rattled frighteningly fast over sand-drifted rails, and the great pistons and wheels were a blur.

Wide-eyed, Hunter and Sary leapt for the regulator, easing the speed to a ladylike stroll in the park. Grinning like maniacs, Sary and Hunter rapturously hugged, watching a luminous smoke-shadow sail away in tatters and their silhouette hurtle across the dunes, relishing the *clackety-clack* and pounding of the giant pistons churning out the miles ever northward.

"We did it, Sary girl!"

Now when they caught each other's eye, looks and hands lingered, bonding over coal-black hands, with sooty, wind-whipped hair. Their kisses tasted of coal dust and couldn't have been sweeter.

Chapter 72
Water Tower

The tower stood out for miles.

They hung out side windows as the train rattled up to the squat tower with its hose clipped to the side. Hunter pulled the whistle cord and slowed the locomotive until it was a waiting, hissing beast.

Hunter scrambled up the ladder, struggled with the lid, and gave a thumbs up, while Sary took the hose below overtopping the boiler.

Hunter watched Sary working in ripped trousers and a shirt held with one button. Her body was bronzed, her hair sun-bleached almost white and in a long pigtail. Shading her eyes, she grinned up at him like a hoyden. He felt his arousal grow. Never was she more appealing.

"Can see forever up here! Come on! You need a good scrub." Hunter laughed, flinging wet hair, making rainbows, his own body coppery and beaded with water, his hair bleached the same, teeth white and grinning. His eyes shone like aquamarines in the frame of his tanned good looks.

Sary suddenly felt sooty and grimy, yearning to feel his wet naked body against hers. With a lust that could not be crushed, she scrambled up the ladder. She plunged beneath the cool water—a second later, her trousers and shirt flew from the tower. The wetness felt delicious on her skin as the hot air played on it.

So good to be joyous and free and on our way! Nothing can go awry now. Perhaps it was the joy they were truly saved. *As long as the coal holds out.*

A strong hand jerked her down. It was dark inside the tower as she plunged under, shocked and vaguely frightened, reviewing images of Ratchet and her near-death in the San Francisco Bay years ago. Sary bobbed up, sputtering, "Sugar!"

She laughed, admiring Hunter spewing water, doing a comic backstroke in the circular confines, flinging diamonds of sparkling water from his brown muscled arms and bronzed hair grown long.

"Modest wench. Imagine, not removing your underpinnings in this veritable fountain of youth." His arms were outspread along the rim, as were hers on the opposite side, teasing with proximity but not touching.

Sary splashed him with her toe, bobbing up, revealing rosy nipples as water sheeted down.

"You dirty girl! Remove that dingy corset."

"Not the dirty sort *you* fancy, I fancy. I'm a good girl, I am," she teased. Never had she felt so childlike and giddy.

He turned serious, cocking his head. A cloud passed over the sun.

"Actually, why keep it on? Hiding some'at?" He flashed a grin and with one sweep of a muscular brown arm was by her side, covering her mouth with his, while pulling at the strings.

Sary stubbornly gripped his wrists, fancying she could not breathe. He seemed to have a fixation on her corset, matched by her determination not to give in. Some part of her was appalled at his obsession, not seeing her own.

Did it matter? She wished they could stay acting as children, making rainbows and sharing wet kisses without a morrow or a care.

"Don't be childish. You should be sick of that grubby thing. What is it? What are you hiding? A scar? A tattoo that'd make a sailor blush?"

"No. It would sink to the bottom." She laughed instead of showing the anger that rose.

"And a good place for it, too."

Then Hunter shrugged, his playful mood returned. "Your dirty little secret." He chuckled. "What sort of secrets could you have?"

Sary looked through lashes with green eyes made wicked. *You'd be surprised. Or would you?*

"Mad wench. No better than a scullery maid."

Quicker than she could react, Hunter tore the rotted strings. The thing separated from her, floating free, and he flung it out of the tower. "There!" he announced, showing strong white teeth with boyish triumph.

"No!" Sary reached out, realizing how eccentric her concern must seem. All the same, she felt his delicious hands about her thinner waist, almost spanning it, and in a moment she forgot all about her errant corset. *It does feel delightfully freeing to not have the blasted thing pinching my side. Besides, there are no diamonds—no mine, no anything.*

Hunter pinned her, bracing his hard body while she pretended to fight, turning her head.

When he entered her, he was cool and slippery-delicious.

Sary swooned with sensation while they took turns kissing every exposed inch. Sary nuzzled Hunter's jaw, nipped his ear, and licked water from his throat where the pulse pounded. He kissed her breasts, her mouth, plunged underwater and nuzzled every other part of her, and he came to the surface gasping. After, they rested on the rim, still eyeing each other with wet hot desire.

The first time was too good to not sample a second watery lovemaking. When at last they rode to a gasping, sputtering halt amid sloshing waves, Sary involuntarily shuddered, while they hung on the rim and drank in the slowly rising red moon.

"They call that a harvest moon, back home…" Sary murmured. A furrow creased her brow.

He didn't ask, "Oh, and where is that?" but gazed back along the tracks. "Come. Or you will catch your death."

Both were suddenly conscious of the untended boiler and the chiller air. He climbed out first. Sary couldn't help but admire his sleek, water-streaked body and all his masculine features.

When Sary descended, she saw him watching her pale bottom before turning to the waiting locomotive. As he did so, Sary scooped up her poor tattered undergarment, feeling for the bump in the lining.

With that gesture, Sary realized she had not given up her quest, no matter how vainglorious.

Chapter 73
The Handsome Con

The devilishly handsome swindler and con artist with the fox-red hair rummaged his elegant backside deeper into the gracefully worn green leather wingback in the gentleman's club, swiveling with satisfaction bordering on smugness.

He was a tomcat owning the whole cow, not just the cream, as he reveled in the room's centuries-old-money patina.

His eye grandly roved the hefty silver urns and serving pieces, the inch-thick Waterford, oiled walnut, linen-fold panels, the generous fire cheerily amusing his ears.

"Ahhhh!" He screwed his bottom deeper, languidly held the snifter to light, turning to his companion with a wicked smile plastered on his face as one who had just told a bawdy story.

"So you never felt a *soupçon* of contrition over your avaricious escapade." The admirer widened his mouth to leer.

The con smirked, studying his snifter's swirl of amber, properly warmed, of course. Then his face took on a nostalgic, little-boy cast.

"There was *one*. Not too long ago. Last fall. A feistiness about her. Eyes even you could drown in. Curious eyes. Changeable green to yellow like a cat's, calculating, with a cat's eye stare one moment, the next liquid and warm as sunlight on a limpid pond." He spread his hands in wonder.

The other man slapped his knee. "Poetry from you! You *have* lost your sticky-fingered touch."

"Pshaaaa!" The con lit a cherry brandy-soaked cigar, blowing perfumed smoke. "Never fear. I didn't melt under her mesmerizing green gaze—yet..." He looked off.

His friend had never seen the fabled con discomfited in the slightest, even while fleecing near-destitute dowager countesses or new widows with suckling babies.

"What was it? The insurance scam? Or...?" He left the question hanging.

"Railroads!" The con grinned. "More romantic and believable, railroads. That coupled with diamond mines. I lightened the bucolic colonial lass by five hundred thousand quid." He lifted his glass, winking at his admiring guest.

"Come, come, old friend, there's a story here. I intend to winkle it out, if only to cadge another snifter of this fine brandy, courtesy of the mysterious green-eyed, apparently *simple,* lovely."

The con grinned. "You've caught me out." He turned grave. "Not simple, but more...looking for a new adventure, like a dewy-eyed maiden, yet I had the oddest feeling she'd been through much misadventure in her time." He stared long into the fire, lost in memory. "I do have a glowing cinder where a beating heart once lay. I damn near succumbed and reneged, almost threw myself at her like a recalcitrant schoolboy begging forgiveness for fleecing her out of her shoes and shimmy, tossing the money back at her feet."

"This witch was that enchanting!"

"Yes," the con said simply, while his friend waited, disappointed, for more.

He stared at the ceiling. "More than that. Some women I've known biblically or otherwise are boxes of chocolates with pretty pink ribbons, simpering, with set choices of sweet nothings, or froths of lace in which one can smother and go nowhere one wishes particularly to go."

He winked. "She was a…" He shrugged, helpless. "*Woman.* A Diana. A Boudica!" He slapped his chair. "And Cleopatra, all rolled into one!"

"Yet you did not help her, though you did have some small remorse, you dog, you. What, pray tell, might that be? I am quite fearful of asking."

The red-haired man grinned wickedly over his snifter. "Ah, yes, I'm quite Jack the lad. I gave the gel a sweetmeat to season her bitter broth upon discovering the pretty documents were fakes."

He upended his glass.

The companion furtively checked the decanter. Almost empty. "And so? This sweetmeat?" he said, impatient.

The con laughed harshly. "A trifle, a scrap of spurious map. Another fake. Something to seek…far, far away"—he bowed at the waist—"from me. In Africa. By that time…?" He shrugged and brooded. "Perhaps, should this gullible wench's path and mine ever cross, we could share a laugh over the folly of our youth."

"You at least *tricked* her in your usual way?" The friend arched brows in wicked peaks.

"No, by Jove! Can you believe it? She fought me fiercer than any general on a battlefield of honor and never once let me breach her precious citadel."

It was true. The con winced at the memory. He'd almost had her, thrusting like an uncouth cowhand in a hayloft or a green schoolboy feverish for his first unsuccessful invasion. He flushed at the recollection.

The friend gawped. "Well, I never! That's a first!"

"Damn right!" The con crossed his legs, swinging one foot in frustration at the affront.

The friend savored his brandy, willing it to last. "Heard there was a spot of trouble over there—a pestilence."

The con snorted. "It *is* Africa."

"No. I mean plague. We suffered it back in 1640 or thereabouts. The Black Death."

The con laughed, sloshing brandy. "Wager the joke's on me. *The plague!* Well, plague take it!" He guffawed. "Do hope she's faring well."

****

In far-off Africa, in the evening chill far removed from the cozy gentleman's club, Sary sat up in a dark locomotive cabin, shivering.

A goose has walked over my grave.

Chapter 74
Penitence

The con sobered. "There is one thing." He motioned the steward to replenish his friend's snifter and leaned close.

"I did have second thoughts."

"But I—?"

"No, *these* second thoughts concerned the map. I thought, 'Damn me, perhaps the joke really is on me. Suppose that scrap is the genuine article? And she, the cunning vixen, lured me with her sex?' "

"But how would she—?"

"Know? Doesn't matter, sir. The map could have been real."

The red-haired man sat up, filled with umbrage.

"So." He tapped his head. "I wired my old friend. No, not you, but a man practically born and bred in Africa. The buggered last son of the last son of a titled gent, that sort."

He laughed. "Fancies himself an archeologist! His papa sent him there; or rather, he banished himself. Handsome rascal. Could not have been more perfect!"

"Yes, do get on."

"Met him once in Deauville in the train of a thrice-widowed duchess endowed with a huge mole and a huger fortune. Quite a ripe crowd at these horse events. He was tiring of the steeplechase *she* led him. Harry

271

Swallow, he's called. He could lend her a helping hand, and one to *moi*, with either the map or any serendipitous findings."

"Fortuitous."

"Yes, wasn't it?"

"So?"

"Haven't heard a dickey bird." The con shrugged.

"Wonder what happened to her—or him?"

He hefted himself from the comfy chair. "Come, let us dine. I could fancy the hind leg of something or druther."

Chapter 75
Unknown Territory

"What troubles you, Hunter?" Sary asked, anxious.

Hunter balanced wide-legged in the jolting cabin, holding the shovel. Sweaty, brawny, coal dust on his nose, a bandanna holding burnished hair, so damnably appealing she had to swallow hard.

"Hunter? What is out there?" She checked the tracks. Nothing alarming she could see.

He thrust hands through long reddish hair. "Should have come to Middelburg long ago. The tracks veered the wrong way back there—we're heading due west."

"But where—?"

"De Aar." He snapped.

"D—De...*Aar?*"

"An outpost. A crossing that connects to the Kimberley line."

"Does it matter? Anyplace will do."

He looked at her oddly. "Kimberley's *best*..."

Hunter set the brake. The train squealed short with a mighty blast of steam. They had not done this before—backed up.

Sary didn't breathe, waiting for pistons to reverse tortuously past the Y juncture. The locomotive ground back past the De Aar sign struggling above the sand.

"There, see?" More tracks veered roughly north. "But how do we get the train on that track?"

Hunter jumped down while the train sat huffing steam, manually tugging the rail-switcher, ballasted by a hefty weight.

Muscles straining, veins popping, he jerked, twisted, and stood on it; wiping his forehead, he gripped it again, and Sary placed her smaller hands next to his big scarred ones and tugged with him.

The rail switcher gave a rusty wail and moved sluggishly, chunking into a new alignment.

Sary kept glancing at De Aar for signs of life as they chucked lumps of coal into the tender from a pile by the tracks. Wandering chickens, blowing papers, and a flock of goats were the only movement.

The small station boasted a Western Union. The window was open. As she approached, flies grew to a heavy drone. With the shift of hot breeze, Sary knew she'd see sights she wished not to.

The slumped operator had became one in death with the Morse code pad, his mummified hand glued to the keys.

Sary turned sick. Hunter supported her until she threw his arm off. "I've seen worse."

Hunter rolled his eyes.

"Hunter?"

"Yeah?"

"If death is here, how—how far, do you think…?" She left it unfinished.

"Has the scourge traveled on up the line? Every car since the first sickened sailor went portside could have brought it up."

Sary was silent.

"Hunter? No matter what happens next, I want you to know this has been—"

"Yes, for me too."

They did not look at each other as the train chugged north and on to their future.

****

The way the locomotive hurtled, Sary fancied the train was a horse knowing the stable was closer, with fresh coal and water.

Coal dwindled again until there was only a sad heap. Sary said nothing, feeding the greedy firebox with parsimonious offerings.

"We could walk faster," Hunter grumbled as the train labored up a small elevation Hunter swore separated them from the Vaal valley spread out below. Sary prayed that was true.

"Should have broken up the seats. The varnish would make fine tinder."

"If we had wings, we could fly..." Sary gave his arm a squeeze.

Chapter 76
Iron Horse

Their green dragon steamed its reluctant way to the last rise. Days ago, upon reaching the tall face of the escarpment, they slid through a narrow jagged rill, one of many scarring the tall ridge, holding their breath, mentally shoving the slowing train up—*up* before it backslid.

Stirring visions of peaks, terraces, gorges, and lime-green valleys showed from the higher terraces. Every turn showed new fascinations of line and color, deposits of ages past, spread over the face of the land, descending the mountain flanks.

Hunter pointed out craggy hills—points called *spit kopjes,* volcanic eruptions rising in jagged fantastic shapes, like walls forming narrow ridges of greenstone which their small train snaked past.

Chapter 77
Vaal

The engine hovered at the top, then gathered speed grudgingly to rattle scarifyingly downslope. By careful braking, Hunter barely kept it from careening off hairpin curves as it hurtled to the valley.

Hunter stole Sary a look, as they seemed to barrel into empty space. Sary's jaws clenched as tight as her fists, her eyes sparkled from the wind, her teeth showed, and her hair was blown to hell and back.

She was breathtaking.

He laughed with her. Sand was a blur. Ribbons of racing dun and green and the great muddy ribbon of the Vaal, lined with cottonwoods, wound at last through a wide panorama of flatland, below, dotted with crude settlements.

Sary's throat closed. She turned from Hunter, smearing her eyes. These were tears of joy and thanksgiving. But she would not let him see how terrified she had been, how close to despair. Yet joy turned to confusion as she showed him a glad face.

What now?

She had been safe on the train, in a never-never world with an enigmatic man who shivered her spine. Now she must think, and do, and plan. The change was so sudden.

How can he be so calm?

Chapter 78
Panners

Click-click, tap-tap, clank-clank. The distant discordant ring, metal on metal. A babble of voices carried with the vagaries of hot wind.

"There, Sary! The Vaal!" Hunter waved as if he were responsible for the wide brown river moving sluggishly below.

It didn't look like much. Sary couldn't appreciate that "Vaal" meant "dun, muddy gray."

She shaded her eyes. From the distance, chaos reigned all along messy banks on both sides of the wide river, it seemed; odd workings, honeycombs of deep holes, all sorts of rickety machines. Some recognizable as the same shaker boxes she and her long-lost brother had used back in Big Bear.

Hunter was jovial. "Ah, Sary, we did it!"

The train bucked, throwing them hard against the throttle and sliding to a gritty halt amid oily brass, dripping copper, and a dead boiler.

The engine halted for good a half mile from all this activity, and no one seemed to care or notice, saving them from explanations or suspicion.

Sary and Hunter stepped from the dead train. It was surreal, not to be bucketing back and forth with their back teeth jolted, needing to brace themselves. The silence and flatness seemed boring and uneventful.

The river was in walking distance when the train, with its empty coal tender and depleted boiler, gave its last gasp. Toward dusk, they walked the tracks to the first panners, communally jostling picks side by side, barely missing each other as, pans glaring in the setting sun, they worked until dark. She and Hunter dropped flat. They knew to be quiet and unnoticed till they figured out the climate.

She pointed across the river. "The real town must be over there."

On the other side, low white buildings and what seemed to be a stubby church spire in the midst of canvas and mud huts intermingled with raw, newer ones, with proper porches and windows and no apparent planning. Sary's eyes glowed, catching the fever of industry and the exhilaration of discovery not made...*yet*.

They both ducked at once. Two figures with rifles stood either side of the tracks. Sary picked others out, all facing outward in a jagged line.

Hunter nudged. "The sickness hasn't arrived here; they're making damned sure it doesn't. Once we mingle, we'll blend."

"How?" *No money, no food, no clothes.*

"Have you seen us?" Hunter rose boldly and walked past them arm and arm with Sary. He nodded at a sentry. Then Sary felt a gun in her back. There was another one in Hunter's. "Get down, the both a ya!"

Hunter turned with a careless grin. "What? A feller can't get off to do a little private canoodlin'?" He laughed and patted Sary's fanny. *Bastard!* Sary gave a sick grin and plastered her hand on Hunter's chest.

"Whatcha think? We walked here?" Hunter

laughed incredulously and pulled Sary along, feigning drunkenness, breaking into a bawdy song.

Already Sary felt an odd departure from Hunter in this strange atmosphere, aware of restlessness, an unease. She looked back. One of the sentries grinned foolishly; the other had his rifle to his shoulder. Sary felt the bullet at her back.

"Keep walking. Don't look back."

They hit the first campfire, wandered past groups of people, families, and loners, one a solitary woman. They were on the fringes now. *How could Tommy suppose I am here? Where did that notion come from?*

Still her heart quickened at each tall, dark-haired man or the sound of the prattle of a young child as they walked among low tents and lean-tos. She and Hunter were just two more diamond-thirsty diggers, as dun-colored as the sluggish Vaal, no one giving them more than the odd glance. The only time folks lingered was when they figured Sary was more than a boy under the rags and sunburnt skin.

Evening meals were being prepared. The smell of biscuits, beans, fat back, and coffee drove them mad.

Sary noticed the oddest medley of dress: woolen, linen, and white cotton shirts; checked or pinstriped trimmed jackets; riding breeches, laced army leggings; hand-me-downs from the cheapest ready-made to coarse brown corduroy to a preacher's raggedy coat; and what were clearly town folk—schoolmarm types or shopkeeper's daughters and farmer's wives—in prim calico. Everyone had set up rude camps.

Sary's knees buckled. She hung on a tent rigging, breathing in the aroma of fish frying in cornmeal and hot fat. Her last meal had been six raisins that morning.

"Food. Where do you suppose...?"

Sary knew they looked lean, hungry, and desperate. Folks turned away from their needy faces.

Hunter nodded to the river without conviction. "Fish. Maybe a chap will lend us a line if we can't beg or steal. We need work," he continued.

"A job?" Somehow that seemed permanent—a left-hand turn from where she needed to go, what she needed to do.

Oh, yes, and what is that—precisely?

A map, a monastery? Drunken traders and renegade dukes! Somehow find Tommy and Jude?

She sighed. *A mad, half-recalled dream.*

"I'm not above stealing," Sary avowed.

Then a woman tossed scraps to her dogs. They fell on them, elbowing the baying hounds aside, snatching bones with shreds of meat and half an enormous biscuit with dried egg, gratefully wolfing it down, aware of curses and thrown rocks as they ducked between tents.

"Better," she muffled. "Now, water."

"So this is the mighty Vaal," she commented up close. "Seen laundry water more appetizing." She poked a stick in the slow-moving river boiled up with gravel and dirt from the panners.

"No worries. You're immune after our little adventures." Hunter laughed carelessly, lapping up handfuls. "Jump in. We'll dry fast."

The water was like warm soup, but she felt cleaner. Sary smoothed her hair, replaiting it, and straightened her ragged clothes to dry on her body, wincing, feeling her old friend the corset chafing her ribs. A woman looked up from her campfire. She scooped something and walked to Sary, holding out two burnt flapjacks on

281

a spatula. "Just goin' ta toss 'em; you may as well have 'em."

"Thank you…" But the woman had already turned, motioning with a brush of her hand—*away.*

Chapter 79
Klip Drift

Nibbling the cakes, Sary and Hunter strolled the Vaal, winding through a line of willows and cottonwoods. They came up to the end of a chaotic line—a clustering of wagons, oxen, and horses, all waiting to cross.

Again, no end of variety, from pale-skinned ladies who never dirtied their hands to rough country boys, old soldiers, farmers, and African natives, all waiting for the swell of the river to drop.

She heard snatches of talk as they forced their way through. "...blindin' dust storms...cain't breathe with all the grit and powder...rain so fast, river filled with torrents of mud...already waited forty days..."

Fortune hunters forced to outwait the swollen river. Sary sensed dangerous impatience beneath.

Hunter pointed. "The Klip Drift. A rocky place to ford. A Dutch farmer's boy found a twenty-two-carat diamond near here, and in '69, an eighty-three-carat diamond caused all this."

Hunter waved at the mad scene. "You wouldn't be schooled in any of that, would you now, Sary?" As he studied her, Hunter's eyes were flat, gray-brown as the Vaal.

Words stuck in her throat.

Chapter 80
Passion and Pain

"The largest mine is Colesberg Kopje—or Hill—the Kimberley. The Big Hole. The wealth there is *unimaginable*," Hunter said with a ferocity that unnerved her.

Why were you not there, then, Hunter, instead of digging up old bones?

Her own breath quickened. Yet she had no desire to join the masses of frantic diggers along the bank. *Not when I have my own secret.* "What now?"

"We wait." He regarded her with an expression she knew well, feeling her own breath quicken.

"But not like them," he whispered huskily. "I have a much better idea." Hunter led her into a quiet oasis of scrub, where he dropped to the sand, dragging her with him.

Hunter stroked her clean, sun-washed hair from her face.

She felt suddenly shy.

"Sarabande. My dear little monkey-face. When this is over, and we—"

She placed a swift hand against his mouth. *No, don't say it.*

"My darling, precious Sary. This is not the time, nor the place, yet I must speak. Who knows about tomorrow? Sary, you are the most perplexing hoyden,

284

the most delectable dirty beggar, the most appealing, delightful, unanticipated female I've ever had providence to…"

She couldn't help it. Sary felt her mouth stretching.

Hunter watched, transfixed. When Sary smiled, her lovely mouth formed a perfect curve—stunningly beautiful. With her pale tresses whipping around her face and green eyes gazing mysteriously as if, through a curtain, with one strand stuck to her full bottom lip, she was an enchantress. He longed to pluck it away and stared mesmerized at her mouth, until she shifted, apprehensive.

What can it hurt, one last time to be with this man? One last time for all of our—adventures. No tears. Then good-bye.

"I even rummaged this." Hunter held a bruised mango as large as a football.

Juice run down their chins between mango-sweet kisses. She roved his broad shoulders, fingering his back as if memorizing it, his burly ribs and belly, taut flanks, down his muscular legs. Hunter explored every inch of her, kissing sweet stickiness from her breasts, her throat, her lips.

They made love, lingering for hours, resting, renewing passion with a strange fever, and on Sary's part, a sweet bitterness she could not shake.

Hunter's body—the silkiness of his muscles, the tickle of chest hair, his hot-blooded aggression, the invasion, the weight of him—was a drug Sary needed with the same desperate passion as the first time—*for the last*.

She awoke with a start, with an odd sense of loss.

The air was still balmy. But she felt chill. A long

while till dawn.

Hunter wasn't there.

She looked over.

Hunter…going through her few rags of clothing.

"What are you doing? Again, Hunter?" Sary cried, bewildered. Forced bewilderment. She knew.

He looked up with a face swimming with guilt, chagrin, even—*hatred?* "You have it! I know you do!"

He shook her grubby garments at her.

"You despise removing everything. Practically have to rip things off, as if you were a virginal bride or an ignorant maid of thirteen. Even when we are most intimate!"

It would seem comical outrage had his face not been so cold. A stone hurled could be no more painful.

Sary covered herself with her hands.

"Oh, here!" he snarled. "Take them!" He flung the corset and rags aside.

"It's not in this grubby thing you are so fond of, is it? I've searched your pockets." He raced back, naked, to grip her skull with two large hands.

"Is it true what Ratchet said, you have it all in your head? Tell me! Tell, or I will crush it out of you like picking walnuts! I can't lose. I *never* lose! I really loved you, Sary. Don't you see? I did, and it's tearing me up. I will not go back, tail between my legs, like some damned village idiot, and prove my sneering brothers and doting father right and have my friend laugh at me."

A cross between a groan and a laugh, harsh and crazed, erupted.

Quite mad.

He cocked his head. "You see, Sary? My old

friend. My old friend, the "railroad magnate," that carrot-top fop, holds something over me, Sary. I rather admire him, he's so fiendishly foxy and clever." He looked down. Almost sulky.

"I didn't really mean to hurt that girl. I was fond of her in my way…"

"Get away from me," she said with the flatness of a skipping stone, all the while dressing haphazardly as she held his eyes with her own.

Hunter narrowed his when she chastely laced her dirty corselet back on.

He slowly began following her like a feral dog as she backed toward the mass of people waiting to cross. Turning to run, Sary picked up speed. With dawning intelligence, Hunter did too.

"You have it!" he snarled, racing after her like a mad dog.

Chapter 81
Flight

As Sary reached the safety of people, the crowd surged as if from one signal, pouring onto flat-bottomed boats and rafts. Wagons and cattle collided with men crossing in rowboats clustered at the ford.

Horses raced the bank and reared, bucking, as riders checked their bits. Oxen forged ahead of long straining lines, swaying creaking wagons, and cracking whips. Ponderous canvas schooners swayed over quaking sands to the bank.

Separately, Hunter and Sary jostled along with this dangerous tide. She could hear cursing and calling. Sary ran to a wagon carrying an elderly couple and what seemed to be grandchildren—age no deterrence for panning.

"Please? Help me? Let me aboard!"

Sary looked back at Hunter bellowing, "Sary! What do you think you are doing—*wife*! You can't run from me!"

The woman assessed her stonily. "Made your bed, young missy, now lay in it, messy as it may be," she sniffed.

The farmer grunted. "Don't mix ourselves in other's God-given marital rights. Go back to your husband…"

"But he's not—!"

Sary saw the stiffening of both backs. *No help here.*

And Hunter dragged her from the wheel hub, shaking her like a rag doll.

Sary turned on him. "Stop it!" To onlookers Sary realized they seemed like any other sordid battling couple as he dragged her off.

"No one will aid you. Only me!" he roared. "Haven't I seen you through hell? Aren't we companions—and *more?*"

"And then you hold out on me. So what if I know Old Foxy? Aren't you the lily-white one, here?"

Sary felt her cheeks flame. "You know *nothing*! Who are you—really?"

"Told you. Don't you listen? Harry Swallow!" He yanked her to the sidelines of the surging crowd as it knocked them about.

That struck an echo. His voice. His bearing. Very much to-the-manor-born. "No," she said thoughtfully. "I don't think you are."

He doffed an imaginary plumed hat, making a mocking bow. "Never said you were dimwitted. Too right. Fourth bastard son. At your service."

Sary backed.

"Conversant in French?"

She shook her head no.

"Hirondelle?"

She shook her head. "I scarce care."

" 'Hirondelle' is French for 'swallow.' In English, 'Arundel.' The Duke of Norfolk's ancestral home is the village of Arundel south of London. Get it?"

He pulled her back. "I was dubbed Harry Swallow. While close in blood, I will never be a true Arundel.

Born the fourth son on the wrong side of the sheets, whelped by the same godforsaken lady, my gullible whore of a mother, by the same true heir in line, and even he is only third."

"I don't give a flaming fig."

He snorted. "Tut-tut. I aim to make my fortune and make them eat their bloody titles. When Alfred told me to follow you, I saw a glittering opportunity I won't let slip. You, my darling girl, were the gilding on the lily, the cinnamon sugar on my slice of tart. And I intend to make it a huge slice, if I need to throttle it out of you! But enough. Where is it? I will help you, you clever trollop."

He placed both large hands, the ones she had adored on her body, around her long neck.

Sary held his gaze. "Do your worst. You think you can get away with it? Here? And then where would you be?"

He threw the lessening mob a look. "In this lawless state? Hah! But of course. Where would I be with you dead at my feet?" His gaze was just as deadly. 'You don't scare."

Sary was not listening. Her attention was on the dust, the chaos of hooves, the straggle of a crowd tensed to cross at the first sign of returning ferries, all the lumbering carts, oxen, horses, and humanity already stampeding ahead, champing at the bit.

"You'll think clearer on the other side," he snarled, grasping her arm before she could lose herself in the scene before them.

Chapter 82
Welcome to hell

Swallow—she could no longer think of him as "Hunter"—never losing his hold on her, prodded Sary, up to her waist in the muddy Vaal, to the back of a barge canted over with shifting weight.

In the dark, he heaved himself aboard and grabbed her hand, helped by a scurrilous youth also stealing a ride. Sary looked back at the bank.

"Don't be stupid."

The barge dragged her through the wake, her head below water. Breaking through at last, she hauled up on the edge with muddy wet hair draining in her face as the ferry poled across.

They slipped off on the opposite side. Sary, drawn to a campfire, wrung out her clothes, while owners looked on, incurious, and Hunter studied their situation.

She eyed a pot of something boiling. Its owners looked the other way, studiously ladling out bowls, offering none.

And over there—a low clapboard building labeled Diamond Assay, much like the gold assayer's office in Big Bear, among a polyglot of rickety churches, tents, wooden shacks, and more deep holes gouging the bank, with a beehive of workers slaving by lantern light. White-topped wagons and camp tents perched on every conceivable place—an insane asylum turned loose on the beach.

Still wet and dripping, Sary fretfully watched the hustling crowd, all knowing their destinations and what commerce interested them.

First, I must lose him. She felt sickened. She'd lost it all on a silly foible. Tommy, Jude, her own nature, sabotaging herself. She *must* lose him. Her only chance lay in the direction of her folly, yet she couldn't think while the turncoat hawked her.

As Sary had discovered to her bitter regret, it was all too soon to write the end to Hunter or Swallow or whatever his name was.

Sary studied her surroundings for any hints as to her next step. "Clean up, find food, and work," she muttered to herself. She looked down at her rags. *Have to snitch some. Somewhere. I'll make it good.*

Her eyes wandered the crowd, hopeless. Everywhere she looked she saw Tommy. Tommy's slender, elegant figure. Every man taller than six feet, with dark hair, be they young or old, she thought was Tommy until they turned. It wasn't logical, yet her wayward mind kept her sidetracked when she should be looking for help. Later she would move heaven and earth to find Tommy and Jude…if they wanted to be found.

Chapter 83
Erstwhile Wife

A striking pale face under a mass of curls glossy as licorice stood head and shoulders above the mob.

Tommy is tall like that... No, it wouldn't be.

Black eyes glittered beneath wicked brows like crow's wings. He looked right at Sary—her heart lurched. Tommy! And rushed, to her bewilderment, not at her but at Hunter, booming, "Harry—Harry *Swallow!* You old fraud! What an amazing happenstance. Haven't clapped eyes on you since boarding school."

"*Tommy...*" Sary whispered, dirty, wet, and miserable at his side. She looked up at him, willing him to see her. *Am I a ghost?*

Sary felt a lump in her throat as big as a darning egg and bit her lip hard to keep from total dissolve. Then an overwhelming rush of gladness, redemption, and relief flooded her. Her skin flushed with the emotion too long tamped into a crazy place between weeping and laughing. "Tommy," she whispered. *He doesn't even notice me.*

Tommy slapped Hunter on the back. "Harry, you old swindler, what disruption are you up to in this part of the globe? And how good to see a face I know!"

"*Tommy!*" Sary raised her voice, which came out a hoarse caw. Tommy looked down at the interruption, back at Hunter, and slowly returned.

Blank.

Sary's heart felt like a lump of the coal they had thrown in the firebox—a burnt-out cinder.

"Tommy? Don't you see me?" She felt the break in her voice.

Tommy looked her over. Her face was burnt brown, her hair darkened by mud and water. Slowly his expression changed.

"Sary?" Faint. Then Tommy's face lit up. "Sary! I've come to every ferry crossing! I almost gave up."

Then he absorbed the sodden hair still dripping mud down her transparent rag of a shirt, her breasts strongly outlined, the smeared grimy cheeks, her face a bit gaunter, and the rail-thin waist. "*My poor Sary...*"

"'Fraid not, old man…"

Hunter stepped in front of her. "A poor specimen of a female, I grant you. And one you must know, or *think* you do, from another life."

He looked quizzically at her and gave her a familiar squeeze. "Yet this little ragamuffin cleans up well." Hunter clapped Sary closer. "I so enjoyed"—he winked broadly—"this feisty gel's company, whilst in the forced familiarity of the desert. Oh, but the nights do get cold and lonely in the Karroo—but that's another tale told out of school."

He winked again.

"Harry? What is this, Sary? *Sary?*" Tommy asked dangerously.

Sary tried to speak. She couldn't get words out. Yet no matter how serious Thomas's bombast, borrowed heavily from Shakespeare or Marley, it was still tinged with playacting, as if he observed himself from an audience.

"'Fraid she's mine, old chap. Trifle on the rough side, I grant you, not up to my usual standard in feminine companions, yet—"

He kissed Sary's muddy forehead. Sary shoved him off with all her remaining strength.

"Don't, Hunter. Don't you dare! Tommy, this isn't..."

Hunter grabbed her back with a dangerous smirk.

Tommy waded in. She twisted free, biting Hunter's hand where it clasped her other arm.

Hunter grimaced but held on.

"As they say in the Bible, this little mudhen"—he grunted with pain—"is worth more than gold, old chum."

Tommy eyed him coldly. "She's my *wife.*"

Hunter's jaw dropped before catching himself. "That's an old saw. Whenever you spotted a pretty wench, as I recall, or perhaps in this case a chance at a *fortune*, you always claimed it."

He backed with his hand about Sary's neck. "May be your wife," he sneered, "but she is *my* bed mate."

"Hunter! Stop!"

As if he had put a brand on her, staining her forever, Sary could neither own it nor deny it. Shaking her head, she looked beseechingly at Tommy.

"Keep your tales to yourself, Swallow." Tommy's mood turned leaden. He was never quick to anger, but when he did... He looked coldly at Sary. "Is this who you ran off with—or to?" he asked, his tone dangerously soft.

"No. It is not like that! Please!" *No time for all of this.* "Where—how is Jude?" Sary looked about, desperate. Sary could not and would not justify herself now, not for any man.

"Good enough for me," Tommy declared. "Sorry, *old bean.*" Tommy jerked Sary away.

Hunter, fists clenched, furiously rounded on them, insane with the rage of being denied. Sary sensed Hunter had never experienced much rejection. *He will now*. He was red-faced and sputtering.

"She's a whore. She had both of us. Ratchet too."

Tommy's stride hitched. He darted a glance at Sary. *Ratchet?*

"No." She shook her head with a look only couples with long histories could translate—"Tell you later— not true—Hunter is a con and a murdering bastard." All said in a look, shrug, and a lifted brow.

Tommy spun back, and his fist rammed Hunter's jaw sideways. A front tooth flew. He would never be as handsome again. The two rolled on the ground, Tommy bashing the bulkier Hunter with newfound authority. Her old Tommy was gone. As more punches were thrown, they drew a careless crowd. A common sight. Sary felt a shiver of thrill.

But where is Jude? Frantic, her eyes roved the crowd, and she placed her hands between her knees to keep from shaking.

"Jude? Tommy, stop!"

She waded in between them, pushing elbows and hands against straining chests and heated faces, screaming, "He's not worth it, Tommy. Where's my boy?" Sary demanded in panic.

Tommy threw one last punch, going down with it as it sailed by Hunter's ear. Hunter brushed himself off with bravado, but his nose leaked like the result of a schoolboy scuffle. Tommy had red knuckles, and a cut bisecting his wicked brow.

The new Tommy rounded on her. "*Now* you care about your son?"

"Son?" Hunter looked on, nonplussed, as Tommy dragged Sary away. Sary, unsure of her motive, was ashamed she hadn't told him.

Tommy, scowling as he pulled her along, growled, "There is an elucidation due here. But now is not the time."

"Oh, Tommy, where is he? Is he—?"

"With Ruth," Tommy snapped.

Sary paled beneath her burn. "Ruth?"

"No worries, my faithful little *'wife.'* Ruth is the vicar's spouse."

"Vicar?"

Hunter trailed after them at a safe distance. "We could be partners," he called.

Sary looked back with disbelief.

Tommy's stride slowed, and then he walked on.

Hunter called again. "I said we could be *partners*. I would be a valuable asset." It came out a funny lisp with the missing tooth.

Tommy urged her on. "Damn you, Sary."

"Dammit yourself, Tommy! Jude? How is he?"

"Spoiled rotten by the vicar's hefty thirteen-year-old daughter. Come. Let us show Jude his *loving mother* isn't with the angels, as said daughter so often suggests as she looks me over."

"I want to clean up first."

He remained stubborn, even punitive, demanding she enter in her reduced state. His lips twitched, though. "On second thought, you might contaminate a pig. But no, let us not make Jude wait longer."

Chapter 84
Vicarage

Ruth, a waif of a thing with soft brown eyes and a tiny sweet mouth, looked Sary over without seeming to, leading her off without fuss.

The sturdy daughter, with two budding lumps in front, entered, scowling at Sary. "He's abed," she said sullenly.

The wife smiled. "Soon," she said and gently scrubbed Sary in a tub of water turning the shade of coffee.

"We get so dirty here," she murmured kindly.

"In more ways than one," Sary replied.

"Well, we here are all washed clean."

The wife held up Sary's corset by a string. "Ohhh, I'm afraid this is beyond help, but I am not certain any of mine fit."

"No!" Sary said, and then more gently, "No. It is a…memento. It has sentimental value."

"I see." Ruth watched Sary carefully for signs of madness. "I'll just wash it then."

Sary had never seen a filthy corset get so much unwarranted attention. She held onto it. "I'll do it later; you've already done so much."

"Poor soul," she heard the wife say to her husband, as she closed the door on Sary. "She's quite touched."

Chapter 85
Jude

Sary had a loving reunion with Jude, who had grown sturdier and above her knee now. He was matter-of-fact regarding her absence, plunging headlong into a detailed story, in rather an anticlimax of the reunion Sary had dreamed of.

"'ook, Mummy!" He ran to her as if he'd seen her only last evening, holding up a carved, lumpy, wood thing. "An e'phant! It nose *bwoke* though."

He still had the lisp. Sary's' heart flip-flopped as she swooped and hugged him, "e'phant" and all.

****

"So you see, Tommy, I wasn't running off— *leaving* you," she explained as they walked around the pastor's yard. She struggled under Jude's weight but would not put him down, until he demanded it.

"When the captain sailed… When I saw the ship leave…" Her face crumpled, reliving the day. "I was so—desperate."

Tommy softened. "I almost swam to shore."

"Except for Jude." They said in unison.

Tommy looked at Sary with her clean hair wafting in the humid breeze and the vicar's wife's prim cotton dress. "Looks like we all found our lost treasures."

Sary's eyes welled, tears spilling. "There nothing between me and that wretched filth of a man," she said vehemently. Too much so. Tommy eyed her, hard.

Not really. It was all sham.

Chapter 86
Corselet

In the corner of the kitchen, Sary pretended to mend; gently picking threads she'd sewn a lifetime ago from her much-abused corset staves. The vicar's wife looked on, perplexed.

"My dear, I'm uncertain if any of mine would fit you, but I might be able to find a clean corset from my"—she blushed—"last confinement."

Sary smiled foolishly, clinging to the muddy, stained cotton, and said brightly, "This will do nicely. You've been so generous."

"Well, if you are certain…" Ruth backed out.

She must think me a lunatic.

Well, aren't you? Still holding on to a lunatic fantasy?

Yet the dream of diamonds, still stubbornly burned. Perhaps the fuel was pride.

The last stitches parted to reveal the leather scraps tightly wound around the staves just above the waist—a natural contour to the casual observer. The rest of the abused corselet fell in shreds of silk and cotton.

Sary unwrapped the pieces of damp stained leather from the steel ribs, gently unrolling them. The leather was pliable and soft, now. She laid them flat on newsprint, carefully fitting the two halves of the map together. They appeared cleanly sliced with a sharp knife. Flicks of mud showered off. *Soil from the trickster's boots.*

The dampness came from her immersion in the railroad water tank and the dunking in the Vaal last night; the scribbles, though faded, seemed indelible…most likely bloodstains.

She teased the rest, brushing gently, straining to see in the lamplight, for that was all the vicarage had.

The wife reentered, again bewildered. "My dear, is anything wrong?" she asked, perplexed at the sodden scraps. "If you need anything—embroidery? Perhaps something edifying to read?" She reached for a book of psalms beside a mantel clock. "This can be soothing to a troubled soul."

Sary stared, both giddy and annoyed. "Oh…" She laughed shakily. "All is most *wonderfully* right. I *have* something to read. I mean that I *must* read." Sary gathered her things and left Ruth gazing after.

"The poor, poor soul. As I live and breathe."

Sary felt anything but poor. She yearned to tell Tommy, but he was on a jaunt with Jude. *Gotten quite chummy, those two.* She felt a prod of green monsters.

Back in the room the kind couple, though cramped themselves, had allotted them, Sary lit the sheep-fat lamp and spread the map again, in time sitting back satisfied.

True, a tiny portion of the map was yet missing—or at least she hoped it was only a tiny bit—but this was a panorama with compass points in the left corner. And here, letters spelling—'c-a-v-e-s, and suggestions of mountains scratched in dark brown, unmistakably dried blood. Sary could visualize a monk bent over a bird quill pen painstakingly scratching away, perhaps pricking his finger for writing ink.

A squiggly line she thought was the Vaal intersected another labeled *ORNGE*. *"Orange,"* she whispered. She compared a map the vicar's wife had lent her, learning they were no more than a mile from the Orange River and with it the Kimberley mine...*and either a cache of diamonds or a handful of pixie dust.*

She scrutinized the scraps from an angle. Tiny flat-bottomed domes dotted beneath what seemed to be mountains close to a big letter K.

Kimberley Mines, of course. She smiled at the unknown monk's simplicity.

With the vicar's magnifying lens, the round-topped shapes seemed to indicate perhaps cave mouths. One had a large X. There were too many of these odd marks, though. Some sideways so the flat part lay on the side—a few were upside-down, all higgledy-piggledy.

She sat back. "A scatter of what looks like tiny letter Ds. A scatter of *diamonds!*" Capital Ds. It could mean no other.

Sary traced her finger south. She looked more closely, swiping away more mud, holding the map to the light, alternately putting her nose to it.

"If it is K for Kimberley, what is this small k that was covered with stain? Little Kay? Little Kimberley? Doesn't make sense." *Unless...* "No," Sary argued, "there is only one Kimberley mine."

She next squinted at a smudge overlaying darker lines that turned into a crude square, with a pyramid on top, and a cross. "An abbey or a monastery. What did the duke say, back in Cape Town?" *Outside a monastery.*

"Are you well? Would you care for cool

buttermilk?" Ruth called through the door.

Sary started. "Quite well. Just recalled something amusing." She heard footsteps going away and recalled the banished duke's words: *"The monk's dwelling, and the church that went with it. A monastery."*

Sary's heart thumped. She must show this to Tommy. *He will be convinced. Why? The wretch didn't believe me. Should I just leave now and—and...*

Sary sat back with a plonk.

What is happening to me? I already tried that. I've done enough damage. Tommy would have to dig deep to forgive me. Still...? Even if I left a note?

Sary carved a smile. She'd love to shower Tommy and Jude with diamonds so brilliant they'd need to squint. "There. I was right. I was wrongheaded and selfish, but I restored our fortune," she'd say.

Sary flushed. Shaking her head, her chagrin interrupted once more by the vicar's wife's slow sweet voice. "My dear, are you certain you would not care for a nice cup of warm lamb broth?"

Assuring the good woman she did not require a cup of warm lamb broth, Sary bent back and soon was happily lost in deciphering the rest of the tale writ in blood.

She turned the map, holding it close to the light. Why had they not restored the monastery? Perhaps they did. One of the Ds was larger, drawn under cone-shapes which *must* indicate mountain ranges or hills.

"But how far?" Sary fretted. "There is no distance indicator. Could be five feet or fifty bloody miles." The larger D was filled in—*like a cave mouth?*

Hunter's words floated back: *"Before the Kimberley, panners mined the streams. The largest stones tumbled down, at first overlooked until they figured those dull pebbles were diamonds damned near big as goose eggs. Before you could spit, the whole bank was honeycombed..."*

Sary's eyes glistened.

"Yes. And that trader in Port Elizabeth. The man was half drunk. He kept saying, "Little Kay. My sweet beautiful Little Kay. I left her and can't find her again..."

"Lordy, it wasn't a lost sweetheart. He meant a small mine, or a cave he named 'little k,' where he stashed diamonds from the river banks. A small mine, like the Kimberley, or a cache of panner's diamonds squirreled away."

She could see them gleaming in the dark fastness of a cave.

Chapter 87
Desperate Devices

Tommy's Irish eyes gleamed with mischief.

They sat on the edge of the vicar's shallow porch, digging toes in the dust, long after the good folk, who were surely tiring of them, were abed.

"Or at least a cache of some sort." Sary punched him lightly when Tommy didn't respond. "Doubting Thomas! You are the mule in *A Midsummer Night's Dream*. I swear! You *do* understand! Say you are excited." She saw a twitch in the corner of his mouth.

He looked at the night sky. "Why the Hades not?"

Sary—the Queen of Sheba in a corona of platinum braids and a drab brown borrowed dress with a tiny brown pansy print—climbed on Tommy's lap.

It had been a long time between intimacies, their forced proximity with the good vicar and his wife, and the thin walls, especially vexing.

"Let's make some quiet sin," Sary whispered.

Tommy scooped her up, stumbled through the dark kitchen, and kicked the door closed.

Their lovemaking was shy and awkward, compounded with need and recalled lust, and saved by the flawlessness of the way their bodies melded and responded—the bed creaked and groaned.

The vicar's wife smiled in the dark. It seemed their troubled guests were finding a light heart at last.

Chapter 88
Hunting the Will-o-the-Wisp

They left early, with the money Tommy had earned as a street busker in that amusement-starved settlement. Sary shook her head when she heard Jude had been his partner in crime, garbed as either a miniature clown or a strong man, the talented little rogue, while she wandered the Karroo desert on a fool's errand.

They also left with a too generous, considering the vicar's circumstances, bundle of supplies, although no more than a day or two's rations for the two of them and a growing boy.

They left also with promises of reimbursement for the kindnesses of the vicar and his wife, who smiled uncertainly while their lumpy daughter looked on, sullen, and tried for a kiss from Jude, who wiped his cheek afterwards.

****

Tommy held Jude on his knee, his arm securing Sary's waist, on the tailgate of a wagon jolting roughly south.

Sary left in the same bedraggled clothing as she'd worn on arrival, mended the best she could, not wishing to soil Ruth's modest dresses.

Chapter 89
Perseverance

Sary fed a grouchy Jude a morsel of ham and biscuit by the side of the road, hoping he'd not be *too* ravenous, putting the rest aside. Tommy and she split an orange and pounced on a discarded melon, a brown banana, and a heel of bread wrapped in waxed paper, left by the wayside out of some worker's lunch.

Last year I was one of the fabled wealthy. This year I'm living on rat cheese.

After tumbling off the barge taking them as far as the Orange/Vaal junction, they followed workers and townspeople down a well-traveled road. It seemed all roads led to the vast Kimberley mine, however, and when at last they reached the fabled Kimberley, they lingered, awed by the vast open hole like the mouth of a spent volcano riddled with pits, plank bridges, struts and scaffolding, and what seemed a million worker bees.

Closer to the edge, keeping a tight hold on Jude, Sary scanned the open wound—an enormous five-story hollow, chockablock with pulleys big as barrels, open cage elevators, hefty braces propping thick wooden roofs, white overseers with clipboards and bull horns, and black laborers.

Suddenly she feared how fairytale her plans were against such a vast industry as they crept past, as if every eye scrutinized them, aware of what they were thinking.

"Should we at least inquire about the monastery?"

"We dare not," Sary snapped. "It would be a—a giveaway."

"I doubt it. No one would credit it. Besides, I don't see a furious stampede monastery-bound or a jewel-crazed monk anywhere about, for that matter."

Sary fought tears of frustration and weariness and, yes, hurt, at Tommy's continual heckling and teasing.

As if reading her, he softened. "Courage."

He pronounced it the French way—cour-*ahge.*

Chapter 90
Derelict Monastery

Sary and Tommy hitched another ride with a young couple with five stepladder boys. Jude had to be torn away from them as they giggled, slapped, pinched, and tickled each other. Hopping down stiffly as dusk neared, Tommy pointed to where whitewashed buildings loomed, ghostly, beyond cottonwood trees.

Dark, low, whitewashed buildings. No courtyard activity. A simple whitish church and a spire.

Sary nodded.

As he switched the ox onward, the husband looked back at the three set down oddly in the middle of nowhere.

"Let's wait a while…" Tommy scanned the church from a thicket across the road, doling out half of a thick wurst sandwich the vicar's wife had provided. Sary vowed again to repay their generosity.

Not quite dark. Sary wondered how long monks or friars, whatever they were, would remain incurious of the three strangers "picnicking" across from them.

Low hills sheltered the buildings in the waning sun. She pictured the monks already slumbering. Still—no candlelit procession as she'd imagined. It looked neither habituated nor thriving. It just *was.*

They waited till full dark. Still no light. Sary laid out her large shawl and settled a sleepy Jude. They too dozed, wrapped around him.

Sary woke when Tommy began to rummage about. "Where are you going?"

"Reconnoiter."

He headed to the road.

"I should." Sary scrambled up. "I understand the map. I can spot things you may not." She didn't want to admit that if they found nothing she wished to be alone.

"It's a big place. Where would you start? We didn't think things out."

"It never happens the way one plans," Sary said, miserable. *So we are here. A monastery. Now what?*

"Man supposes. God disposes? In this case, woman guesses, God jests," Tommy said, with his usual cleverness.

Sary bit her cheek. Why had she not coerced Ruth to look after Jude just for the while? Yet the fear in the vicar's wife's eyes that they meant to leave Jude permanently, while they went their merry way, had made it impossible.

Tommy grinned. "I can just see an innocent, unshriven monk scared out of his ecclesiastical knickers, if not his holy vows, at the sight of you skulking about half-dressed."

'I don't skulk. I will be alert. Besides, monks sleep with the chickens."

"Literally?" Tommy raised wicked brows.

Sary primmed her mouth. "They bed early and get up at four or something, so we waste time, unless you wish to spend another night outside. Besides, I don't see anyone."

"Oh, go on! Don't expect me rushing to your aid if a clutch of sex-starved friars carry you off."

"I'll be back by first light, if not before."

"Two hours," Tommy warned, "or Jude and I will come after you, making as much noise as possible."

But Tommy addressed the dark, watching long after gloom enveloped her figure.

Chapter 91
Ruin

Sary wended the moonlit copse of cottonwoods shielding the compound from the road.

It wasn't frightening. Moonlight made the church glimpsed through trees peaceful and mystical, until she thrust through onto a weathered yard of the monastery grounds—stables, odd sheds, privies, a blacksmith shed.

She stepped from the small woods. No sentry or farm dog lazily barking. *Good.* She studied overturned barrels, a broken hayrick, a wagon with three wheels. All derelict. "I can poke about at will," she muttered.

The moon cast her shadow long as she stole from stable to hayrick. Half the stable was charred beams, with the peppery spice of burnt wood. Only a third of the long dormitory was whole, the roof caved in save for the section next to the church.

A candle flared somewhere. She looked again. It was only moonlight on a plain window.

Sary studied the woods behind her, thinking she heard Jude crying, and missed seeing a cross-braced door open and a short plump monk emerge. The yawning, long-skirted monk meandered barefoot to an outhouse, sat, and after a time shook his robes down and nipped back inside.

Sary turned, frowning, as the door closed. She

eased to the caved-in dormitory, peeked in narrow windows—all dark—and eventually rounded a corner and stood on steps leading to the sanctuary's arched double doors, where she stood gazing thoughtfully at the fortress-like thickness.

A clever man might hide treasure here as a jest. Something about building treasures on earth.

Sary checked the moon. Still high. *Why not here? Why not now*? She tugged the heavy doors. One opened easily, the other stuck from disuse. Inside, an echo of incense mingled with dust, old bindings, and ancient flowers cloaked her as she stepped onto cold flagstones. The church windows threw icy blue shadows on her pale hair.

Her newly-gained ethereal beauty did not go unnoticed by the chubby monk creeping pew to pew, column to column, of the lofty, not-quite cathedral.

Was she a saint? A holy vision? Or Satan's temptress sent in her unholy comeliness to snare him into a doomed and hellish temptation?

The portly monk felt the devil's campfire licking his toes in their rope sandals and turning his fat to rendered lard. His jowls quivered with rage and longing. He was lonely at the bottom. He didn't care what she was, as long as she stayed. He decided to tempt Satan.

Sary didn't hear the rustle of stiff sackcloth or brush of footsteps as he padded and watched. Such rare beauty to come to his place of placid sanctity, *his special place,* was singular as double rainbows. A treasure to summon during the hot nights and lonely winters.

Sary padded about, touching things, kneeling,

looking under pews, unconsciously avoiding hidden corners despite the moon; so focused on her search for anomalies she didn't hear his hushed footfalls.

At an insipid statue of Saint Katherine, Sary poked the base and probed the floor around it, even felt all over the statue itself, but nothing indicated a 'little kay,' sweet or not.

She passed Virgin Mary with the crowned infant Jesus, stumbled against a pew, and heard a gasp behind her.

She whirled, sieving the dark, noting several elderly candles about to give up their ghost, if not the wick. How thoughtless not to bring matches. *Must have imagined it, or it was a rat scurrying across the flags.* She was at the arched doors again.

Oh! He longed to touch this ethereal one. He had already reached out a fingertip so many times, almost touching her hair as she moved about.

He could ambush her from a column, or jump out of the confessional in waves of dusty velvet as she passed! That would be nice. Would she vanish in a killing mist? A frost freezing his gonads, his small sacs of shame, accompanied by the Prince of Darkness's pitiless laughter?

Or would she turn, fulsome, rosy-cheeked, and kiss him as if to say, "Oh, how I've longed for someone chaste and pure. I will stay forever your servant and acolyte, satisfying your every bidding. I will…"

His thoughts extinguished with the ponderous thunk of the door as the unholy vision left.

Sary sighed, scrutinizing the barren yard. "Now what?" Gazing blankly at a dead blasted tree, bleak and leafless, suddenly bone weary, she longed to be snugged up with Tommy and Jude, watching the stars wheel overhead, with scented scrub as her pillow.

As resources dwindled, Sary realized she had only a tiny window of time pitted against grandiose dreams to find any wretched treasure before she fell on her face or guilt feelings of motherhood took over.

She dreaded reality without hope. No food, money, shelter. A child to feed and only Tommy's skills as an actor, brilliant as he was... He was still a wandering gypsy. She was forgetting that, at the moment, so was she.

Sary scanned foothills beyond the ruined buildings. Were these the inverted Ws on the map? They seemed a half mile away, not crowding the church as X marks the spot indicated.

A faint moon and mild breeze made monsters of the trees and a skeleton rattle of branches as Sary threaded, despondent, back through the copse. She felt stray hairs fanning her shoulders but resisted the urge to look behind her.

****

Tommy, whistling, paced the edge of the woods with sleeping Jude slung over his shoulder. "Sary? Sary! Is that you?"

He looked at Jude. He had not dared to leave him; he might wake up. But he should have gone with her.

Sary emerged. "Damn you, Sary! It's been too long."

She nodded, rueful. "No letter K. Nothing but that line of hills there."

Sary began collecting things.

Tommy steadied her.

She looked up, weary and dazed.

"Are you daft? It's near dawn. We can't make it, love." He waved at the church. "Anybody about? Maybe an egg or two."

Sary shook her head no and fell rather than lay down, snoring softly. Tommy shook his head. Never had he loved her more.

Chapter 92
The Unearthing

Tommy squinted against a sun throwing butterscotch beams over the green hills Sary had seen the night before. A long way on an empty stomach. This was the end. He knew it. But how to convince the intractable love of his life?

Suddenly he stiffened, blinked, and cried out, "I see it, Sary. I think that's it!"

Sary looked up, cross. Her hair was matted, eyes puffy. Jude was grizzling and pawing through their skimpy provisions. She felt empty. All her planning, scheming, and expectations had dwindled down to this ill-thought risk. She wanted sleep, "to knit up the raveled sleeve of care," as Sir Thomas would put it, she thought grumpily.

She sat up instead, swatting hair from her face. "Oh, what is it, Tommy?" She squinted where he pointed. "Where? I don't see anything," she had begun …when she did. Sleep forgotten, she clapped hands over her mouth and, hopping, got her boots on. "It can't be. Oh, Tommy!"

Sary swung Jude about. "What does that look like, punkin?" She pointed. "Remember your alphabet? A, B, C, D?" She laughed and held her arm rigid, straight at an elderly acacia, thick trunked, scarred. Dead, blasted, and just in the nick. In another year, the clue would vanish, thanks to storms and insects.

"'Ook 'ike a *kay*, Mummy. It letter—K!" Jude crowed. "A-b-c-d-e-f-g-h-i-j—*KAY*!" he yelled, triumphant.

"Out of the mouths of babes."

Tommy paced, studying the dead tree from every angle. He knelt down, squinting. "Can only be seen from this one direction."

Sary saw the tree's central trunk stabbed the sky. Two dead branches spiked off it. One up, the other pointing to the ground.

"I saw that tree last night. From there, it looked like it had no branches at all."

In daylight, the chapel resembled the crude drawings—white box, stubby spire, a simple cross—its whitewash charred and grubby.

"S'pose if we do stumble on something, it belongs to them." Tommy jerked his head at the church.

"It seemed empty." She recalled the dead leaves and mouse droppings…and the little monk in the courtyard. No lights burned. Still no industry of any sort.

They walked their side of the road, Jude on Tommy's shoulders, until out of sight, crossed, and approached the dead tree from the south.

She ducked, dragging Tommy down with her.

The friar or monk wandered from the chapel.

Tommy flattened as the monk plodded, focused on prayer or the inner workings of his stomach.

"We're playing a game, Jude," Sary whispered. "You can't let him know we see him."

Jude crawled behind a tree, then peeked out crowing, "I spy!"

"Jude. Shhhh."

"Okay, Mummie. One. Two. Three, here I come."

"Jude, shush!"

But the monk gazed about now, fretfully wringing his hands. "Hettie?" He scratched his head and wandered back to the chapel. They heard the plaintive echo, "Hettie?"

"Perhaps he's deaf?"

"Oh, Sary, this is too good. I shall have to write a comic farce around this whole—ha-ha! *Hettie*!" Tommy subsided in rude chortles.

"Oh, do be quiet, Tommy." Sary bit back tears, from hunger mostly. In the night, Jude had eaten all the biscuits, not that she blamed him.

"Here." Tommy handed her a morsel. "Managed to save a crumb from the little beggar. Today tells the tale. 'Much Ado About Nothing,' or…"

" 'A Comedy of Errors,' " Sary finished, nibbling the biscuit.

****

They played in the grass with Jude, and slept occasionally, until evening. In the building they watched, a lone candle flared, extinguished immediately. Sary scrambled up. Tommy lifted Jude, who grizzled to waken the dead. "Shhhh, pumpkin— quiet as a lamb."

"Want down!" Suddenly irritable, his voice could be stentorian when called upon.

"Oh, Jude, sweeting. Do be quiet." Sary put fingers to lips, looking helplessly at Tommy.

"Don't *wike* this game." Jude puckered up. "Want *supper*. Want *down*!"

Feeling the lump in her throat, Sary felt she

dragged robes of shame behind her.

"You go again," Tommy whispered. He nodded to the tree shaped like a K.

"No! It's all of us or no one."

"Obviously we can't all three go. It *is* your show. Your starring role. We are only supporting players." *Again the theater. My triumph or failure.*

"No one around, beyond that one monk, and God knows when he will pop out again. You'll be safe as long as you're discreet."

He nodded ruefully at Jude. "A quality your son lacks. Besides, they probably bed early."

"With Hettie." Sary giggled. She felt lightheaded, as if her feet did not touch the ground.

Tommy solemnly gave her a trowel taken from the vicarage. Her face crinkled at the absurdity.

"A trowel, Tommy?"

"Look what I saved back. Emergency rations." He held a sweets sack. "Barley sugar." He handed a lump to Jude.

Jude immediately stuck it in his mouth, happily sucking.

Sary dug one out.

"Afraid?"

"If I had any sense." She looked at the full disk of platinum moon, just rising as the sun set. "No time like now. Even the moon's helping." She raised on tiptoe and kissed them both, lingering on Tommy.

"I'll whistle if I see anything, and I will see you the entire time." He watched the pale gleam of her hair as she flew across. He cuddled Jude close.

"Where Mummy going?"

"God knows, Jude…"

Sary knelt gingerly at the base, gnarled and blackened, bark flaking, but the ancient acacia thorns were still lethal.

On her map, burned into her memory, the monk or whoever it was had drawn the filled-in D directly over an X, at the base of the small letter k. It *had* to mean this lifeless tree so close to the church and spire.

She scraped rootbound soil, feeling the spiky tree loom larger than most acacia, alien without leaves and other branches. She fancied an evil aura, as if the tree guarded its own deep secret.

Dig, Sary, DIG!

With her hair hanging in her face like a witch, Sary squatted on her haunches and savagely thrust the trowel in. *How far out? A foot this way? Or two feet that way?* She could not help fretting. Her mind seemed wrapped in gauze, and it was hard to think, difficult to recall the urgency, wondering how she'd duped herself into believing this fool's game. It had seemed so bloody possible. *When I had food.*

The roots were tangles of iron under leathery grass. She desperately thrust the rusty old trowel between roots, wedging them apart to get to the sandy dirt beneath, feeling her vitality leach with each thrust.

A light touch. On her shoulder. Her blood thrummed with shock.

The monk touched her again.

Her shriek pierced the dark, cut off as she swiveled, trowel in hand, directly into the face of the portly monk in a ragged habit.

He bent with benign but interested expression like an inquisitive dog. She scooted back, nearly falling in the hole.

"*Was machts du?*"

His words were Dutch or German, she figured, but she understood it. He had a wandering eye. One looked west, one straight ahead.

"Are—are you alone?" Sary stuttered.

He cocked his head again, watching her with at least one of his eyes. He waved a chubby arm in a raveled sleeve. His stained and torn habit had not received any care for how long a time? She couldn't guess.

"*Nein. Das ist alles meins.* Alone, *Ja.* I keep holy sanctuary light."

"I see." *Oh, go away!* Sary was anxious, keeping an eye on the church door, not sure whether to leave or to keep digging.

He hitched his shoulders. "Church burn. I not go. Besides, my chickens need me," he said simply.

"Chickens?"

"*Ja.* Keep them safe, me. I take eggs but not eat them, das chickens."

"You are the protector of the flame and the chickens." *Oh, Lord, please leave.*

A grin split the simple moon face. "*Jawohl.*" He struggled to his knees. "Now, must find Hettie." He blushed. "My favorite."

He wasn't curious about what she did—no awareness of a map. Sary watched him waddle off, a poor soul happy in his innocence.

She dug the trowel viciously.

Seconds later, another tap on her shoulder. Sary had managed a foot-deep hole. She drooped. "Yes?"

She saw the leading edge of a rusty shovel over her shoulder.

The monk nudged her gently aside. "I vill help."

He reached deep in his habit and brought out a hardboiled egg and a bit of coarse bread.

Sary sat back, biting the egg, shell and all, near tears as the little monk thrust and heaved dirt like a man twice his size.

Time drifted on with the moon's passage. Sary drifted with it. She wondered if Tommy worried. She wondered if they could beg more food? She must beg some for Jude, at least. Somehow she could not move. The night was pitch black. How long had it been? Possibly no more than an hour. Out of her mist, she heard a puzzled voice.

"Something here? Ja?" The monk. She'd almost forgotten him.

Sary blinked. Knee deep in the hole, the frowning monk stomped a sandal-clad foot. In place of the tamp of dirt, a dull thump or thud sounded. Also a grating, like gravel grinding together on something.

The monk climbed out and stood, hands on waist, scowling down at the hole.

Sary crawled over.

She laid a soothing hand on his arm and reached, bottom up, almost over-tipping. Mildew and rot reached her nose. She felt something spongy, hard, and shifting all at the same time.

She flattened, inching down, slowly cupping her hands around and cradling a large leather sack of hard rattling lumps. She lifted, grunting with effort, the mildewed bag—*Hefty. Shifting*—dragging it up the side inch by inch. For once, the small monk did not help, and she was unaware he was even there—and then the bag was out of the hole.

Leather knots of a drawstring separated like rotten cheese as Sary yanked them apart, and the bag fell away into a tri-corner shape, spilling out...*diamonds,* not the sharp, clattering glitter of cut prisms, but the pearly sheen of uncut stones translucent in the sudden shaft of moon.

Sary couldn't speak.

Must be seventy-five pounds of uncut diamonds, wallowing in mildewed rotten leather.

It was all *real.*

She wanted to call Tommy but feared if she turned away the diamonds would change into moonbeams and fairy dust—or gravel.

She wonderingly sorted shapes—most like large hen's eggs, none smaller than a good-sized lump of butter—fumbling and scattering them about with numbed fingers and a disbelieving mind, even though she heard their liquid tinkle and crisp clatter.

Suddenly it was all too much. Was it worth it? Sary was too weak even to call Tommy.

The monk she'd forgotten about picked up an egg-sized stone, chortling.

Sary wasn't so numbed as to not make the comparison. It reminded him of a hen's egg. She saw the rightness in it.

"Yes." Sary stood, shaking out her rags, and gently closed his hand about it.

"*Ja.* Egg!" A nest egg. An egg to place in a nest to encourage the hen's laying. He nodded and waddled toward the sanctuary.

"Wait!" She pantomimed hefting a bag over her shoulder.

Smiling, he carefully stuffed his diamond egg in

325

his habit. With the monk helping, Sary swiftly gathered the stones, knotting them again in the musty rawhide.

She grinned—for a second she saw where the original map had been cut from the bag's material. *Thrifty monks.*

Chapter 93
Bad Pennies & Bloody Diamonds

Sary stumbled on the road when the moon chose to hide behind a cloud the shade of old bed sheets against the darker sky. Trailed by the monk, she ran into a nervously pacing Tommy with sleeping Jude thrown over his shoulder.

"Damn me, Sary! Damn you! And you damned near scared me witless," he sputtered. "Never again! I will—"

She gently turned him.

Tommy stopped mid-reproof as he noticed the monk waddling behind her, struggling with a large, bulky bag.

"Meet my monk, Tommy." Sary laughed. "Keeper of the sanctuary and the chickens. His brothers abandoned him. Tommy, you will never believe—"

"No truer words," Tommy snapped. "I am certain you have another tall tale for me to chase."

"Tommy! We did it! We bloody well, jolly well, absolutely found the whole bloody lot."

Sary laughed, giddy, grabbing his arm to keep from falling.

Tommy looked, baleful, back to the monk gently settling the bag at Sary's feet, then to Sary.

"Look, Tommy." Sary untied the bag in the middle of the road. She could not wait. The monk held up his "egg." The rough stone gleamed iridescent under the pearly light.

Setting Jude gently down, Tommy slowly, reverently, dropped by the side of the smelly bag. Jude awoke and had no compunction about thrusting his hands into the bag's contents, chortling, tossing into the air rocks that glowed with inner light—some pearlescent, some dull opaque, a few nearly clear like isinglass.

"Jude, darling, you're tossing away thousands!" Sary was giggly and lightheaded. That did not stop her from noting a scatter of blood-red, glints of green, and notes of deep blue amid the shower of pebbles.

Interesting.

Tommy held up double handfuls. "Sary? These are *real*—not a jest?"

"Yes. Diamonds, Tommy. *Tons* of them. We are rich again."

The voice hissed through the dark, like the slither of a snake through sand. "Knew you'd come through, by jingo. And how thoughtful! But you didn't have to do all that just for me."

Sary and Tommy froze. Sary cranked her head round, and there was Hunter.

"Well done, for an *ac*-tor and a gullible female."

Sitting high on a horse, Hunter cradled a long rifle. He slid off and strode sideways to the rotted leather bag, keeping them in sight, his eyes glittering with black light. With a sardonic eye cocked, he scooped rocks, trickling them through his fingers and tossing them back into the bag.

"Oh, me, oh, my. I do believe I've outconned that ginger-haired bastard. How clever of me."

"Hunter!" Sary swung her arm with her remaining strength, slapping him on the face. She half-closed her hand in a fist so it was more of a sock, but the noise rang in the clear air.

His eyes flared. He touched his cheek. His rifle pointed directly at Tommy and Jude.

Tommy thrust Jude behind him, but his advance was stopped by the gun barrel in his chest.

Hunter ignored Tommy and studied Sary, all familiarity gone.

How had she ever thought his brutish face handsome?

"I think…I, ah, rather think…I *fear*…" Harry Swallow looked down sadly. "I might have to leave you here. Truly, I am grieved it has to be like this. However, I cannot have you blathering and sobbing and telling tales, now, can I? You do see, Sary?" He challenged her, with a hint of muddling nostalgia.

"Don't harm Jude. He is an innocent. Take the blasted stones!"

"Oh, I shall." He mock-frowned as if stunned by the notion he might leave them. "But what *of* Jude? There's the conundrum. I cannot *leave him*—alone out here? And I do despise wee ones. All that clabbered milk smell, and grubby little hands…"

He ignored the pathetic monk standing forlorn and uncomprehending, as beneath notice.

"Nor can I take him, unless I could teach the brat the fine arts of chicanery—*fast*. Until that happy day, he'd be a troublesome horror. Besides, I do not trust children. Too clever by half. No, I am dreadfully afraid you will remain a family unit, no matter how regretful the outcome."

Swallow looked off while Sary felt Tommy tensing beside her, ready to spring.

"Ah, Sary, we did have some adventures. Now, if you will just"—he twirled his finger—"turn your backs. Hide the child's face. It will go easier." He raised his rifle.

Sary's mind raced, as no doubt did Tommy's, fists clenched so tight his knuckles popped.

He gritted low, "Rush him. We must."

Sary barely nodded.

Hunter shrugged and sighed. "You won't turn?" Hunter sighted down his rifle, interrupted by a loud *squawk!*

Sary jerked her head, zeroing in on a fat, ruffled-up hen trussed by the legs to Hunter's pommel.

Hunter looked distracted, even chagrined, however only just so, keeping the rifle steady.

"My apologies. This excellent fat bird has all the earmarks of a fine dinner. I—"

Sary was barely aware of a silver blur before Hunter fell over the bag of diamonds, with a sold thunk on his head sounding like a melon dropping off a table.

It had happened so fast.

A sharp shovel, silvered on the edge from its stint in the ground, had taken half of Hunter's bronze curls away, sailing off in the dark with a spray of blood.

Hunter fell with a meaty thud and a surprised look on his face. The sand beneath him spread a dark river.

The mild monk stood over him, heaving with wrath, triumph, and a bloody shovel in hand. Then, weeping and calling, "Hettie!" he dropped the shovel and rushed to the startled horse. Removing a small knife from his voluminous pockets, he severed the bonds and freed poor Hettie.

As he cradled the fat bird under his chin, the plump little monk crooned, *"Hettie! Hettie!"*

Sary finally turned to go toward Hunter.

Tommy held her back. "It's over." Sary hid her face in his arms.

Tenderly cradling the bird, the monk continued fussing, kissing Hettie's feathers, stroking the handsome bird's head as he hustled her back to the sanctuary.

Already forgotten, Tommy and Sary, starving and sleep-deprived, gazed disoriented at each other. Jude peeked out and for once was quiet.

They had enough strength to drag Hunter to the blasted tree, where they dug the hole deeper somehow, folded him up, and without a tear Sary helped tuck him in for his long night where the diamonds had lain so long.

Who knew? Perhaps there were still a few buried in the dirt to keep him company.

"He was going to kill us," she said simply.

Tommy climbed on the horse. "Come!" He held a hand out to Sary, who first lifted Jude, then the bag, and finally herself. She held the bag between her thighs, riding shotgun behind Tommy, with Jude before him, back to the Vaal River, just as a new dawn arose.

Epilogue

Sary climbed to the forecastle as the sun spread a crimson quilt over the wrinkled sheet of sea and a pattern of stars heralded a breeze.

Tommy and she had endured much; he'd been there in the shadows, coming into the light when she needed him most, as no other man—even Jonathon—before or after him. She desired Tommy with a body that had no intellect, only a fever in her blood, and their made-up quarrels nigh broke the thermometer.

Sary paced. She owed Tommy for loyalty, enduring love, patience.

Perhaps life on the open road would be the best antidote for her avarice and stubborn pride. Where else would she go? Back to the mindless pleasures of European courts? Sary curled her beautiful lip.

Searching out the scoundrel who had sold her the empty shares? Not worth her time.

With the diamonds, they could well fund a magnificent traveling theatrical troupe. She smiled, walking faster. It felt right.

Tommy had even bashfully mentioned Ethel Barrymore, first actress of the American stage, it was said, as a possible star of his fantasy troupe.

Why not? Diamonds were as good as gold.

She reached their cabin door. Marshalling herself like a general in a sheer cotton shift in place of epaulets,

Sary prepared for an onslaught of intimate pleasure.

She eyed Tommy.

Their cabin was palatial now, their ship, sleek and fueled by steam, top of the line. Little Jude had his own quarters next door, with his own nanny, the vicar's sullen, red-haired daughter that Jude had taken a puzzling fancy to. She even seemed happy. Sary grinned. Perhaps showing the girl the world was the way to put a pleasant aspect on her face.

They were alone.

Tommy's long gypsy lashes fanned newly bronzed cheeks, overlaying his natural pale Irish skin, his hair curling in heat more than ever like a rough Gitano or Italian.

She studied him with pure shivering pleasure in the candlelight. *Must ask Tommy from whence he came.* She was vaguely aware he'd traveled the English countryside with his troupe before showing up in Big Bear that fateful day, sealing both their futures. She smiled faintly. The rough mining town had been as entranced as she.

Her eyes flared green, her breath caught, and her lips smiled in preparation. Perhaps they wouldn't make a baby, but not for lack of trying.

Tommy awoke; black fire burned as he roughly pulled her down, grasping her slim naked waist, drawing her to him breast to chest, his hardness against hers…

They lay there, softly kissing, drawing the pleasure out, mending fractured affections, while she whispered their future.

He grinned up, exuberant, as she rested her fanny on his thighs and her sex on his manhood. She leant, brushing full breasts shed of the hated corselet, now kept in a glass case, unbuttoning his shirt, slow and teasing, running her slim hands over him, her small palms covering his tiny nipples so absurd on a man but endearing nonetheless. She bit one gently.

She sighed when he slid in, and rode him down…

Sary gazed, blind with passion, far into the night.

Perhaps there would be a little brother or sister for Jude…

****

Somewhere in Africa, a fat man wobbled up to the bar, ever hopeful against all odds or reality heretofore. Perhaps today the bartender would invite him for a drink. His hands trembled. Instead of being shuttled off, miracle of miracles, he was beckoned.

He looked over his chubby shoulder. No. He meant him. Expecting a blow, the fat man leaned to listen. His eyes grew so wide they threatened his cheeks.

"Truly?"

The bartender spread his hands as if to say, *I don't understand it either*. "Truth. Free booze. The best I have—no tab for the rest of your days, mate."

Privately, as he polished a glass, the bartender thought that might not be far in the future.

"But…who?"

The bartender shrugged and poured him his first. Pale as honey, sweet as wine, the whiskey slid down.

For some reason, a face with glowing green eyes and windblown blonde hair wafted across the fat man's mind as he accepted his second libation of many.

****

In a modest vicarage, a woman stared speechless at a gleaming pump organ—the finest made, fruitwood, filigreed, scrolled, and painted with gold and roses. The keys were ivory, the round seat plush velvet and heavily fringed.

When she wonderingly sat to play, a disappointing *thunk* came from the sound board.

Lifting the lid, she rescued a large irregular, clear stone.

With a catch in her throat, she held it to the light and called to the vicar.

****

In a half-burned-out monastery, a small plump monk smiled endearingly at his hen and placed an egg-shaped stone in Hettie's nest of sweet clover and straw. Perhaps it would encourage his Hettie...

A word about the author...

Sharon writes her novels and scripts on the coast of California and Big Bear Mountain.

Her first script, *Sary's Gold*, captured ScriptPimp's Grand Prize, and is now published as a novel by The Wild Rose Press, Inc.

Her other novels, published elsewhere, include: *Beast in the Moon*, an erotic, dystopian Sci-Fi, and *The Monster Factory*, an adult coming-of-age horror.